I0764566

Lucy Maud Montgomery

Short Stories, 1907-1908

By

Lucy Maud Montgomery

Cover Artwork: goddessofchocolate

ISBN: 978-1-78139-243-0

Contents

A Millionaire's Proposal 7
A Substitute Journalist 20
Anna's Love Letters 27
Aunt Caroline's Silk Dress 36
Aunt Susanna's Thanksgiving Dinner. 44
By Grace of Julius Caesar 53
By the Rule of Contrary 60
Fair Exchange and No Robbery 64
Four Winds 72
Marcella's Reward 107
Margaret's Patient 114
Matthew Insists on Puffed Sleeves 120
Missy's Room 128
Ted's Afternoon Off 136
The Doctor's Sweetheart 142
The End of the Young Family Feud 149
The Genesis of the Doughnut Club 156
The Girl Who Drove the Cows 163
The Growing Up of Cornelia 169
The Old Fellow's Letter 181
The Parting of The Ways 187
The Promissory Note 191

The Revolt of Mary Isabel 199
The Twins and a Wedding 212

A Millionaire's Proposal

Thrush Hill, Oct. 5, 18—.

It is all settled at last, and in another week I shall have left Thrush Hill. I am a little bit sorry and a great bit glad. I am going to Montreal to spend the winter with Alicia.

Alicia—it used to be plain Alice when she lived at Thrush Hill and made her own dresses and trimmed her own hats—is my half-sister. She is eight years older than I am. We are both orphans, and Aunt Elizabeth brought us up here at Thrush Hill, the most delightful old country place in the world, half smothered in big willows and poplars, every one of which I have climbed in the early tomboy days of gingham pinafores and sun-bonnets.

When Alicia was eighteen she married Roger Gresham, a man of forty. The world said that she married him for his money. I dare say she did. Alicia was tired of poverty.

I don't blame her. Very likely I shall do the same thing one of these days, if I get the chance—for I too am tired of poverty.

When Alicia went to Montreal she wanted to take me with her, but I wanted to be outdoors, romping in the hay or running wild in the woods with Jack.

Jack Willoughby—Dr. John H. Willoughby, it reads on his office door—was the son of our nearest neighbour. We were chums always, and when he went away to college I was heartbroken.

The vacations were the only joy of my life then.

I don't know just when I began to notice a change in Jack, but when he came home two years ago, a full-fledged M.D.—a great, tall, broad-shouldered fellow, with the sweetest moustache, and lovely thick black hair, just made for poking one's fingers through—I realized it to the full. Jack was grown up. The dear old days of bird-nesting and nutting and coasting and fishing and general delightful goings-on were over forever.

I was sorry at first. I wanted "Jack." "Dr. Willoughby" seemed too distinguished and far away.

I suppose he found a change in me, too. I had put on long skirts and wore my hair up. I had also found out that I had a complexion, and that sunburn was not becoming. I honestly thought I looked pretty, but Jack surveyed me with decided disapprobation.

"What have you done to yourself? You don't look like the same girl. I'd never know you in that rig-out, with all those flippery-trippery curls all over your head. Why don't you comb your hair straight back, and let it hang in a braided tail, like you used to?"

This didn't suit me at all. When I expect a compliment and get something quite different I always get snippy. So I said, with what I intended to be crushing dignity, "that I supposed I wasn't the same girl; I had grown up, and if he didn't like my curls he needn't look at them. For my part, I thought them infinitely preferable to that horrid, conceited-looking moustache he had grown."

"I'll shave it off if it doesn't suit you," said Jack amiably.

Jack is always so provokingly good-humoured. When you've taken pains and put yourself out—even to the extent of fibbing about a moustache—to exasperate a person, there is nothing more annoying than to have him keep perfectly angelic.

But after a while Jack and I adjusted ourselves to the change in each other and became very good friends again. It was quite a different friendship from the old, but it was very pleasant. Yes, it was; I *will* admit that much.

I was provoked at Jack's determination to settle down for life in Valleyfield, a horrible, humdrum, little country village.

"You'll never make your fortune there, Jack," I said spitefully. "You'll just be a poor, struggling country doctor all your life, and you'll be grey at forty."

"I don't expect to make a fortune, Kitty," said Jack quietly. "Do you think that is the one desirable thing? I shall never be a rich man. But riches are not the only thing that makes life pleasant."

"Well, I think they have a good deal to do with it, anyhow," I retorted. "It's all very well to pretend to despise wealth, but it's generally a case of sour grapes. *I* will own up honestly that I'd *love* to be rich."

It always seems to make Jack blue and grumpy when I talk like that. I suppose that is one reason why he never asked me to settle down in life as a country doctor's wife. Another was, no doubt, that I always nipped his sentimental sproutings religiously in the bud.

Three weeks ago Alicia wrote to me, asking me to spend the winter with her. Her letters always make me just gasp with longing for the life they describe.

Jack's face, when I told him about it, was so woebegone that I felt a stab of remorse, even in the heyday of my delight.

"Do you really mean it, Kitty? Are you going away to leave me?"

"You won't miss me much," I said flippantly—I had a creepy, crawly presentiment that a scene of some kind was threatening—"and I'm awfully tired of Thrush Hill and country life, Jack. I suppose it is horribly ungrateful of me to say so, but it is the truth."

"I shall miss you," he said soberly.

Somehow he had my hands in his. *How* did he ever get them? I was sure I had them safely tucked out of harm's way behind me. "You know, Kitty, that I love you. I am a poor man—perhaps I may never be anything else—and this may seem to you very presumptuous. But I cannot let you go like this. Will you be my wife, dear?"

Wasn't it horribly straightforward and direct? So like Jack! I tried to pull my hands away, but he held them fast. There was nothing to do but answer him. That "no" I had determined to say must be said, but, oh! how woefully it did stick in my throat!

And I honestly believe that by the time I got it out it would have been transformed into a "yes," in spite of me, had it not been for a certain paragraph in Alicia's letter which came providentially to my mind:

> Not to flatter you, Katherine, you are a beauty, my dear—if your photo is to be trusted. If you have not discovered that fact before—how should you, indeed, in a place like Thrush Hill?—you soon will in Montreal. With your face and figure you will make a sensation.
>
> There is to be a nephew of the Sinclairs here this winter. He is an American, immensely wealthy, and will be the catch of the season. A word to the wise, etc. Don't get into any foolish entanglement down there. I have heard some gossip of you and our old playfellow, Jack Willoughby. I hope it is nothing but gossip. You can do better than that, Katherine.

That settled Jack's fate, if there ever had been any doubt.

"Don't talk like that, Jack," I said hurriedly. "It is all nonsense. I think a great deal of you as a friend and—and—all that, you know. But I can never marry you."

"Are you sure, Kitty?" said Jack earnestly. "Don't you care for me at all?"

It was horrid of Jack to ask that question!

"No," I said miserably, "not—not in that way, Jack. Oh, don't ever say anything like this to me again."

He let go of my hands then, white to the lips.

"Oh, don't look like that, Jack," I entreated.

"I can't help it," he said in a low voice. "But I won't bother you again, dear. It was foolish of me to expect—to hope for anything of the sort. You are a thousand times too good for me, I know."

"Oh, indeed I'm not, Jack," I protested. "If you knew how horrid I am, really, you'd be glad and thankful for your escape. Oh, Jack, I wish people never grew up."

Jack smiled sadly.

"Don't feel badly over this, Kitty. It isn't your fault. Good night, dear."

He turned my face up and kissed me squarely on the mouth. He had never kissed me since the summer before he went away to college. Somehow it didn't seem a bit the same as it used to; it was—nicer now.

After he went away I came upstairs and had a good, comfortable howl. Then I buried the whole affair decently. I am not going to think of it any more.

I shall always have the highest esteem for Jack, and I hope he will soon find some nice girl who will make him happy. Mary Carter would jump at him, I know. To be sure, she is as homely as she can be and live. But, then, Jack is always telling me how little he cares for beauty, so I have no doubt she will suit him admirably.

As for myself—well, I am ambitious. I don't suppose my ambition is a very lofty one, but such as it is I mean to hunt it down. Come. Let me put it down in black and white, once for all, and see how it looks:

I mean to marry the rich nephew of the Sinclairs.

There! It is out, and I feel better. How mercenary and awful it looks written out in cold blood like that. I wouldn't have Jack or Aunt Elizabeth—dear, unworldly old soul—see it for the world. But I wouldn't mind Alicia.

Poor dear Jack!

Montreal, Dec. 16, 18—.

This is a nice way to keep a journal. But the days when I could write regularly are gone by. That was when I was at Thrush Hill.

I am having a simply divine time. How in the world did I ever contrive to live at Thrush Hill?

To be sure, I felt badly enough that day in October when I left it. When the train left Valleyfield I just cried like a baby.

Alicia and Roger welcomed me very heartily, and after the first week of homesickness—I shiver yet when I think of it—was over, I settled down to my new life as if I had been born to it.

Alicia has a magnificent home and everything heart could wish for—jewels, carriages, servants, opera boxes, and social position. Roger is a model husband apparently. I must also admit that he is a model brother-in-law.

I could feel Alicia looking me over critically the moment we met. I trembled with suspense, but I was soon relieved.

"Do you know, Katherine, I am glad to see that your photograph didn't flatter you. Photographs so often do, I am positively surprised at the way you have developed, my dear; you used to be such a scrawny little brown thing. By the way, I hope there is nothing between you and Jack Willoughby?"

"No, of course not," I answered hurriedly. I had intended to tell Alicia all about Jack, but when it came to the point I couldn't.

"I am glad of that," said Alicia, with a relieved air. "Of course, I've no doubt Jack is a good fellow enough. He was a nice boy. But he would not be a suitable husband for you, Katherine."

I knew that very well. That was just why I had refused him. But it made me wince to hear Alicia say it. I instantly froze up—Alicia says dignity is becoming to me—and Jack's name has never been mentioned between us since.

I made my bow to society at an "At Home" which Alicia gave for that purpose. She drilled me well beforehand, and I think I acquitted myself decently. Charlie Vankleek, whose verdict makes or mars every debutante in his set, has approved of me. He called me a beauty, and everybody now believes that I am one, and greets me accordingly.

I met Gus Sinclair at Mrs. Brompton's dinner. Alicia declares it was a case of love at first sight. If so, I must confess that it was all on one side.

Mr. Sinclair is undeniably ugly—even Alicia has to admit that—and can't hold a candle to Jack in point of looks, for Jack, poor boy, was handsome, if he were nothing else. But, as Alicia does not fail to remind me, Mr. Sinclair's homeliness is well gilded.

Apart from his appearance, I really liked him very much. He is a gentlemanly little fellow—his head reaches about to my shoulder—

cultured and travelled, and can talk splendidly, which Jack never could.

He took me into dinner at Mrs. Brompton's, and was very attentive. You may imagine how many angelic glances I received from the other candidates for his favour.

Since then I have been having the gayest time imaginable. Dances, dinners, luncheons, afternoon teas, "functions" to no end, and all delightful.

Aunt Elizabeth writes to me, but I have never heard a word from Jack. He seems to have forgotten my existence completely. No doubt he has consoled himself with Mary Carter.

Well, that is all for the best, but I must say I did not think Jack could have forgotten me so soon or so absolutely. Of course it does not make the least difference to me.

The Sinclairs and the Bromptons and the Curries are to dine here tonight. I can see myself reflected in the long mirror before me, and I really think my appearance will satisfy even Gus Sinclair's critical eye. I am pale, as usual, I never have any colour. That used to be one of Jack's grievances. He likes pink and white milkmaidish girls. My "magnificent pallor" didn't suit him at all.

But, what is more to the purpose, it suits Gus Sinclair. He admires the statuesque style.

Montreal, Jan. 20, 18—.

Here it is a whole month since my last entry. I am sitting here decked out in "gloss of satin and glimmer of pearls" for Mrs. Currie's dance. These few minutes, after I emerge from the hands of my maid and before the carriage is announced, are almost the only ones I ever have to myself.

I am having a good time still. Somehow, though, it isn't as exciting as it used to be. I'm afraid I'm very changeable. I believe I must be homesick.

I'd love to get a glimpse of dear old Thrush Hill and Aunt Elizabeth, and J—but, no! I will not write that.

Mr. Sinclair has not spoken yet, but there is no doubt that he soon will. Of course, I shall accept him when he does, and I coolly told Alicia so when she just as coolly asked me what I meant to do.

"Certainly, I shall marry him," I said crossly, for the subject always irritates me. "Haven't I been laying myself out all winter to catch him? That is the bold, naked truth, and ugly enough it is. My dearly beloved sister, I mean to accept Mr. Sinclair, without any hesitation, whenever I get the chance."

"I give you credit for more sense than to dream of doing anything else," said Alicia in relieved tones. "Katherine, you are a very lucky girl."

"Because I am going to marry a rich man for his money?" I said coldly.

Sometimes I get snippy with Alicia these days.

"No," said my half-sister in an exasperated way. "Why will you persist in speaking in that way? You are very provoking. It is not likely I would wish to see you throw yourself away on a poor man, and I'm sure you must like Gus."

"Oh, yes, I like him well enough," I said listlessly. "To be sure, I did think once, in my salad days, that liking wasn't quite all in an affair of this kind. I was absurd enough to imagine that love had something to do with it."

"Don't talk so nonsensically," said Alicia sharply. "Love! Well, of course, you ought to love your husband, and you will. He loves you enough, at all events."

"Alicia," I said earnestly, looking her straight in the face and speaking bluntly enough to have satisfied even Jack's love of straightforwardness, "you married for money and position, so people say. Are you happy?"

For the first time that I remembered, Alicia blushed. She was very angry.

"Yes, I did marry for money," she said sharply, "and I don't regret it. Thank heaven, I never was a fool."

"Don't be vexed, Alicia," I entreated. "I only asked because—well, it is no matter."

Montreal, Jan. 25, 18—.

It is bedtime, but I am too excited and happy and miserable to sleep. Jack has been here—dear old Jack! How glad I was to see him.

His coming was so unexpected. I was sitting alone in my room this afternoon—I believe I was moping—when Bessie brought up his card. I gave it one rapturous look and tore downstairs, passing Alicia in the hall like a whirlwind, and burst into the drawing-room in a most undignified way.

"Jack!" I cried, holding out both hands to him in welcome.

There he was, just the same old Jack, with his splendid big shoulders and his lovely brown eyes. And his necktie was crooked, too; as soon as I could get my hands free I put them up and straightened it out for him. How nice and old-timey that was!

"So you are glad to see me, Kitty?" he said as he squeezed my hands in his big strong paws.

"'Deed and 'deed I am, Jack. I thought you had forgotten me altogether. And I've been so homesick and so—so everything," I said incoherently. "And, oh, Jack, I've so many questions to ask I don't know where to begin. Tell me all the Thrush Hill and Valleyfield news, tell me everything that has happened since I left. How many people have you killed off? And, oh, why didn't you come to see me before?"

"I didn't think I should be wanted, Kitty," Jack answered quietly. "You seemed to be so absorbed in your new life that old friends and interests were crowded out."

"So I was at first," I answered penitently. "I was dazzled, you know. The glare was too much for my Thrush Hill brown. But it's different now. How did you happen to come, Jack?"

"I had to come to Montreal on business, and I thought it would be too bad if I went back without coming to see what they had been doing in Vanity Fair to my little playmate."

"Well, what do you think they have been doing?" I asked saucily.

I had on a particularly fetching gown and knew I was looking my best. Jack, however, looked me over with his head on one side.

"Well, I don't know, Kitty," he said slowly. "That is a stunning sort of dress you have on—not so pretty, though, as that old blue muslin you used to wear last summer—and your hair is pretty good. But you look rather disdainful and, after all, I believe I prefer Thrush Hill Kitty."

How like Jack that was. He never thought me really pretty, and he is too honest to pretend he does.

But I didn't care. I just laughed, and we sat down together and had a long, delightful, chummy talk.

Jack told me all the Valleyfield gossip, not forgetting to mention that Mary Carter was going to be married to a minister in June. Jack didn't seem to mind it a bit, so I guess he couldn't have been particularly interested in Mary.

In due time Alicia sailed in. I suppose she had found out from Bessie who my caller was, and felt rather worried over the length of our tête-à-tête.

She greeted Jack very graciously, but with a certain polite condescension of which she is past mistress. I am sure Jack felt it, for, as soon as he decently could, he got up to go. Alicia asked him to remain to dinner.

"We are having a few friends to dine with us, but it is quite an informal affair," she said sweetly.

I felt that Jack glanced at me for the fraction of a second. But I remembered that Gus Sinclair was coming too, and I did not look at him.

Then he declined quietly. He had a business engagement, he said.

I suppose Alicia had noticed that look at me, for she showed her claws.

"Don't forget to call any time you are in Montreal," she said more sweetly than ever. "I am sure Katherine will always be glad to see any of her old friends, although some of her new ones *are* proving very absorbing—one, in especial. Don't blush, Katherine, I am sure Mr. Willoughby won't tell any tales out of school to your old Valleyfield friends."

I was not blushing, and I was furious. It was really too bad of Alicia, although I don't see why I need have cared.

Alicia kept her eye on us both until Jack was fairly gone. Then she remarked in the patronizing tone which I detest:

"Really, Katherine, Jack Willoughby has developed into quite a passable-looking fellow, although he is rather shabby. But I suppose he is poor."

"Yes," I answered curtly, "he is poor, in everything except youth and manhood and goodness and truth! But I suppose those don't count for anything."

Whereupon Alicia lifted her eyebrows and looked me over.

Just at dusk a box arrived with Jack's compliments. It was full of lovely white carnations, and must have cost the extravagant fellow more than he has any business to waste on flowers. I was beast enough to put them on when I went down to listen to another man's lovemaking.

This evening I sparkled and scintillated with unusual brilliancy, for Jack's visit and my consequent crossing of swords with Alicia had produced a certain elation of spirits. When Gus Sinclair was leaving he asked if he might see me alone tomorrow afternoon.

I knew what that meant, and a cold shiver went up and down my backbone. But I looked down at him—spick-and-span and glossy—*his* neckties are never crooked—and said, yes, he might come at three o'clock.

Alicia had noticed our aside—when did anything ever escape her?—and when he was gone she asked, significantly, what secret he had been telling me.

"He wants to see me alone tomorrow afternoon. I suppose you know what that means, Alicia?"

"Ah," purred Alicia, "I congratulate you, my dear."

"Aren't your congratulations a little premature?" I asked coldly. "I haven't accepted him yet."

"But you will?"

"Oh, certainly. Isn't it what we've schemed and angled for? I'm very well satisfied."

And so I am. But I wish it hadn't come so soon after Jack's visit, because I feel rather upset yet. Of course I like Gus Sinclair very much, and I am sure I shall be very fond of him.

Well, I must go to bed now and get my beauty sleep. I don't want to be haggard and hollow-eyed at that important interview tomorrow—an interview that will decide my destiny.

Thrush Hill, May 6, 18—.

Well, it did decide it, but not exactly in the way I anticipated. I can look back on the whole affair quite calmly now, but I wouldn't live it over again for all the wealth of Ind.

That day when Gus Sinclair came I was all ready for him. I had put on my very prettiest new gown to do honour to the occasion, and Alicia smilingly assured me I was looking very well.

"And *so* cool and composed. Will you be able to keep that up? Don't you really feel a little nervous, Katherine?"

"Not in the least," I said. "I suppose I ought to be, according to traditions, but I never felt less flustered in my life."

When Bessie brought up Gus Sinclair's card Alicia dropped a pecky little kiss on my cheek, and pushed me toward the door. I went down calmly, although I'll admit that my heart *was* beating wildly. Gus Sinclair was plainly nervous, but I was composed enough for both. You would really have thought that I was in the habit of being proposed to by a millionaire every day.

"I suppose you know what I have come to say," he said, standing before me, as I leaned gracefully back in a big chair, having taken care that the folds of my dress fell just as they should.

And then he proceeded to say it in a rather jumbled-up fashion, but very sincerely.

I remember thinking at the time that he must have composed the speech in his head the night before, and rehearsed it several times, but was forgetting it in spots.

When he ended with the self-same question that Jack had asked me three months before at Thrush Hill he stopped and took my hands.

I looked up at him. His good, homely face was close to mine, and in his eyes was an unmistakable look of love and tenderness.

I opened my mouth to say yes.

And then there came over me in one rush the most awful realization of the sacrilege I was going to commit.

I forgot everything except that I loved Jack Willoughby, and that I could never, never marry anybody in the world except him.

Then I pulled my hands away and burst into hysterical, undignified tears.

"I beg your pardon," said Mr. Sinclair. "I did not mean to startle you. Have I been too abrupt? Surely you must have known—you must have expected—"

"Yes—yes—I knew," I cried miserably, "and I intended right up to this very minute to marry you. I'm so sorry—but I can't—I can't."

"I don't understand," he said in a bewildered tone. "If you expected it, then why—why—don't you care for me?"

"No, that's just it," I sobbed. "I don't love you at all—and I do love somebody else. But he is poor, and I hate poverty. So I refused him, and I meant to marry you just because you are rich."

Such a pained look came over his face. "I did not think this of you," he said in a low tone.

"Oh, I know I have acted shamefully," I said. "You can't think any worse of me than I do of myself. How you must despise me!"

"No," he said, with a grim smile, "if I did it would be easier for me. I might not love you then. Don't distress yourself, Katherine. I do not deny that I feel greatly hurt and disappointed, but I am glad you have been true to yourself at last. Don't cry, dear."

"You're very good," I answered disconsolately, "but all the same the fact remains that I have behaved disgracefully to you, and I know you think so. Oh, Mr. Sinclair, please, please, go away. I feel so miserably ashamed of myself that I cannot look you in the face."

"I am going, dear," he said gently. "I know all this must be very painful to you, but it is not easy for me, either."

"Can you forgive me?" I said wistfully.

"Yes, my dear, completely. Do not let yourself be unhappy over this. Remember that I will always be your friend. Goodbye."

He held out his hand and gave mine an earnest clasp. Then he went away.

I remained in the drawing-room, partly because I wanted to finish out my cry, and partly because, miserable coward that I was, I didn't dare face Alicia. Finally she came in, her face wreathed with anticipatory smiles. But when her eyes fell on my forlorn, crumpled self she fairly jumped.

"Katherine, what is the matter?" she asked sharply. "Didn't Mr. Sinclair—"

"Yes, he did," I said desperately. "And I've refused him. There now, Alicia!"

Then I waited for the storm to burst. It didn't all at once. The shock was too great, and at first quite paralyzed my half-sister.

"Katherine," she gasped, "are you crazy? Have you lost your senses?"

"No, I've just come to them. It's true enough, Alicia. You can scold all you like. I know I deserve it, and I won't flinch. I did really intend to take him, but when it came to the point I couldn't. I didn't love him."

Then, indeed, the storm burst. I never saw Alicia so angry before, and I never got so roundly abused. But even Alicia has her limits, and at last she grew calmer.

"You have behaved disgracefully," she concluded. "I am disgusted with you. You have encouraged Gus Sinclair markedly right along, and now you throw him over like this. I never dreamed that you were capable of such unwomanly behaviour."

"That's a hard word, Alicia," I protested feebly.

She dealt me a withering glance. "It does not begin to be as hard as your shameful conduct merits. To think of losing a fortune like that for the sake of sentimental folly! I didn't think you were such a consummate fool."

"I suppose you absorbed all the sense of our family," I said drearily. "There now, Alicia, do leave me alone. I'm down in the very depths already."

"What do you mean to do now?" said Alicia scornfully. "Go back to Valleyfield and marry that starving country doctor of yours, I suppose?"

I flared up then; Alicia might abuse me all she liked, but I wasn't going to hear a word against Jack.

"Yes, I will, if he'll have me," I said, and I marched out of the room and upstairs, with my head very high.

Of course I decided to leave Montreal as soon as I could. But I couldn't get away within a week, and it was a very unpleasant one. Alicia treated me with icy indifference, and I knew I should never be reinstated in her good graces.

To my surprise, Roger took my part. "Let the girl alone," he told Alicia. "If she doesn't love Sinclair, she was right in refusing him. I, for one, am glad that she has got enough truth and womanliness in her to keep her from selling herself."

Then he came to the library where I was moping, and laid his hand on my head.

"Little girl," he said earnestly, "no matter what anyone says to you, never marry a man for his money or for any other reason on earth except because you love him."

This comforted me greatly, and I did not cry myself to sleep that night as usual.

At last I got away. I had telegraphed to Jack: "Am coming home Wednesday; meet me at train," and I knew he would be there. How I longed to see him again—dear, old, badly treated Jack.

I got to Valleyfield just at dusk. It was a rainy evening, and everything was slush and fog and gloom. But away up I saw the home light at Thrush Hill, and Jack was waiting for me on the platform.

"Oh, Jack!" I said, clinging to him, regardless of appearances. "Oh, I'm so glad to be back."

"That's right, Kitty. I knew you wouldn't forget us. How well you are looking!"

"I suppose I ought to be looking wretched," I said penitently. "I've been behaving very badly, Jack. Wait till we get away from the crowd and I'll tell you all about it."

And I did.

I didn't gloss over anything, but just confessed the whole truth. Jack heard me through in silence, and then he kissed me.

"Can you forgive me, Jack, and take me back?" I whispered, cuddling up to him.

And he said—but, on second thought, I will not write down what he said.

We are to be married in June.

A Substitute Journalist

Clifford Baxter came into the sitting-room where Patty was darning stockings and reading a book at the same time. Patty could do things like that. The stockings were well darned too, and Patty understood and remembered what she read.

Clifford flung himself into a chair with a sigh of weariness. "Tired?" queried Patty sympathetically.

"Yes, rather. I've been tramping about the wharves all day gathering longshore items. But, Patty, I've got a chance at last. Tonight as I was leaving the office Mr. Harmer gave me a real assignment for tomorrow—two of them in fact, but only one of importance. I'm to go and interview Mr. Keefe on this new railroad bill that's up before the legislature. He's in town, visiting his old college friend, Mr. Reid, and he's quite big game. I wouldn't have had the assignment, of course, if there'd been anyone else to send, but most of the staff will be away all day tomorrow to see about that mine explosion at Midbury or the teamsters' strike at Bainsville, and I'm the only one available. Harmer gave me a pretty broad hint that it was my chance to win my spurs, and that if I worked up a good article out of it I'd stand a fair show of being taken on permanently next month when Alsop leaves. There'll be a shuffle all round then, you know. Everybody on the staff will be pushed up a peg, and that will leave a vacant space at the foot."

Patty threw down her darning needle and clapped her hands with delight. Clifford gazed at her admiringly, thinking that he had the prettiest sister in the world—she was so bright, so eager, so rosy.

"Oh, Clifford, how splendid!" she exclaimed. "Just as we'd begun to give up hope too. Oh, you must get the position! You must hand in a good write-up. Think what it means to us."

"Yes, I know." Clifford dropped his head on his hand and stared rather moodily at the lamp. "But my joy is chastened, Patty. Of course I want to get the permanency, since it seems to be the only possible thing, but you know my heart isn't really in newspaper work. The plain truth is I don't like it, although I do my best. You know Father always said I was a born mechanic. If I only could get a position somewhere among machinery—that would be my choice. There's one vacant in the Steel and Iron Works at Bancroft—but of course I've no chance of getting it."

"I know. It's too bad," said Patty, returning to her stockings with a sigh. "I wish I were a boy with a foothold on the *Chronicle*. I firmly believe that I'd make a good newspaper woman, if such a thing had ever been heard of in Aylmer."

"That you would. You've twice as much knack in that line as I have. You seem to know by instinct just what to leave out and put in. I never do, and Harmer has to blue-pencil my copy mercilessly. Well, I'll do my best with this, as it's very necessary I should get the permanency, for I fear our family purse is growing very slim. Mother's face has a new wrinkle of worry every day. It hurts me to see it."

"And me," sighed Patty. "I do wish I could find something to do too. If only we both could get positions, everything would be all right. Mother wouldn't have to worry so. Don't say anything about this chance to her until you see what comes of it. She'd only be doubly disappointed if nothing did. What is your other assignment?"

"Oh, I've got to go out to Bancroft on the morning train and write up old Mr. Moreland's birthday celebration. He is a hundred years old, and there's going to be a presentation and speeches and that sort of thing. Nothing very exciting about it. I'll have to come back on the three o'clock train and hurry out to catch my politician before he leaves at five. Take a stroll down to meet my train, Patty. We can go out as far as Mr. Reid's house together, and the walk will do you good."

The Baxters lived in Aylmer, a lively little town with two newspapers, the *Chronicle* and the *Ledger*. Between these two was a sharp journalistic rivalry in the matter of "beats" and "scoops." In the preceding spring Clifford had been taken on the *Chronicle* on trial, as a sort of general handyman. There was no pay attached to the position, but he was getting training and there was the possibility of a permanency in September if he proved his mettle. Mr. Baxter had died two years before, and the failure of the company in which Mrs. Baxter's money was invested had left the little family dependent on their own resources. Clifford, who had cherished dreams of a course in mechanical engineering, knew that he must give them up and go to the first work that offered itself, which he did staunchly and uncomplainingly. Patty, who hitherto had had no designs on a "career," but had been sunnily content to be a home girl and Mother's right hand, also realized that it would be well to look about her for something to do. She was not really needed so far as the work of the little house went, and the whole burden must not be allowed to fall on Clifford's eighteen-year-old shoulders. Patty was his senior by a year, and ready to do her part unflinchingly.

The next afternoon Patty went down to meet Clifford's train. When it came, no Clifford appeared. Patty stared about her at the hurrying throngs in bewilderment. Where was Clifford? Hadn't he come on the train? Surely he must have, for there was no other until seven o'clock. She must have missed him somehow. Patty waited until everybody had left the station, then she walked slowly homeward. As the *Chronicle* office was on her way, she dropped in to see if Clifford had reported there.

She found nobody in the editorial offices except the office boy, Larry Brown, who promptly informed her that not only had Clifford not arrived, but that there was a telegram from him saying that he had missed his train. Patty gasped in dismay. It was dreadful!

"Where is Mr. Harmer?" she asked.

"He went home as soon as the afternoon edition came out. He left before the telegram came. He'll be furious when he finds out that nobody has gone to interview that foxy old politician," said Larry, who knew all about Clifford's assignment and its importance.

"Isn't there anyone else here to go?" queried Patty desperately.

Larry shook his head. "No, there isn't a soul in. We're mighty shorthanded just now on account of the explosion and the strike."

Patty went downstairs and stood for a moment in the hall, rapt in reflection. If she had been at home, she verily believed she would have sat down and cried. Oh, it was too bad, too disappointing! Clifford would certainly lose all chance of the permanency, even if the irate news editor did not discharge him at once. What could she do? Could she do anything? She *must* do something.

"If I only could go in his place," moaned Patty softly to herself.

Then she started. Why not? Why not go and interview the big man herself? To be sure, she did not know a great deal about interviewing, still less about railroad bills, and nothing at all about politics. But if she did her best it might be better than nothing, and might at least save Clifford his present hold.

With Patty, to decide was to act. She flew back to the reporters' room, pounced on a pencil and tablet, and hurried off, her breath coming quickly, and her eyes shining with excitement. It was quite a long walk out to Mr. Reid's place and Patty was tired when she got there, but her courage was not a whit abated. She mounted the steps and rang the bell undauntedly.

"Can I scc Mr.—Mr.—Mr.—" Patty paused for a moment in dismay. She had forgotten the name. The maid who had come to the door looked her over so superciliously that Patty flushed with indignation. "The gentleman who is visiting Mr. Reid," she said crisply. "I can't remember his name, but I've come to interview him on behalf of the *Chronicle*. Is he in?"

"If you mean Mr. Reefer, he is," said the maid quite respectfully. Evidently the *Chronicle*'s name carried weight in the Reid establishment. "Please come into the library. I'll go and tell him."

Patty had just time to seat herself at the table, spread out her paper imposingly, and assume a businesslike air when Mr. Reefer came in. He was a tall, handsome old man with white hair, jet-black eyes, and a mouth that made Patty hope she wouldn't stumble on any questions he wouldn't want to answer. Patty knew she would waste her breath if she did. A man with a mouth like that would never tell anything he didn't want to tell.

"Good afternoon. What can I do for you, madam?" inquired Mr. Reefer with the air and tone of a man who means to be courteous, but has no time or information to waste.

Patty was almost overcome by the "Madam." For a moment, she quailed. She couldn't ask that masculine sphinx questions! Then the thought of her mother's pale, careworn face flashed across her mind, and all her courage came back with an inspiriting rush. She bent forward to look eagerly into Mr. Reefer's carved, granite face, and said with a frank smile:

"I have come to interview you on behalf of the *Chronicle* about the railroad bill. It was my brother who had the assignment, but he has missed his train and I have come in his place because, you see, it is so important to us. So much depends on this assignment. Perhaps Mr. Harmer will give Clifford a permanent place on the staff if he turns in a good article about you. He is only handyman now. I just couldn't let him miss the chance—he might never have another. And it means so much to us and Mother."

"Are you a member of the *Chronicle* staff yourself?" inquired Mr. Reefer with a shade more geniality in his tone.

"Oh, no! I've nothing to do with it, so you won't mind my being inexperienced, will you? I don't know just what I should ask you, so won't you please just tell me everything about the bill, and Mr. Harmer can cut out what doesn't matter?"

Mr. Reefer looked at Patty for a few moments with a face about as expressive as a graven image. Perhaps he was thinking about the bill, and perhaps he was thinking what a bright, vivid, plucky little girl this was with her waiting pencil and her air that strove to be businesslike, and only succeeded in being eager and hopeful and anxious.

"I'm not used to being interviewed myself," he said slowly, "so I don't know very much about it. We're both green hands together, I imagine. But I'd like to help you out, so I don't mind telling you what I think about this bill, and its bearing on certain important interests."

Mr. Reefer proceeded to tell her, and Patty's pencil flew as she scribbled down his terse, pithy sentences. She found herself asking questions too, and enjoying it. For the first time, Patty thought she might rather like politics if she understood them—and they did not seem so hard to understand when a man like Mr. Reefer explained them. For half an hour he talked to her, and at the end of that time Patty was in full possession of his opinion on the famous railroad bill in all its aspects.

"There now, I'm talked out," said Mr. Reefer. "You can tell your news editor that you know as much about the railroad bill as Andrew Reefer knows. I hope you'll succeed in pleasing him, and that your brother will get the position he wants. But he shouldn't have missed that train. You tell him that. Boys with important things to do mustn't miss trains. Perhaps it's just as well he did in this case though, but tell him not to let it happen again."

Patty went straight home, wrote up her interview in ship-shape form, and took it down to the *Chronicle* office. There she found Mr. Harmer, scowling blackly. The little news editor looked to be in a rather bad temper, but he nodded not unkindly to Patty. Mr. Harmer knew the Baxters well and liked them, although he would have sacrificed them all without a qualm for a "scoop."

"Good evening, Patty. Take a chair. That brother of yours hasn't turned up yet. The next time I give him an assignment, he'll manage to be on hand in time to do it."

"Oh," cried Patty breathlessly, "please, Mr. Harmer, I have the interview here. I thought perhaps I could do it in Clifford's place, and I went out to Mr. Reid's and saw Mr. Reefer. He was very kind and—"

"Mr. who?" fairly shouted Mr. Harmer.

"Mr. Reefer—Mr. Andrew Reefer. He told me to tell you that this article contained all he knew or thought about the railroad bill and—"

But Mr. Harmer was no longer listening. He had snatched the neatly written sheets of Patty's report and was skimming over them with a practised eye. Then Patty thought he must have gone crazy. He danced around the office, waving the sheets in the air, and then he dashed frantically up the stairs to the composing room.

Ten minutes later, he returned and shook the mystified Patty by the hand.

"Patty, it's the biggest beat we've ever had! We've scooped not only the *Ledger*, but every other newspaper in the country. How did you do it? How did you ever beguile or bewitch Andrew Reefer into giving you an interview?"

"Why," said Patty in utter bewilderment, "I just went out to Mr. Reid's and asked for the gentleman who was visiting there—I'd forgotten his name—and Mr. Reefer came down and I told him my brother had been detailed to interview him on behalf of the *Chronicle* about the bill, and that Clifford had missed his train, and wouldn't he let me interview him in his place and excuse my inexperience—and he did."

"It wasn't Andrew Reefer I told Clifford to interview," laughed Mr. Harmer. "It was John C. Keefe. I didn't know Reefer was in town, but even if I had I wouldn't have thought it a particle of use to send a man to him. He has never consented to be interviewed before on any known subject, and he's been especially close-mouthed about this bill, although men from all the big papers in the country have been after him. He is notorious on that score. Why, Patty, it's the biggest journalistic fish that has ever been landed in this office. Andrew Reefer's opinion on the bill will have a tremendous influence. We'll run the interview as a leader in a special edition that is under way already. Of course, he must have been ready to give the information to the public or nothing would have induced him to open his mouth. But to think that we should be the first to get it! Patty, you're a brick!"

Clifford came home on the seven o'clock train, and Patty was there to meet him, brimful of her story. But Clifford also had a story to tell and got his word in first.

"Now, Patty, don't scold until you hear why I missed the train. I met Mr. Peabody of the Steel and Iron Company at Mr. Moreland's and got into conversation with him. When he found out who I was, he was greatly interested and said Father had been one of his best friends when they were at college together. I told him about wanting to get the position in the company, and he had me go right out to the works and see about it. And, Patty, I have the place. Goodbye to the grind of newspaper items and fillers. I tried to get back to the station at Bancroft in time to catch the train but I couldn't, and it was just as well, for Mr. Keefe was suddenly summoned home this afternoon, and when the three-thirty train from town stopped at Bancroft he was on it. I found that out and I got on, going to the next station with him and getting my interview after all. It's here in my notebook, and I must hurry up to the office and hand it in. I suppose Mr. Harmer will be very much vexed until he finds that I have it."

"Oh, no. Mr. Harmer is in a very good humour," said Patty with dancing eyes. Then she told her story.

The interview with Mr. Reefer came out with glaring headlines, and the *Chronicle* had its hour of fame and glory. The next day Mr. Harmer sent word to Patty that he wanted to see her.

"So Clifford is leaving," he said abruptly when she entered the office. "Well, do you want his place?"

"Mr. Harmer, are you joking?" demanded Patty in amazement.

"Not I. That stuff you handed in was splendidly written—I didn't have to use the pencil more than once or twice. You have the proper journalist instinct all right. We need a lady on the staff anyhow, and if you'll take the place it's yours for saying so, and the permanency next month."

"I'll take it," said Patty promptly and joyfully.

"Good. Go down to the Symphony Club rehearsal this afternoon and report it. You've just ten minutes to get there," and Patty joyfully and promptly departed.

Anna's Love Letters

"Are you going to answer Gilbert's letter tonight, Anna?" asked Alma Williams, standing in the pantry doorway, tall, fair, and grey-eyed, with the sunset light coming down over the dark firs, through the window behind her, and making a primrose nimbus around her shapely head.

Anna, dark, vivid, and slender, was perched on the edge of the table, idly swinging her slippered foot at the cat's head. She smiled wickedly at Alma before replying.

"I am not going to answer it tonight or any other night," she said, twisting her full, red lips in a way that Alma had learned to dread. Mischief was ripening in Anna's brain when that twist was out.

"What do you mean?" asked Alma anxiously.

"Just what I say, dear," responded Anna, with deceptive meekness. "Poor Gilbert is gone, and I don't intend to bother my head about him any longer. He was amusing while he lasted, but of what use is a beau two thousand miles away, Alma?"

Alma was patient—outwardly. It was never of any avail to show impatience with Anna.

"Anna, you are talking foolishly. Of course you are going to answer his letter. You are as good as engaged to him. Wasn't that practically understood when he left?"

"No, no, dear," and Anna shook her sleek black head with the air of explaining matters to an obtuse child. "*I* was the only one who understood. Gil *mis*understood. He thought that I would really wait for him until he should have made enough money to come home and pay off the mortgage. I let him think so, because I hated to hurt his little feelings. But now it's off with the old love and on with a new one for me."

"Anna, you cannot be in earnest!" exclaimed Alma.

But she was afraid that Anna was in earnest. Anna had a wretched habit of being in earnest when she said flippant things.

"You don't mean that you are not going to write to Gilbert at all—after all you promised?"

Anna placed her elbows daintily on the top of the rocking chair, dropped her pointed chin in her hands, and looked at Alma with black demure eyes.

"I—do—mean—just—that," she said slowly. "I never mean to marry Gilbert Murray. This is final, Alma, and you need not scold or coax, because it would be a waste of breath. Gilbert is safely out of the way, and now I am going to have a good time with a few other delightful men creatures in Exeter."

Anna nodded decisively, flashed a smile at Alma, picked up her cat, and went out. At the door she turned and looked back, with the big black cat snuggled under her chin.

"If you think Gilbert will feel very badly over his letter not being answered, you might answer it yourself, Alma," she said teasingly. "There it is"—she took the letter from the pocket of her ruffled apron and threw it on a chair. "You may read it if you want to; it isn't really a love letter. I told Gilbert he wasn't to write silly letters. Come, pussy, I'm going to get ready for prayer meeting. We've got a nice, new, young, good-looking minister in Exeter, pussy, and that makes prayer meeting *very* interesting."

Anna shut the door, her departing laugh rippling mockingly through the dusk. Alma picked up Gilbert Murray's letter and went to her room. She wanted to cry, since she could not shake Anna. Even if she could have shook her, it would only have made her more perverse. Anna was in earnest; Alma knew that, even while she hoped and believed that it was but the earnestness of a freak that would pass in time. Anna had had one like it a year ago, when she had cast Gilbert off for three months, driving him distracted by flirting with Charlie Moore. Then she had suddenly repented and taken him back. Alma thought that this whim would run its course likewise and leave a repentant Anna. But meanwhile everything might be spoiled. Gilbert might not prove forgiving a second time.

Alma would have given much if she could only have induced Anna to answer Gilbert's letter, but coaxing Anna to do anything was a very sure and effective way of preventing her from doing it.

Alma and Anna had lived alone at the old Williams homestead ever since their mother's death four years before. Exeter matrons thought this hardly proper, since Alma, in spite of her grave ways, was only twenty-four. The farm was rented, so that Alma's only responsibilities were the post office which she kept, and that harum-scarum beauty of an Anna.

The Murray homestead adjoined theirs. Gilbert Murray had grown up with Alma; they had been friends ever since she could remember. Alma loved Gilbert with a love which she herself believed to be purely sisterly, and which nobody else doubted could be, since she had been at pains to make a match—Exeter matrons' phrasing—between Gil and Anna, and was manifestly delighted when Gilbert obligingly fell in love with the latter.

There was a small mortgage on the Murray place which Mr. Murray senior had not been able to pay off. Gilbert determined to get rid of it, and his thoughts turned to the west. His father was an active, hale old man, quite capable of managing the farm in Gilbert's absence. Alexander MacNair had gone to the west two years previously and got work on a new railroad. He wrote to Gilbert to come too, promising him plenty of work and good pay. Gilbert went, but before going he had asked Anna to marry him.

It was the first proposal Anna had ever had, and she managed it quite cleverly, from her standpoint. She told Gilbert that he must wait until he came home again before settling that, meanwhile, they would be *very* good friends—emphasized with a blush—and that he might write to her. She kissed him goodbye, and Gilbert, honest fellow, was quite satisfied. When an Exeter girl had allowed so much to be inferred, it was understood to be equivalent to an engagement. Gilbert had never discerned that Anna was not like the other Exeter girls, but was a law unto herself.

Alma sat down by her window and looked out over the lane where the slim wild cherry trees were bronzing under the autumn frosts. Her lips were very firmly set. Something must be done. But what?

Alma's heart was set on this marriage for two reasons. Firstly, if Anna married Gilbert she would be near her all her life. She could not bear the thought that some day Anna might leave her and go far away to live. In the second and largest place, she desired the marriage because Gilbert did. She had always been desirous, even in the old, childish play-days, that Gilbert should get just exactly what he wanted. She had always taken a keen, strange delight in furthering his wishes.

Anna's falseness would surely break his heart, and Alma winced at the thought of his pain.

There was one thing she could do. Anna's tormenting suggestion had fallen on fertile soil. Alma balanced pros and cons, admitting the risk. But she would have taken a tenfold larger risk in the hope of holding secure Anna's place in Gilbert's affections until Anna herself should come to her senses.

When it grew quite dark and Anna had gone lilting down the lane on her way to prayer meeting, Alma lighted her lamp, read Gilbert's letter—and answered it. Her handwriting was much like Anna's. She signed the letter "A. Williams," and there was nothing in it that might not have been written by her to Gilbert; but she knew that Gilbert would believe Anna had written it, and she intended him so to believe. Alma never did a thing halfway when she did it at all. At first she wrote rather constrainedly but, reflecting that in any case Anna would have written a merely friendly letter, she allowed her thoughts to run freely, and the resulting epistle was an excellent one of its kind. Alma had the gift of expression and more brains than Exeter people had ever imagined she possessed. When Gilbert read that letter a fortnight later he was surprised to find that Anna was so clever. He had always, with a secret regret, thought her much inferior to Alma in this respect, but that delightful letter, witty, wise, fanciful, was the letter of a clever woman.

When a year had passed Alma was still writing to Gilbert the letters signed "A. Williams." She had ceased to fear being found out, and she took a strange pleasure in the correspondence for its own sake. At first she had been quakingly afraid of discovery. When she smuggled the letters addressed in Gilbert's handwriting to Miss Anna Williams out of the letter packet and hid them from Anna's eyes, she felt as guilty as if she were breaking all the laws of the land at once. To be sure, she knew that she would have to confess to Anna some day, when the latter repented and began to wish she had written to Gilbert, but that was a very different thing from premature disclosure.

But Anna had as yet given no sign of such repentance, although Alma looked for it anxiously. Anna was having the time of her life. She was the acknowledged beauty of five settlements, and she went forward on her career of conquest quite undisturbed by the jealousies and heart-burnings she provoked on every side.

One moonlight night she went for a sleigh-drive with Charlie Moore of East Exeter—and returned to tell Alma that they were married!

"I knew you would make a fuss, Alma, because you don't like Charlie, so we just took matters into our own hands. It was so much more romantic, too. I'd always said I'd never be married in any of your dull, commonplace ways. You might as well forgive me and be nice right off, Alma, because you'd have to do it anyway, in time. Well, you do look surprised!"

Alma accepted the situation with an apathy that amazed Anna. The truth was that Alma was stunned by a thought that had come to her even while Anna was speaking.

"Gilbert will find out about the letters now, and despise me."

Nothing else, not even the fact that Anna had married shiftless Charlie Moore, seemed worth while considering beside this. The fear and shame of it haunted her like a nightmare; she shrank every morning from the thought of all the mail that was coming that day, fearing that there would be an angry, puzzled letter from Gilbert. He must certainly soon hear of Anna's marriage; he would see it in the home paper, other correspondents in Exeter would write him of it. Alma grew sick at heart thinking of the complications in front of her.

When Gilbert's letter came she left it for a whole day before she could summon courage to open it. But it was a harmless epistle after all; he had not yet heard of Anna's marriage. Alma had at first no thought of answering it, yet her fingers ached to do so. Now that Anna was gone, her loneliness was unbearable. She realized how much Gilbert's letters had meant to her, even when written to another woman. She could bear her life well enough, she thought, if she only had his letters to look forward to.

No more letters came from Gilbert for six weeks. Then came one, alarmed at Anna's silence, anxiously asking the reason for it; Gilbert had heard no word of the marriage. He was working in a remote district where newspapers seldom penetrated. He had no other correspondent in Exeter now; except his mother, and she, not knowing that he supposed himself engaged to Anna had forgotten to mention it.

Alma answered that letter. She told herself recklessly that she would keep on writing to him until he found out. She would lose his friendship anyhow, when that occurred, but meanwhile she would have the letters a little longer. She could not learn to live without them until she had to.

The correspondence slipped back into its old groove. The harassed look which Alma's face had worn, and which Exeter people had attributed to worry over Anna, disappeared. She did not even feel lonely, and reproached herself for lack of proper feeling in missing Anna so little. Besides, to her horror and dismay, she detected in herself a strange undercurrent of relief at the thought that Gilbert could never marry Anna now! She could not understand it. Had not that marriage been her dearest wish for years? Why then should she feel this strange gladness at the impossibility of its fulfilment? Altogether, Alma feared that her condition of mind and morals must be sadly askew. Perhaps, she thought mournfully, this perversion of proper feeling was her punishment for the deception she had practised. She had deliberately done evil that good might come, and now the very imaginations of her heart were stained by that evil. Alma cried herself to sleep many a night in her repentance, but she kept on writing to Gilbert, for all that.

The winter passed, and the spring and summer waned, and Alma's outward life flowed as smoothly as the currents of the seasons, broken only by vivid eruptions from Anna, who came over often from East Exeter, glorying in her young matronhood, "to cheer Alma up." Alma, so said Exeter people, was becoming unsociable and old maidish. She lost her liking for company, and seldom went anywhere among her neighbours. Her once frequent visits across the yard to chat with old Mrs. Murray became few and far between. She could not bear to hear the old lady talking about Gilbert, and she was afraid that some day she would be told that he was coming home. Gilbert's home-coming was the nightmare dread that darkened poor Alma's whole horizon.

One October day, two years after Gilbert's departure, Alma, standing at her window in the reflected glow of a red maple outside, looked down the lane and saw him striding up it! She had had no warning of his coming. His last letter, dated three weeks back, had not hinted at it. Yet there he was—and with him Alma's Nemesis.

She was very calm. Now that the worst had come, she felt quite strong to meet it. She would tell Gilbert the truth, and he would go away in anger and never forgive her, but she deserved it. As she went downstairs, the only thing that really worried her was the thought of the pain Gilbert would suffer when she told him of Anna's faithlessness. She had seen his face as he passed under her window, and it was the face of a blithe man who had not heard any evil tidings. It was left to her to tell him; surely, she thought apathetically, that was punishment enough for what she had done.

With her hand on the doorknob, she paused to wonder what she should say when he asked her why she had not told him of Anna's marriage when it occurred—why she had still continued the deception when it had no longer an end to serve. Well, she would tell him the truth—that it was because she could not bear the thought of giving up writing to him. It was a humiliating thing to confess, but that did not matter—nothing mattered now. She opened the door.

Gilbert was standing on the big round door-stone under the red maple—a tall, handsome young fellow with a bronzed face and laughing eyes. His exile had improved him. Alma found time and ability to reflect that she had never known Gilbert was so fine-looking.

He put his arm around her and kissed her cheek in his frank delight at seeing her again. Alma coldly asked him in. Her face was still as pale as when she came downstairs, but a curious little spot of fiery red blossomed out where Gilbert's lips had touched it.

Gilbert followed her into the sitting-room and looked about eagerly.

"When did you come home?" she said slowly. "I did not know you were expected."

"Got homesick, and just came! I wanted to surprise you all," he answered, laughing. "I arrived only a few minutes ago. Just took time to hug my mother, and here I am. Where's Anna?"

The pent-up retribution of two years descended on Alma's head in the last question of Gilbert's. But she did not flinch. She stood straight before him, tall and fair and pale, with the red maple light streaming in through the open door behind her, staining her light house-dress and mellowing the golden sheen of her hair. Gilbert reflected that Alma Williams was really a very handsome girl. These two years had improved her. What splendid big grey eyes she had! He had always wished that Anna's eyes had not been quite so black.

"Anna is not here," said Alma. "She is married."

"Married!"

Gilbert sat down suddenly on a chair and looked at Alma in bewilderment.

"She has been married for a year," said Alma steadily. "She married Charlie Moore of East Exeter, and has been living there ever since."

"Then," said Gilbert, laying hold of the one solid fact that loomed out of the mist of his confused understanding, "why did she keep on writing letters to me after she was married?"

"She never wrote to you at all. It was I that wrote the letters."

Gilbert looked at Alma doubtfully. Was she crazy? There was something odd about her, now that he noticed, as she stood rigidly there, with that queer red spot on her face, a strange fire in her eyes, and that weird reflection from the maple enveloping her like an immaterial flame.

"I don't understand," he said helplessly.

Still standing there, Alma told the whole story, giving full explanations, but no excuses. She told it clearly and simply, for she had often pictured this scene to herself and thought out what she must say. Her memory worked automatically, and her tongue obeyed it promptly. To herself she seemed like a machine, talking mechanically, while her soul stood on one side and listened.

When she had finished there was a silence lasting perhaps ten seconds. To Alma it seemed like hours. Would Gilbert overwhelm her with angry reproaches, or would he simply rise up and leave her in unutterable contempt? It was the most tragic moment of her life, and her whole personality was strung up to meet it and withstand it.

"Well, they were good letters, anyhow," said Gilbert finally; "interesting letters," he added, as if by way of a meditative afterthought.

It was so anti-climactic that Alma broke into an hysterical giggle, cut short by a sob. She dropped into a chair by the table and flung her hands over her face, laughing and sobbing softly to herself. Gilbert rose and walked to the door, where he stood with his back to her until she regained her self-control. Then he turned and looked down at her quizzically.

Alma's hands lay limply in her lap, and her eyes were cast down, with tears glistening on the long fair lashes. She felt his gaze on her.

"Can you ever forgive me, Gilbert?" she said humbly.

"I don't know that there is much to forgive," he answered. "I have some explanations to make too and, since we're at it, we might as well get them all over and have done with them. Two years ago I did honestly think I was in love with Anna—at least when I was round where she was. She had a taking way with her. But, somehow, even then, when I wasn't with her she seemed to kind of grow dim and not count for so awful much after all. I used to wish she was more like you—quieter, you know, and not so sparkling. When I parted from her that last night before I went west, I did feel very bad, and she seemed very dear to me, but it was six weeks from that before her—your—letter came, and in that time she seemed to have faded out of my thoughts. Honestly, I wasn't thinking much about her at all. Then came the letter—and it was a splendid one, too. I had never thought that Anna could write a letter like that, and I was as pleased as Punch about it. The letters kept coming, and I kept on looking for them more and more all the time. I fell in love all over again—with the writer of those letters. I thought it was Anna, but since you wrote the letters, it must have been with you, Alma. I thought it was because she was growing more womanly that she could write such letters. That was why I came home. I wanted to get acquainted all over again, before she grew beyond me altogether—I wanted to find the real Anna the letters showed me. I—I—didn't expect this. But I don't care if Anna is married, so long as the girl who wrote those letters isn't. It's you I love, Alma."

He bent down and put his arm about her, laying his cheek against hers. The little red spot where his kiss had fallen was now quite drowned out in the colour that rushed over her face.

"If you'll marry me, Alma, I'll forgive you," he said.

A little smile escaped from the duress of Alma's lips and twitched her dimples.

"I'm willing to do anything that will win your forgiveness, Gilbert," she said meekly.

Aunt Caroline's Silk Dress

Patty came in from her walk to the post office with cheeks finely reddened by the crisp air. Carry surveyed her with pleasure. Of late Patty's cheeks had been entirely too pale to please Carry, and Patty had not had a very good appetite. Once or twice she had even complained of a headache. So Carry had sent her to the office for a walk that night, although the post office trip was usually Carry's own special constitutional, always very welcome to her after a weary day of sewing on other people's pretty dresses.

Carry never sewed on pretty dresses for herself, for the simple reason that she never had any pretty dresses. Carry was twenty-two—and feeling forty, her last pretty dress had been when she was a girl of twelve, before her father had died. To be sure, there was the silk organdie Aunt Kathleen had sent her, but that was fit only for parties, and Carry never went to any parties.

"Did you get any mail, Patty?" she asked unexpectantly. There was never much mail for the Lea girls.

"Yes'm," said Patty briskly. "Here's the *Weekly Advocate*, and a patent medicine almanac with all your dreams expounded, *and* a letter for Miss Carry M. Lea. It's postmarked Enfield, and has a suspiciously matrimonial look. I'm sure it's an invitation to Chris Fairley's wedding. Hurry up and see, Caddy."

Carry, with a little flush of excitement on her face, opened her letter. Sure enough, it contained an invitation "to be present at the marriage of Christine Fairley."

"How jolly!" exclaimed Patty. "Of course you'll go, Caddy. You'll have a chance to wear that lovely organdie of yours at last."

"It was sweet of Chris to invite me," said Carry. "I really didn't expect it."

"Well, I did. Wasn't she your most intimate friend when she lived in Enderby?"

"Oh, yes, but it is four years since she left, and some people might forget in four years. But I might have known Chris wouldn't. Of course I'll go."

"And you'll make up your organdie?"

"I shall have to," laughed Carry, forgetting all her troubles for a moment, and feeling young and joyous over the prospect of a festivity. "I haven't another thing that would do to wear to a wedding. If I hadn't that blessed organdie I couldn't go, that's all."

"But you have it, and it will look lovely made up with a tucked skirt. Tucks are so fashionable now. And there's that lace of mine you can have for a bertha. I want you to look just right, you see. Enfield is a big place, and there will be lots of grandees at the wedding. Let's get the last fashion sheet and pick out a design right away. Here's one on the very first page that would be nice. You could wear it to perfection, Caddy you're so tall and slender. It wouldn't suit a plump and podgy person like myself at all."

Carry liked the pattern, and they had an animated discussion over it. But, in the end, Carry sighed, and pushed the sheet away from her, with all the brightness gone out of face.

"It's no use, Patty. I'd forgotten for a few minutes, but it's all come back now. I can't think of weddings and new dresses, when the thought of that interest crowds everything else out. It's due next month—fifty dollars—and I've only ten saved up. I can't make forty dollars in a month, even if I had any amount of sewing, and you know hardly any-one wants sewing done just now. I don't know what we shall do. Oh, I suppose we can rent a couple of rooms in the village and *exist* in them. But it breaks my heart to think of leaving our old home."

"Perhaps Mr. Kerr will let us have more time," suggested Patty, not very hopefully. The sparkle had gone out of her face too. Patty loved their little home as much as Carry did.

"You know he won't. He has been only too anxious for an excuse to foreclose, this long time. He wants the land the house is on. Oh, if I only hadn't been sick so long in the summer—just when everybody had sewing to do. I've tried so hard to catch up, but I couldn't." Carry's voice broke in a sob.

Patty leaned over the table and patted her sister's glossy dark hair gently.

"You've worked too hard, dearie. You've just gone to skin and bone. Oh, I know how hard it is! I can't bear to think of leaving this dear old spot either. If we could only induce Mr. Kerr to give us a year's grace! I'd be teaching then, and we could easily pay the interest and some of the principal too. Perhaps he will if we both go to him and coax very hard. Anyway, don't worry over it till after the wedding. I want you to go and have a good time. You never have good times, Carry."

"Neither do you," said Carry rebelliously. "You never have anything that other girls have, Patty—not even pretty clothes."

"Deed, and I've lots of things to be thankful for," said Patty cheerily. "Don't you fret about me. I'm vain enough to think I've got some brains anyway, and I'm a-meaning to do something with them too. Now I think I'll go upstairs and study this evening. It will be warm enough there tonight, and the noise of the machine rather bothers me."

Patty whisked out, and Carry knew she should go to her sewing. But she sat a long while at the table in dismal thought. She was so tired, and so hopeless. It had been such a hard struggle, and it seemed now as if it would all come to naught. For five years, ever since her mother's death, Carry had supported herself and Patty by dressmaking. They had been a hard five years of pinching and economizing and going without, for Enderby was only a small place, and there were two other dressmakers. Then there was always the mortgage to devour everything. Carry had kept it at bay till now, but at last she was conquered. She had had typhoid fever in the spring and had not been able to work for a long time. Indeed, she had gone to work before she should. The doctor's bill was yet unpaid, but Dr. Hamilton had told her to take her time. Carry knew she would not be pressed for that, and next year Patty would be able to help her. But next year would be too late. The dear little home would be lost then.

When Carry roused herself from her sad reflections, she saw a crumpled note lying on the floor. She picked it up and absently smoothed it out. Seeing Patty's name at the top she was about to lay it aside without reading it, but the lines were few, and the sense of them flashed into Carry's brain. The note was an invitation to Clare Forbes's party! The Lea girls had known that the Forbes girls were going to give a party, but they had not expected that Patty would be invited. Of course, Clare Forbes was in Patty's class at school and was always very nice and friendly with her. But then the Forbes set was not the Lea set.

Carry ran upstairs to Patty's room. "Patty, you dropped this on the floor. I couldn't help seeing what it was. Why didn't you tell me Clare had invited you?"

"Because I knew I couldn't go, and I thought you would feel badly over that. Caddy, I wish you hadn't seen it."

"Oh, Patty, I *do* wish you could go to the party. It was so sweet of Clare to invite you, and perhaps she will be offended if you don't go—she won't understand. Clare Forbes isn't a girl whose friendship is to be lightly thrown away when it is offered."

"I know that. But, Caddy dear, it is impossible. I don't think that I have any foolish pride about clothes, but you know it is out of the question to think of going to Clare Forbes's party in my last winter's plaid dress, which is a good two inches too short and skimpy in proportion. Putting my own feelings aside, it would be an insult to Clare. There, don't think any more about it."

But Carry did think about it. She lay awake half the night wondering if there might not be some way for Patty to go to that party. She knew it was impossible, unless Patty had a new dress, and how could a new dress be had? Yet she did so want Patty to go. Patty never had any good times, and she was studying so hard. Then, all at once, Carry thought of a way by which Patty might have a new dress. She had been tossing restlessly, but now she lay very still, staring with wide-open eyes at the moonlit window, with the big willow boughs branching darkly across it. Yes, it was a way, but could she? *Could* she? Yes, she could, and she would. Carry buried her face in her pillow with a sob and a gulp. But she had decided what must be done, and how it must be done.

"Are you going to begin on your organdic today?" asked Patty in the morning, before she started for school.

"I must finish Mrs. Pidgeon's suit first," Carry answered. "Next week will be time enough to think about my wedding garments."

She tried to laugh and failed. Patty thought with a pang that Carry looked horribly pale and tired—probably she had worried most of the night over the interest. "I'm so glad she's going to Chris's wedding," thought Patty, as she hurried down the street. "It will take her out of herself and give her something nice to think of for ever so long."

Nothing more was said that week about the organdie, or the wedding, or the Forbes's party. Carry sewed fiercely, and sat at her machine for hours after Patty had gone to bed. The night before the party she said to Patty, "Braid your hair tonight, Patty. You'll want it nice and wavy to go to the Forbes's tomorrow night."

Patty thought that Carry was actually trying to perpetrate a weak joke, and endeavoured to laugh. But it was a rather dreary laugh. Patty, after a hard evening's study, felt tired and discouraged, and she was really dreadfully disappointed about the party, although she wouldn't have let Carry suspect it for the world.

"You're going, you know," said Carry, as serious as a judge, although there was a little twinkle in her eyes.

"In a faded plaid two inches too short?" Patty smiled as brightly as possible.

"Oh, no. I have a dress all ready for you." Carry opened the wardrobe door and took out—the loveliest girlish dress of creamy organdie, with pale pink roses scattered over it, made with the daintiest of ruffles and tucks, with a bertha of soft creamy lace, and a girdle of white silk. "This is for you," said Carry.

Patty gazed at the dress with horror-stricken eyes. "Caroline Lea, *that is your organdie!* And you've gone and made it up for *me*! Carry Lea, what are you going to wear to the wedding?"

"Nothing. I'm not going."

"You are—you must—you shall. I won't take the organdie."

"You'll have to now, because it's made to fit you. Come, Patty dear, I've set my heart on your going to that party. You mustn't disappoint me—you *can't*, for what good would it do? I can never wear the dress now."

Patty realized that. She knew she might as well go to the party, but she did not feel much pleasure in the prospect. Nevertheless, when she was ready for it the next evening, she couldn't help a little thrill of delight. The dress was so pretty, and dainty, and becoming.

"You look sweet," exclaimed Carry admiringly. "There, I hear the Browns' carriage. Patty, I want you to promise me this—that you'll not let any thought of me, or my not going to the wedding, spoil your enjoyment this evening. I gave you the dress that you might have a good time, so don't make my gift of no effect."

"I'll try," promised Patty, flying downstairs, where her next-door neighbours were waiting for her.

At two o'clock that night Carry was awakened to see Patty bending over her, flushed and radiant. Carry sat sleepily up. "I hope you had a good time," she said.

"I had—oh, I had—but I didn't waken you out of your hard-earned slumbers at this wee sma' hour to tell you that. Carry, I've thought of a way for you to go to the wedding. It just came to me at supper. Mrs. Forbes was sitting opposite to me, and her dress suggested it. You must make over Aunt Caroline's silk dress."

"Nonsense," said Carry, a little crossly; even sweet-tempered people are sometimes cross when they are wakened up for—as it seemed—nothing.

"It's good plain sense. Of course, you must make it over and—"

"Patty Lea, you're crazy. I wouldn't dream of wearing that hideous thing. Bright green silk, with huge yellow brocade flowers as big as cabbages all over it! I think I see myself in it."

"Caddy, listen to me. You know there's enough of that black lace of mother's for the waist, and the big black lace shawl of Grandmother Lea's will do for the skirt. Make it over—"

"A plain slip of the silk," gasped Carry, her quick brain seizing on all the possibilities of the plan. "Why didn't I think of it before? It will be just the thing, the greens and yellow will be toned down to a nice shimmer under the black lace. And I'll make cuffs of black velvet with double puffs above—and just cut out a wee bit at the throat with a frill of lace and a band of black velvet ribbon around my neck. Patty Lea, it's an inspiration."

Carry was out of bed by daylight the next morning and, while Patty still slumbered, she mounted to the garret, and took Aunt Caroline's silk dress from the chest where it had lain forgotten for three years. Carry held it up at arm's length, and looked at it with amusement.

"It is certainly ugly, but with the lace over it it will look very different. There's enough of it, anyway, and that skirt is stiff enough to stand alone. Poor Aunt Caroline, I'm afraid I wasn't particularly grateful for her gift at the time, but I really am now."

Aunt Caroline, who had given the dress to Carry three years before, was, an old lady of eighty, the aunt of Carry's father. She had once possessed a snug farm but in an evil hour she had been persuaded to deed it to her nephew, Edward Curry, whom she had brought up. Poor Aunt Caroline had lived to regret this step, for everyone in Enderby knew that Edward Curry and his wife had repaid her with ingratitude and greed.

Carry, who was named for her, was her favourite grandniece and often went to see her, though such visits were coldly received by the Currys, who always took especial care never to leave Aunt Caroline alone with any of her relatives. On one occasion, when Carry was there, Aunt Caroline had brought out this silk dress.

"I'm going to give this to you, Carry," she said timidly. "It's a good silk, and not so very old. Mr. Greenley gave it to me for a birthday present fifteen years ago. Maybe you can make it over for yourself."

Mrs. Edward, who was on duty at the time, sniffed disagreeably, but she said nothing. The dress was of no value in her eyes, for the pattern was so ugly and old-fashioned that none of her smart daughters would have worn it. Had it been otherwise, Aunt Caroline would probably not have been allowed to give it away.

Carry had thanked Aunt Caroline sincerely. If she did not care much for the silk, she at least prized the kindly motive behind the gift. Perhaps she and Patty laughed a little over it as they packed it away in the garret. It was so very ugly, but Carry thought it was sweet of Aunt Caroline to have given her something. Poor old Aunt Caroline had died soon after, and Carry had not thought about the silk dress again. She had too many other things to think of, this poor worried Carry.

After breakfast Carry began to rip the skirt breadths apart. Snip, snip, went her scissors, while her thoughts roamed far afield—now looking forward with renewed pleasure to Christine's wedding, now dwelling dolefully on the mortgage. Patty, who was washing the dishes, knew just what her thoughts were by the light and shadow on her expressive face.

"Why!—what?" exclaimed Carry suddenly. Patty wheeled about to see Carry staring at the silk dress like one bewitched. Between the silk and the lining which she had just ripped apart was a twenty-dollar bill, and beside it a sheet of letter paper covered with writing in a cramped angular hand, both secured very carefully to the silk.

"Carry Lea!" gasped Patty.

With trembling fingers Carry snipped away the stitches that held the letter, and read it aloud.

> "My dear Caroline," it ran, "I do not know when you will find this letter and this money, but when you do it belongs to you. I have a hundred dollars which I always meant to give you because you were named for me. But Edward and his wife do not know I have it, and I don't want them to find out. They would not let me give it to you if they knew, so I have thought of this way of getting it to you. I have sewed five twenty-dollar bills under the lining of this skirt, and they are all yours, with your Aunt Caroline's best love. You were always a good girl, Carry, and you've worked hard, and I've given Edward enough. Just take this money and use it as you like.
>
> "Aunt Caroline Greenley."

"Carry Lea, are we both dreaming?" gasped Patty.

With crimson cheeks Carry ripped the other breadths apart, and there were the other four bills. Then she slipped down in a little heap on the sofa cushions and began to cry—happy tears of relief and gladness.

"We can pay the interest," said Patty, dancing around the room, "and get yourself a nice new dress for the wedding."

"Indeed I won't," said Carry, sitting up and laughing through her tears. "I'll make over this dress and wear it out of gratitude to the memory of dear Aunt Caroline."

Aunt Susanna's Thanksgiving Dinner.

"Here's Aunt Susanna, girls," said Laura who was sitting by the north window—nothing but north light does for Laura who is the artist of our talented family.

Each of us has a little pet new-fledged talent which we are faithfully cultivating in the hope that it will amount to something and soar highly some day. But it is difficult to cultivate four talents on our tiny income. If Laura wasn't such a good manager we never could do it.

Laura's words were a signal for Kate to hang up her violin and for me to push my pen and portfolio out of sight. Laura had hidden her brushes and water colors as she spoke. Only Margaret continued to bend serenely over her Latin grammar. Aunt Susanna frowns on musical and literary and artistic ambitions but she accords a faint approval to Margaret's desire for an education. A college course, with a tangible diploma at the end, and a sensible pedagogic aspiration is something Aunt Susanna can understand when she tries hard. But she cannot understand messing with paints, fiddling, or scribbling, and she has only unmeasured contempt for messers, fiddlers, and scribblers. Time was when we had paid no attention to Aunt Susanna's views on these points; but ever since she had, on one incautious day when she was in high good humor, dropped a pale, anemic little hint that she might send Margaret to college if she were a good girl we had been bending all our energies towards securing Aunt Susanna's approval. It was not enough that Aunt Susanna should approve of Margaret; she must approve of the whole four of us or she would not help Margaret. That is Aunt Susanna's way. Of late we had been growing a little discouraged. Aunt Susanna had recently read a magazine article which stated that the higher education of women was ruining our country and that a woman who was a B.A. couldn't, in the very nature of things, ever be a housewifely, cookly creature. Consequently, Margaret's chances looked a little foggy; but we hadn't quite given up hope. A very little thing might sway Aunt Susanna one way or the other, so that we walked very softly and tried to mingle serpents' wisdom and doves' harmlessness in practical portions.

When Aunt Susanna came in Laura was crocheting, Kate was sewing, and I was poring over a recipe book. That was not deception at all, since we did all these things frequently—much more frequently, in fact, than we painted or fiddled or wrote. But Aunt Susanna would never believe it. Nor did she believe it now.

She threw back her lovely new sealskin cape, looked around the sitting-room and then smiled—a truly Aunt Susannian smile.

"What a pity you forgot to wipe that smudge of paint off your nose, Laura," she said sarcastically. "You don't seem to get on very fast with your lace. How long is it since you began it? Over three months, isn't it?"

"This is the third piece of the same pattern I've done in three months, Aunt Susanna," said Laura presently. Laura is an old duck. She never gets cross and snaps back. I do; and it's so hard not to with Aunt Susanna sometimes. But I generally manage it for I'd do anything for Margaret. Laura did not tell Aunt Susanna that she sold her lace at the Women's Exchange in town and made enough to buy her new hats. She makes enough out of her water colors to dress herself.

Aunt Susanna took a second breath and started in again.

"I notice your violin hasn't quite as much dust on it as the rest of the things in this room, Kate. It's a pity you stopped playing just as I came in. I don't enjoy fiddling much but I'd prefer it to seeing anyone using a needle who isn't accustomed to it."

Kate is really a most dainty needlewoman and does all the fine sewing in our family. She colored and said nothing—that being the highest pitch of virtue to which our Katie, like myself, can attain.

"And there's Margaret ruining her eyes over books," went on Aunt Susanna severely. "Will you kindly tell me, Margaret Thorne, what good you ever expect Latin to do you?"

"Well, you see, Aunt Susanna," said Margaret gently—Magsie and Laura are birds of a feather—"I want to be a teacher if I can manage to get through, and I shall need Latin for that."

All the girls except me had now got their accustomed rap, but I knew better than to hope I should escape.

"So you're reading a recipe book, Agnes? Well, that's better than poring over a novel. I'm afraid you haven't been at it very long though. People generally don't read recipes upside down—and besides, you didn't quite cover up your portfolio. I see a corner of it sticking out. Was genius burning before I came in? It's too bad if I quenched the flame."

"A cookery book isn't such a novelty to me as you seem to think, Aunt Susanna," I said, as meekly as it was possible for me. "Why I'm a real good cook—'if I do say it as hadn't orter.'"

I am, too.

"Well, I'm glad to hear it," said Aunt Susanna skeptically, "because that has to do with my errand her to-day. I'm in a peck of troubles. Firstly, Miranda Mary's mother has had to go and get sick and Miranda Mary must go home to wait on her. Secondly, I've just had a telegram from my sister-in-law who has been ordered west for her health, and I'll have to leave on to-night's train to see her before she goes. I can't get back until the noon train Thursday, and that is Thanksgiving, and I've invited Mr. and Mrs. Gilbert to dinner that day. They'll come on the same train. I'm dreadfully worried. There doesn't seem to be anything I can do except get on of you girls to go up to the Pinery Thursday morning and cook the dinner for us. Do you think you can manage it?"

We all felt rather dismayed, and nobody volunteered with a rush. But as I had just boasted that I could cook it was plainly my duty to step into the breach, and I did it with fear and trembling.

"I'll go, Aunt Susanna," I said.

"And I'll help you," said Kate.

"Well, I suppose I'll have to try you," said Aunt Susanna with the air of a woman determined to make the best of a bad business. "Here is the key of the kitchen door. You'll find everything in the pantry, turkey and all. The mince pies are all ready made so you'll only have to warm them up. I want dinner sharp at twelve for the train is due at 11:50. Mr. and Mrs. Gilbert are very particular and I do hope you will have things right. Oh, if I could only be home myself! Why will people get sick at such inconvenient times?"

"Don't worry, Aunt Susanna," I said comfortingly. "Kate and I will have your Thanksgiving dinner ready for you in tiptop style."

"Well I'm sure I hope so. Don't get to mooning over a story, Agnes. I'll lock the library up and fortunately there are no fiddles at the Pinery. Above all, don't let any of the McGinnises in. They'll be sure to be prowling around when I'm not home. Don't give that dog of theirs any scraps either. That is Miranda Mary's one fault. She will feed that dog in spite of all I can do and I can't walk out of my own back door without falling over him."

We promise to eschew the McGinnises and all their works, including the dog, and when Aunt Susanna had gone we looked at each other with mingled hope and fear.

"Girls, this is the chance of your lives," said Laura. "If you can only please Aunt Susanna with this dinner it will convince her that you are good cooks in spite of your nefarious bent for music and literature. I consider the illness of Miranda Mary's mother a Providential interposition—that is, if she isn't too sick."

"It's all very well for you to be pleased, Lolla," I said dolefully. "But I don't feel jubilant over the prospect at all. Something will probably go wrong. And then there's our own nice little Thanksgiving celebration we've planned, and pinched and economized for weeks to provide. That is half spoiled now."

"Oh, what is that compared to Margaret's chance of going to college?" exclaimed Kate. "Cheer up, Aggie. You know we can cook. I feel that it is now or never with Aunt Susanna."

I cheered up accordingly. We are not given to pessimism which is fortunate. Ever since father died four years ago we have struggled on here, content to give up a good deal just to keep our home and be together. This little gray house—oh, how we do love it and its apple trees—is ours and we have, as aforesaid, a tiny income and our ambitions; not very big ambitions but big enough to give zest to our lives and hope to the future. We've been very happy as a rule. Aunt Susanna has a big house and lots of money but she isn't as happy as we are. She nags us a good deal—just as she used to nag father—but we don't mind it very much after all. Indeed, I sometimes suspect that we really like Aunt Susanna tremendously if she'd only leave us alone long enough to find it out.

Thursday morning was an ideal Thanksgiving morning—bright, crisp and sparkling. There had been a white frost in the night, and the orchard and the white birch wood behind it looked like fairyland. We were all up early. None of us had slept well, and both Kate and I had had the most fearful dreams of spoiling Aunt Susanna's Thanksgiving dinner.

"Never mind, dreams always go by contraries, you know," said Laura cheerfully. "You'd better go up to the Pinery early and get the fires on, for the house will be cold. Remember the McGinnises and the dog. Weigh the turkey so that you'll know exactly how long to cook it. Put the pies in the oven in time to get piping hot—lukewarm mince pies are an abomination. Be sure—"

"Laura, don't confuse us with any more cautions," I groaned, "or we shall get hopelessly fuddled. Come on, Kate, before she has time to."

It wasn't very far up to the Pinery—just ten minutes' walk, and such a delightful walk on that delightful morning. We went through the orchard and then through the white birch wood where the loveliness of the frosted boughs awed us. Beyond that there was a lane between ranks of young, balsamy, white-misted firs and then an open pasture field, sere and crispy. Just across it was the Pinery, a lovely old house with dormer windows in the roof, surrounded by pines that were dark and glorious against the silvery morning sky.

The McGinnis dog was sitting on the back-door steps when we arrived. He wagged his tail ingratiatingly, but we ruthlessly pushed him off, went in and shut the door in his face. All the little McGinnises were sitting in a row on their fence, and they whooped derisively. The McGinnis manners are not those which appertain to the caste of Vere de Vere; but we rather like the urchins—there are eight of them—and we would probably have gone over to talk to them if we had not had the fear of Aunt Susanna before our eyes.

We kindled the fires, weighed the turkey, put it in the oven and prepared the vegetables. Then we set the dining-room table and decorated it with Aunt Susanna's potted ferns and dishes of lovely red apples. Everything went so smoothly that we soon forgot to be nervous. When the turkey was done, we took it out, set it on the back of the range to keep warm and put the mince pies in. The potatoes, cabbage and turnips were bubbling away cheerfully, and everything was going as merrily as a marriage bell. Then, all at once, things happened.

In an evil hour we went to the yard window and looked out. We saw a quiet scene. The McGinnis dog was still sitting on his haunches by the steps, just as he had been sitting all the morning. Down in the McGinnis yard everything wore an unusually peaceful aspect. Only one McGinnis was in sight—Tony, aged eight, who was perched up on the edge of the well box, swinging his legs and singing at the top of his melodious Irish voice. All at once, just as we were looking at him, Tony went over backward and apparently tumbled head foremost down his father's well.

Kate and I screamed simultaneously. We tore across the kitchen, flung open the door, plunged down over Aunt Susanna's yard, scrambled over the fence and flew to the well. Just as we reached it, Tony's red head appeared as he climbed serenely out over the box. I don't know whether I felt more relieved or furious. He had merely fallen on the blank guard inside the box: and there are times when I am tempted to think he fell on purpose because he saw Kate and me looking out at the window. At least he didn't seem at all frightened, and grinned most impishly at us.

Kate and I turned on our heels and marched back in as dignified a manner as was possible under the circumstances. Half way up Aunt Susanna's yard we forgot dignity and broke into a run. We had left the door open and the McGinnis dog had disappeared.

Never shall I forget the sight we saw or the smell we smelled when we burst into that kitchen. There on the floor was the McGinnis dog and what was left of Aunt Susanna's Thanksgiving turkey. As for the smell, imagine a commingled odor of scorching turnips and burning mince pies, and you have it.

The dog fled out with a guilty yelp. I groaned and snatched the turnips off. Kate threw open the oven door and dragged out the pies. Pies and turnips were ruined as irretrievably as the turkey.

"Oh, what shall we do?" I cried miserably. I knew Margaret's chance of college was gone forever.

"Do!" Kate was superb. She didn't lose her wits for a second. "We'll go home and borrow the girls' dinner. Quick—there's just ten minutes before train time. Throw those pies and turnips into this basket—the turkey too—we'll carry them with us to hide them."

I might not be able to evolve an idea like that on the spur of the moment, but I can at least act up to it when it is presented. Without a moment's delay we shut the door and ran. As we went I saw the McGinnis dog licking his chops over in their yard. I have been ashamed ever since of my feelings toward that dog. They were murderous. Fortunately I had no time to indulge them.

It is ten minutes walk from the Pinery to our house, but you can run it in five. Kate and I burst into the kitchen just as Laura and Margaret were sitting down to dinner. We had neither time nor breath for explanations. Without a word I grasped the turkey platter and the turnip tureen. Kate caught one hot mince pie from the oven and whisked a cold one out of the pantry.

"We've—got—to have—them," was all she said.

I've always said that Laura and Magsie would rise to any occasion. They saw us carry their Thanksgiving dinner off under their very eyes and they never interfered by word or motion. They didn't even worry us with questions. They realized that something desperate had happened and that the emergency called for deed not words.

"Aggie," gasped Kate behind me as we tore through the birch wood, "the border—of these pies—is crimped—differently—from Aunt Susanna's."

"She—won't know—the difference," I panted. "Miranda—Mary—crimps them."

We got back to the Pinery just as the train whistle blew. We had ten minutes to transfer turkey and turnips to Aunt Susanna's dishes, hide our own, air the kitchen, and get back our breath. We accomplished it. When Aunt Susanna and her guests came we were prepared for them: we were calm—outwardly—and the second mince pie was getting hot in the oven. It was ready by the time it was needed. Fortunately our turkey was the same size as Aunt Susanna's, and Laura had cooked a double supply of turnips, intending to warm them up the next day. Still, all things considered, Kate and I didn't enjoy that dinner much. We kept thinking of poor Laura and Magsie at home, dining off potatoes on Thanksgiving!

But at least Aunt Susanna was satisfied. When Kate and I were washing the dishes she came out quite beamingly.

"Well, my dears, I must admit that you made a very good job of the dinner, indeed. The turkey was done to perfection. As for the mince pies—well, of course Miranda Mary made them, but she must have had extra good luck with them, for they were excellent and heated to just the right degree. You didn't give anything to the McGinnis dog, I hope?"

"No, we didn't give him anything," said Kate.

Aunt Susanna did not notice the emphasis.

When we had finished the dishes we smuggled our platter and tureen out of the house and went home. Laura and Margaret were busy painting and studying and were just as sweet-tempered as if we hadn't robbed them of their dinner. But we had to tell them the whole story before we even took off our hats.

"There is a special Providence for children and idiots," said Laura gently. We didn't ask her whether she meant us or Tony McGinnis or both. There are some things better left in obscurity. I'd have probably said something much sharper than that if anybody had made off with my Thanksgiving turkey so unceremoniously.

Aunt Susanna came down the next day and told Margaret that she would send her to college. Also she commissioned Laura to paint her a water-color for her dining-room and said she'd pay her five dollars for it.

Kate and I were rather left out in the cold in this distribution of favors, but when you come to reflect that Laura and Magsie had really cooked that dinner, it was only just.

Anyway, Aunt Susanna has never since insinuated that we can't cook, and that is as much as we deserve.

By Grace of Julius Caesar

Melissa sent word on Monday evening that she thought we had better go round with the subscription list for cushioning the church pews on Tuesday. I sent back word that I thought we had better go on Thursday. I had no particular objection to Tuesday, but Melissa is rather fond of settling things without consulting anyone else, and I don't believe in always letting her have her own way. Melissa is my cousin and we have always been good friends, and I am really very fond of her; but there's no sense in lying down and letting yourself be walked over. We finally compromised on Wednesday.

I always have a feeling of dread when I hear of any new church-project for which money will be needed, because I know perfectly well that Melissa and I will be sent round to collect for it. People say we seem to be able to get more than anybody else; and they appear to think that because Melissa is an unencumbered old maid, and I am an unencumbered widow, we can spare the time without any inconvenience to ourselves. Well, we have been canvassing for building funds, and socials, and suppers for years, but it is needed now; at least, I have had enough of it, and I should think Melissa has, too.

We started out bright and early on Wednesday morning, for Jersey Cove is a big place and we knew we should need the whole day. We had to walk because neither of us owned a horse, and anyway it's more nuisance getting out to open and shut gates than it is worth while. It was a lovely day then, though promising to be hot, and our hearts were as light as could be expected, considering the disagreeable expedition we were on.

I was waiting at my gate for Melissa when she came, and she looked me over with wonder and disapproval. I could see she thought I was a fool to dress up in my second best flowered muslin and my very best hat with the pale pink roses in it to walk about in the heat and dust; but I wasn't. All my experience in canvassing goes to show that the better dressed and better looking you are the more money you'll get—that is, when it's the men you have to tackle, as in this case. If it had been the women, however, I would have put on the oldest and ugliest things, consistent with decency, I had. This was what Melissa had done, as it was, and she did look fearfully prim and dowdy, except for her front hair, which was as soft and fluffy and elaborate as usual. I never could understand how Melissa always got it arranged so beautifully.

Nothing particular happened the first part of the day. Some few growled and wouldn't subscribe anything, but on the whole we did pretty well. If it had been a missionary subscription we should have fared worse; but when it was something touching their own comfort, like cushioning the pews, they came down handsomely. We reached Daniel Wilson's by noon, and had to have dinner there. We didn't eat much, although we were hungry enough—Mary Wilson's cooking is a by-word in Jersey Cove. No wonder Daniel is dyspeptic; but dyspeptic or not, he gave us a big subscription for our cushions and told us we looked younger than ever. Daniel is always very complimentary, and they say Mary is jealous.

When we left the Wilson's Melissa said, with an air of a woman nerving herself to a disagreeable duty:

"I suppose we might as well go to Isaac Appleby's now and get it over."

I agreed with her. I had been dreading that call all day. It isn't a very pleasant thing to go to a man you have recently refused to marry and ask him for money; and Melissa and I were both in that predicament.

Isaac was a well-to-do old bachelor who had never had any notion of getting married until his sister died in the winter. And then, as soon as the spring planting was over, he began to look round for a wife. He came to me first and I said "No" good and hard. I liked Isaac well enough; but I was snug and comfortable, and didn't feel like pulling up my roots and moving into another lot; besides, Isaac's courting seemed to me a shade too business-like. I can't get along without a little romance; it's my nature.

Isaac was disappointed and said so, but intimated that it wasn't crushing and that the next best would do very well. The next best was Melissa, and he proposed to her after the decent interval of a fortnight. Melissa also refused him. I admit I was surprised at this, for I knew Melissa was rather anxious to marry; but she has always been down on

Isaac Appleby, from principle, because of a family feud on her mother's side; besides, an old beau of hers, a widower at Kingsbridge, was just beginning to take notice again, and I suspected Melissa had hopes concerning him. Finally, I imagine Melissa did not fancy being second choice.

Whatever her reasons were, she refused poor Isaac, and that finished his matrimonial prospects as far as Jersey Cove was concerned, for there wasn't another eligible woman in it—that is, for a man of Isaac's age. I was the only widow, and the other old maids besides Melissa were all hopelessly old-maiden.

This was all three months ago, and Isaac had been keeping house for himself ever since. Nobody knew much about how he got along, for the Appleby house is half a mile from anywhere, down near the shore at the end of a long lane—the lonesomest place, as I did not fail to remember when I was considering Isaac's offer.

"I heard Jarvis Aldrich say Isaac had got a dog lately," said Melissa, when we finally came in sight of the house—a handsome new one, by the way, put up only ten years ago. "Jarvis said it was an imported breed. I do hope it isn't cross."

I have a mortal horror of dogs, and I followed Melissa into the big farmyard with fear and trembling. We were halfway across the yard when Melissa shrieked:

"Anne, there's the dog!"

There was the dog; and the trouble was that he didn't stay there, but came right down the slope at a steady, business-like trot. He was a bull-dog and big enough to bite a body clean in two, and he was the ugliest thing in dogs I had ever seen.

Melissa and I both lost our heads. We screamed, dropped our parasols, and ran instinctively to the only refuge that was in sight—a ladder leaning against the old Appleby house. I am forty-five and something more than plump, so that climbing ladders is not my favorite form of exercise. But I went up that one with the agility and grace of sixteen. Melissa followed me, and we found ourselves on the roof—fortunately it was a flat one—panting and gasping, but safe, unless that diabolical dog could climb a ladder.

I crept cautiously to the edge and peered over. The beast was sitting on his haunches at the foot of the ladder, and it was quite evident he was not short on time. The gleam in his eye seemed to say:

"I've got you two unprincipled subscription hunters beautifully treed and it's treed you're going to stay. That is what I call satisfying."

I reported the state of the case to Melissa.

"What shall we do?" I asked.

"Do?" said Melissa, snappishly. "Why, stay here till Isaac Appleby comes out and takes that brute away? What else can we do?"

"What if he isn't at home?" I suggested.

"We'll stay here till he comes home. Oh, this is a nice predicament. This is what comes of cushioning churches!"

"It might be worse," I said comfortingly. "Suppose the roof hadn't been flat?"

"Call Isaac," said Melissa shortly.

I didn't fancy calling Isaac, but call him I did, and when that failed to bring him Melissa condescended to call, too; but scream as we might, no Isaac appeared, and that dog sat there and smiled internally.

"It's no use," said Melissa sulkily at last. "Isaac Appleby is dead or away."

Half an hour passed; it seemed as long as a day. The sun just boiled down on that roof and we were nearly melted. We were dreadfully thirsty, and the heat made our heads ache, and I could see my muslin dress fading before my very eyes. As for the roses on my best hat—but that was too harrowing to think about.

Then we saw a welcome sight—Isaac Appleby coming through the yard with a hoe over his shoulder. He had probably been working in his field at the back of the house. I never thought I should have been so glad to see him.

"Isaac, oh, Isaac!" I called joyfully, leaning over as far as I dared.

Isaac looked up in amazement at me and Melissa craning our necks over the edge of the roof. Then he saw the dog and took in the situation. The creature actually grinned.

"Won't you call off your dog and let us get down, Isaac?" I said pleadingly.

Isaac stood and reflected for a moment or two. Then he came slowly forward and, before we realized what he was going to do, he took that ladder down and laid it on the ground.

"Isaac Appleby, what do you mean?" demanded Melissa wrathfully.

Isaac folded his arms and looked up. It would be hard to say which face was the more determined, his or the dog's. But Isaac had the advantage in point of looks, I will say that for him.

"I mean that you two women will stay up on that roof until one of you agrees to marry me," said Isaac solemnly.

I gasped.

"Isaac Appleby, you can't be in earnest?" I cried incredulously. "You couldn't be so mean?"

"I am in earnest. I want a wife, and I am going to have one. You two will stay up there, and Julius Caesar here will watch you until one of you makes up her mind to take me. You can settle it between yourselves, and let me know when you have come to a decision."

And with that Isaac walked jauntily into his new house.

"The man can't mean it!" said Melissa. "He is trying to play a joke on us."

"He does mean it," I said gloomily. "An Appleby never says anything he doesn't mean. He will keep us here until one of us consents to marry him."

"It won't be me, then," said Melissa in a calm sort of rage. "I won't marry him if I have to sit on this roof for the rest of my life. You can take him. It's really you he wants, anyway; he asked you first."

I always knew that rankled with Melissa.

I thought the situation over before I said anything more. We certainly couldn't get off that roof, and if we could, there was Julius Caesar. The place was out of sight of every other house in Jersey Cove, and nobody might come near it for a week. To be sure, when Melissa and I didn't turn up the Covites might get out and search for us; but that wouldn't be for two or three days anyhow.

Melissa had turned her back on me and was sitting with her elbows propped up on her knees, looking gloomily out to sea. I was afraid I couldn't coax her into marrying Isaac. As for me, I hadn't any real objection to marrying him, after all, for if he was short of romance he was good-natured and has a fat bank account; but I hated to be driven into it that way.

"You'd better take him, Melissa," I said entreatingly. "I've had one husband and that is enough."

"More than enough for me, thank you," said Melissa sarcastically.

"Isaac is a fine man and has a lovely house; and you aren't sure the Kingsbridge man really means anything," I went on.

"I would rather," said Melissa, with the same awful calmness, "jump down from this roof and break my neck, or be devoured piecemeal by that fiend down there than marry Isaac Appleby."

It didn't seem worth while to say anything more after that. We sat there in stony silence and the time dragged by. I was hot, hungry, thirsty, cross; and besides, I felt that I was in a ridiculous position, which was worse than all the rest. We could see Isaac sitting in the shade of one of his apple trees in the front orchard comfortably reading a newspaper. I think if he hadn't aggravated me by doing that I'd have given in sooner. But as it was, I was determined to be as stubborn as everybody else. We were four obstinate creatures—Isaac and Melissa and Julius Caesar and I.

At four o'clock Isaac got up and went into the house; in a few minutes he came out again with a basket in one hand and a ball of cord in the other.

"I don't intend to starve you, of course, ladies," he said politely, "I will throw this ball up to you and you can then draw up the basket."

I caught the ball, for Melissa never turned her head. I would have preferred to be scornful, too, and reject the food altogether; but I was so dreadfully thirsty that I put my pride in my pocket and hauled the basket up. Besides, I thought it might enable us to hold out until some loophole of escape presented itself.

Isaac went back into the house and I unpacked the basket. There was a bottle of milk, some bread and butter, and a pie. Melissa wouldn't take a morsel of the food, but she was so thirsty she had to take a drink of milk.

She tried to lift her veil—and something caught; Melissa gave it a savage twitch, and off came veil and hat—and all her front hair!

You never saw such a sight. I'd always suspected Melissa wore a false front, but I'd never had any proof before.

Melissa pinned on her hair again and put on her hat and drank the milk, all without a word; but she was purple. I felt sorry for her.

And I felt sorry for Isaac when I tried to eat that bread. It was sour and dreadful. As for the pie, it was hopeless. I tasted it, and then threw it down to Julius Caesar. Julius Caesar, not being over particular, ate it up. I thought perhaps it would kill him, for anything might come of eating such a concoction. That pie was a strong argument for Isaac. I thought a man who had to live on such cookery did indeed need a wife and might be pardoned for taking desperate measures to get one. I was dreadfully tired of broiling on the roof anyhow.

But it was the thunderstorm that decided me. When I saw it coming up, black and quick, from the northwest, I gave in at once. I had endured a good deal and was prepared to endure more; but I had paid ten dollars for my hat and I was not going to have it ruined by a thunderstorm. I called to Isaac and out he came.

"If you will let us down and promise to dispose of that dog before I come here I will marry you, Isaac," I said, "but I'll make you sorry for it afterwards, though."

"I'll take the risk of that, Anne," he said; "and, of course, I'll sell the dog. I won't need him when I have you."

Isaac meant to be complimentary, though you mightn't have thought so if you had seen the face of that dog.

Isaac ordered Julius Caesar away and put up the ladder, and turned his back, real considerately, while we climbed down. We had to go in his house and stay till the shower was over. I didn't forget the object of our call and I produced our subscription list at once.

"How much have you got?" asked Isaac.

"Seventy dollars and we want a hundred and fifty," I said.

"You may put me down for the remaining eighty, then," said Isaac calmly.

The Applebys are never mean where money is concerned, I must say.

Isaac offered to drive us home when it cleared up, but I said "No." I wanted to settle Melissa before she got a chance to talk.

On the way home I said to her:

"I hope you won't mention this to anyone, Melissa. I don't mind marrying Isaac, but I don't want people to know how it came about."

"Oh, I won't say anything about it," said Melissa, laughing a little disagreeably.

"Because," I said, to clinch the matter, looking significantly at her front hair as I said it, "I have something to tell, too."

Melissa will hold her tongue.

By the Rule of Contrary

"Look here, Burton," said old John Ellis in an ominous tone of voice, "I want to know if what that old busybody of a Mary Keane came here today gossiping about is true. If it is—well, I've something to say about the matter! Have you been courting that niece of Susan Oliver's all summer on the sly?"

Burton Ellis's handsome, boyish face flushed darkly crimson to the roots of his curly black hair. Something in the father's tone roused anger and rebellion in the son. He straightened himself up from the turnip row he was hoeing, looked his father squarely in the face, and said quietly,

"Not on the sly, sir, I never do things that way. But I have been going to see Madge Oliver for some time, and we are engaged. We are thinking of being married this fall, and we hope you will not object."

Burton's frankness nearly took away his father's breath. Old John fairly choked with rage.

"You young fool," he spluttered, bringing down his hoe with such energy that he sliced off half a dozen of his finest young turnip plants, "have you gone clean crazy? No, sir, I'll never consent to your marrying an Oliver, and you needn't have any idea that I will."

"Then I'll marry her without your consent," retorted Burton angrily, losing the temper he had been trying to keep.

"Oh, will you indeed! Well, if you do, out you go, and not a cent of my money or a rod of my land do you ever get."

"What have you got against Madge?" asked Burton, forcing himself to speak calmly, for he knew his father too well to doubt for a minute that he meant and would do just what he said.

"She's an Oliver," said old John crustily, "and that's enough." And considering that he had settled the matter, John Ellis threw down his hoe and left the field in a towering rage.

Burton hoed away savagely until his anger had spent itself on the weeds. Give up Madge—dear, sweet little Madge? Not he! Yet if his father remained of the same mind, their marriage was out of the question at present. And Burton knew quite well that his father would remain of the same mind. Old John Ellis had the reputation of being the most contrary man in Greenwood.

When Burton had finished his row he left the turnip field and went straight across lots to see Madge and tell her his dismal story. An hour later Miss Susan Oliver went up the stairs of her little brown house to Madge's room and found her niece lying on the bed, her pretty curls tumbled, her soft cheeks flushed crimson, crying as if her heart would break.

Miss Susan was a tall, grim, angular spinster who looked like the last person in the world to whom a love affair might be confided. But never were appearances more deceptive than in this case. Behind her unprepossessing exterior Miss Susan had a warm, sympathetic heart filled to the brim with kindly affection for her pretty niece. She had seen Burton Ellis going moodily across the fields homeward and guessed that something had gone wrong.

"Now, dearie, what is the matter?" she said, tenderly patting the brown head.

Madge sobbed out the whole story disconsolately. Burton's father would not let him marry her because she was an Oliver. And, oh, what would she do?

"Don't worry, Madge," said Miss Susan comfortingly. "I'll soon settle old John Ellis."

"Why, what can you do?" asked Madge forlornly.

Miss Susan squared her shoulders and looked amused.

"You'll see. I know old John Ellis better than he knows himself. He is the most contrary man the Lord ever made. I went to school with him. I learned how to manage him then, and I haven't forgotten how. I'm going straight up to interview him."

"Are you sure that will do any good?" said Madge doubtfully. "If you go to him and take Burton's and my part, won't it only make him worse?"

"Madge, dear," said Miss Susan, busily twisting her scanty, iron-grey hair up into a hard little knob at the back of her head before Madge's glass, "you just wait. I'm not young, and I'm not pretty, and I'm not in love, but I've more gumption than you and Burton have or ever will have. You keep your eyes open and see if you can learn something. You'll need it if you go up to live with old John Ellis."

Burton had returned to the turnip field, but old John Ellis was taking his ease with a rampant political newspaper on the cool verandah of his house. Looking up from a bitter editorial to chuckle over a cutting sarcasm contained therein, he saw a tall, angular figure coming up the lane with aggressiveness written large in every fold and flutter of shawl and skirt.

"Old Susan Oliver, as sure as a gun," said old John with another chuckle. "She looks mad clean through. I suppose she's coming here to blow me up for refusing to let Burton take that girl of hers. She's been angling and scheming for it for years, but she will find who she has to deal with. Come on, Miss Susan."

John Ellis laid down his paper and stood up with a sarcastic smile.

Miss Susan reached the steps and skimmed undauntedly up them. She did indeed look angry and disturbed. Without any preliminary greeting she burst out into a tirade that simply took away her complacent foe's breath.

"Look here, John Ellis, I want to know what this means. I've discovered that that young upstart of a son of yours, who ought to be in short trousers yet, has been courting my niece, Madge Oliver, all summer. He has had the impudence to tell me that he wants to marry her. I won't have it, I tell you, and you can tell your son so. Marry my niece indeed! A pretty pass the world is coming to! I'll never consent to it."

Perhaps if you had searched Greenwood and all the adjacent districts thoroughly you might have found a man who was more astonished and taken aback than old John Ellis was at that moment, but I doubt it. The wind was completely taken out of his sails and every bit of the Ellis contrariness was roused.

"What have you got to say against my son?" he fairly shouted in his rage. "Isn't he good enough for your girl, Susan Oliver, I'd like to know?"

"No, he isn't," retorted Miss Susan deliberately and unflinchingly. "He's well enough in his place, but you'll please to remember, John Ellis, that my niece is an Oliver, and the Olivers don't marry beneath them."

Old John was furious. "Beneath them indeed! Why, woman, it is condescension in my son to so much as look at your niece—condescension, that is what it is. You are as poor as church mice."

"We come of good family, though," retorted Miss Susan. "You Ellises are nobodies. Your grandfather was a hired man! And yet you have the presumption to think you're fit to marry into an old, respectable family like the Olivers. But talking doesn't signify. I simply won't allow this nonsense to go on. I came here today to tell you so plump and plain. It's your duty to stop it; if you don't I will, that's all."

"Oh, will you?" John Ellis was at a white heat of rage and stubbornness now. "We'll see, Miss Susan, we'll see. My son shall marry whatever girl he pleases, and I'll back him up in it—do you hear that? Come here and tell me my son isn't good enough for your niece indeed! I'll show you he can get her anyway."

"You've heard what I've said," was the answer, "and you'd better go by it, that's all. I shan't stay to bandy words with you, John Ellis. I'm going home to talk to my niece and tell her her duty plain, and what I want her to do, and she'll do it, I haven't a fear."

Miss Susan was halfway down the steps, but John Ellis ran to the railing of the verandah to get the last word.

"I'll send Burton down this evening to talk to her and tell her what *he* wants her to do, and we'll see whether she'll sooner listen to you than to him," he shouted.

Miss Susan deigned no reply. Old John strode out to the turnip field. Burton saw him coming and looked for another outburst of wrath, but his father's first words almost took away his breath.

"See here, Burt, I take back all I said this afternoon. I want you to marry Madge Oliver now, and the sooner, the better. That old cat of a Susan had the face to come up and tell me you weren't good enough for her niece. I told her a few plain truths. Don't you mind the old crosspatch. I'll back you up."

By this time Burton had begun hoeing vigorously, to hide the amused twinkle of comprehension in his eyes. He admired Miss Susan's tactics, but he did not say so.

"All right, Father," he answered dutifully.

When Miss Susan reached home she told Madge to bathe her eyes and put on her new pink muslin, because she guessed Burton would be down that evening.

"Oh, Auntie, how did you manage it?" cried Madge.

"Madge," said Miss Susan solemnly, but with dancing eyes, "do you know how to drive a pig? Just try to make it go in the opposite direction and it will bolt the way you want it. Remember that, my dear."

Fair Exchange and No Robbery

Katherine Rangely was packing up. Her chum and roommate, Edith Wilmer, was sitting on the bed watching her in that calm disinterested fashion peculiarly maddening to a bewildered packer.

"It does seem too provoking," said Katherine, as she tugged at an obstinate shawl strap, "that Ned should be transferred here now, just when I'm going away. The powers that be might have waited until vacation was over. Ned won't know a soul here and he'll be horribly lonesome."

"I'll do my best to befriend him, with your permission," said Edith consolingly.

"Oh, I know. You're a special Providence, Ede. Ned will be up tonight first thing, of course, and I'll introduce him. Try to keep the poor fellow amused until I get back. Two months! Just fancy! And Aunt Elizabeth won't abate one jot or tittle of the time I promised to stay with her. Harbour Hill is so frightfully dull, too."

Then the talk drifted around to Edith's affairs. She was engaged to a certain Sidney Keith, who was a professor in some college.

"I don't expect to see much of Sidney this summer," said Edith. "He's writing another book. He is so terribly addicted to literature."

"How lovely," sighed Katherine, who had aspirations in that line herself. "If only Ned were like him I should be perfectly happy. But Ned is so prosaic. He doesn't care a rap for poetry, and he laughs when I enthuse. It makes him quite furious when I talk of taking up writing seriously. He says women writers are an abomination on the face of the earth. Did you ever hear anything so ridiculous?"

"He is very handsome, though," said Edith, with a glance at his photograph on Katherine's dressing table. "And that is what Sid is not. He is rather distinguished looking, but as plain as he can possibly be."

Edith sighed. She had a weakness for handsome men and thought it rather hard that fate should have allotted her so plain a lover.

"He has lovely eyes," said Katherine comfortingly, "and handsome men are always vain. Even Ned is. I have to snub him regularly. But I think you'll like him."

Edith thought so too when Ned Ellison appeared that night. He was a handsome off-handed young fellow, who seemed to admire Katherine immensely, and be a little afraid of her into the bargain.

"Edith will try to make Riverton pleasant for you while I am away," she told him in their good-bye chat. "She is a dear girl—you'll like her, I know. It's really too bad I have to go away now, but it can't be helped."

"I shall be awfully lonesome," grumbled Ned. "Don't you forget to write regularly, Kitty."

"Of course I'll write, but for pity's sake, Ned, don't call me Kitty. It sounds so childish. Well, bye-bye, dear boy. I'll be back in two months and then we'll have a lovely time."

When Katherine had been at Harbour Hill for a week she wondered how upon earth she was going to put in the remaining seven. Harbour Hill was noted for its beauty, but not every woman can live by scenery alone.

"Aunt Elizabeth," said Katherine one day, "does anybody ever die in Harbour Hill? Because it doesn't seem to me it would be any change for them if they did."

Aunt Elizabeth's only reply to this was a shocked look.

To pass the time Katherine took to collecting seaweeds, and this involved long tramps along the shore. On one of these occasions she met with an adventure. The place was a remote spot far up the shore. Katherine had taken off her shoes and stockings, tucked up her skirt, rolled her sleeves high above her dimpled elbows, and was deep in the absorbing process of fishing up seaweeds off a craggy headland. She looked anything but dignified while so employed, but under the circumstances dignity did not matter.

Presently she heard a shout from the shore and, turning around in dismay, she beheld a man on the rocks behind her. He was evidently shouting at her. What on earth could the creature want?

"Come in," he called, gesticulating wildly. "You'll be in the bottomless pit in another moment if you don't look out."

"He certainly must be a lunatic," said Katherine to herself, "or else he's drunk. What am I to do?"

"Come in, I tell you," insisted the stranger. "What in the world do you mean by wading out to such a place? Why, it's madness."

Katherine's indignation got the better of her fear.

"I do not think I am trespassing," she called back as icily as possible.

The stranger did not seem to be snubbed at all. He came down to the very edge of the rocks where Katherine could see him plainly. He was dressed in a somewhat well-worn grey suit and wore spectacles. He did not look like a lunatic, and he did not seem to be drunk.

"I implore you to come in," he said earnestly. "You must be standing on the very brink of the bottomless pit."

He is certainly off his balance, thought Katherine. He must be some revivalist who has gone insane on one point. I suppose I'd better go in. He looks quite capable of wading out here after me if I don't.

She picked her steps carefully back with her precious specimens. The stranger eyed her severely as she stepped on the rocks.

"I should think you would have more sense than to risk your life in that fashion for a handful of seaweeds," he said.

"I haven't the faintest idea what you mean," said Miss Rangely. "You don't look crazy, but you talk as if you were."

"Do you mean to say you don't know that what the people hereabouts call the Bottomless Pit is situated right off that point—the most dangerous spot along the whole coast?"

"No, I didn't," said Katherine, horrified. She remembered now that Aunt Elizabeth had warned her to be careful of some bad hole along shore, but she had not been paying much attention and had supposed it to be in quite another direction. "I am a stranger here."

"Well, I hardly thought you'd be foolish enough to be out there if you knew," said the other in mollified accents. "The place ought not to be left without warning, anyhow. It is the most careless thing I ever heard of. There is a big hole right off that point and nobody has ever been able to find the bottom of it. A person who got into it would never be heard of again. The rocks there form an eddy that sucks everything right down."

"I am very grateful to you for calling me in," said Katherine humbly. "I had no idea I was in such danger."

"You have a very fine bunch of seaweeds, I see," said the unknown.

But Katherine was in no mood to converse on seaweeds. She suddenly realized what she must look like—bare feet, draggled skirts, dripping arms. And this creature whom she had taken for a lunatic was undoubtedly a gentleman. Oh, if he would only go and give her a chance to put on her shoes and stockings!

Nothing seemed further from his intentions. When Katherine had picked up the aforesaid articles and turned homeward, he walked beside her, still discoursing on seaweeds as eloquently as if he were commonly accustomed to walking with barefooted young women. In spite of herself, Katherine couldn't help listening to him, for he managed to invest seaweeds with an absorbing interest. She finally decided that as he didn't seem to mind her bare feet, she wouldn't either.

He knew so much about seaweeds that Katherine felt decidedly amateurish beside him. He looked over her specimens and pointed out the valuable ones. He explained the best method of preserving and mounting them, and told her of other and less dangerous places along the shore where she might get some new varieties.

When they came in sight of Harbour Hill, Katherine began to wonder what on earth she would do with him. It wasn't exactly permissible to snub a man who had practically saved your life, but, on the other hand, the prospect of walking through the principal street of Harbour Hill barefooted and escorted by a scholarly looking gentleman discoursing on seaweeds was not to be calmly contemplated.

The unknown cut the Gordian knot himself. He said that he must really go back or he would be late for dinner, lifted his hat politely, and departed. Katherine waited until he was out of sight, then sat down on the sand and put on her shoes and stockings.

"Who on earth can he be?" she said to herself. "And where have I seen him before? There was certainly something familiar about his appearance. He is very nice, but he must have thought me crazy. I wonder if he belongs to Harbour Hill."

The mystery was solved when she got home and found a letter from Edith awaiting her.

"I see Ned quite often," wrote the latter, "and I think he is perfectly splendid. You are a lucky girl, Kate. But oh, do you know that Sidney is actually at Harbour Hill, too, or at least quite near it? I had a letter from him yesterday. He has gone down there to spend his vacation, because it is so quiet, and to finish up some horrid scientific book he is working at. He's boarding at some little farmhouse up the shore. I've written to him today to hunt you up and consider himself introduced to you. I think you'll like him, for he's just your style."

Katherine smiled when Sidney Keith's card was brought up to her that evening and went down to meet him. Her companion of the morning rose to meet her.

"You!" he said.

"Yes, me," said Miss Rangely cheerfully and ungrammatically. "You didn't expect it, did you? I was sure I had seen you before—only it wasn't you but your photograph."

When Professor Keith went away it was with a cordial invitation to call again. He did not fail to avail himself of it—in fact, he became a constant visitor at Sycamore Villa. Katherine wrote all about it to Edith and cultivated Professor Keith with a dear conscience.

They got on capitally together. They went on long expeditions up shore after seaweeds, and when seaweeds were exhausted they began to make a collection of the Harbour Hill flora. This involved more long, companionable expeditions. Katherine sometimes wondered when Professor Keith found time to work on his book, but as he made no reference to the subject, neither did she.

Once in a while, when she had time to think of them, she wondered how Ned and Edith were getting on. At first Edith's letters had been full of Ned, but in her last two or three she had said little about him. Katherine wrote and jokingly asked Edith if she and Ned had quarreled. Edith wrote back and said, "What nonsense." She and Ned were as good friends as ever, but he was getting acquainted in Riverton now and wasn't so dependent on her society, etc.

Katherine sighed and went on a fern hunt with Professor Keith. It was getting near the end of her vacation and she had only two weeks more. They were sitting down to rest on the side of the road when she mentioned this fact inconsequently. The professor prodded the harmless dust with his cane. Well, he supposed she would find a return to work pleasant and would doubtless be glad to see her Riverton friends again.

"I'm dying to see Edith," said Katherine.

"And Ned?" suggested Professor Keith.

"Oh yes. Ned, of course," assented Katherine without enthusiasm. There didn't seem to be anything more to say. One cannot talk everlastingly about ferns, so they got up and went home.

Katherine wrote a particularly affectionate letter to Ned that night. Then she went to bed and cried.

When Professor Keith came up to bid Miss Rangely good-bye on the eve of her departure from Harbour Hill, he looked like a man who was being led to execution without benefit of clergy. But he kept himself well in hand and talked calmly on impersonal subjects. After all, it was Katherine who made the first break when she got up to say good-bye. She was in the middle of some conventional sentence when she suddenly stopped short, and her voice trailed off in a babyish quiver.

The professor put out his arm and drew her close to him. His hat dropped under their feet and was trampled on, but I doubt if Professor Keith knows the difference to this day, for he was fully absorbed in kissing Katherine's hair. When she became cognizant of this fact, she drew herself away.

"Oh, Sidney, don't!—think of Edith! I feel like a traitor."

"Do you think she would care very much if I—if you—if we—" hesitated the professor.

"Oh, it would break her heart," cried Katherine with convincing earnestness. "I know it would—and Ned's too. They must never know."

The professor stooped and began hunting for his maltreated hat. He was a long time finding it, and when he did he went softly to the door. With his hand on the knob, he paused and looked back.

"Good-bye, Miss Rangely," he said softly.

But Katherine, whose face was buried in the cushions of the lounge, did not hear him and when she looked up he was gone.

Katharine felt that life was stale, flat and unprofitable when she alighted at Riverton station in the dusk of the next evening. She was not expected until a later train and there was no one to meet her. She walked drearily through the streets to her boarding house and entered her room unannounced. Edith, who was lying on the bed, sprang up with a surprised greeting. It was too dark to be sure, but Katherine had an uncomfortable suspicion that her friend had been crying, and her heart quaked guiltily. Could Edith have suspected anything?

"Why, we didn't think you'd be up till the 8:30 train, and Ned and I were going to meet you."

"I found I could catch an earlier train, so I took it," said Katherine, as she dropped listlessly into a chair. "I am tired to death and I have such a headache. I can't see anyone tonight, not even Ned."

"You poor dear," said Edith sympathetically, beginning a search for the cologne. "Lie down on the bed and I'll bathe your poor head. Did you have a good time at Harbour Hill? And how did you leave Sid? Did he say anything about coming up?"

"Oh, he was quite well," said Katherine wearily. "I didn't hear him say if he intended to come up or not. There, thanks—that will do nicely."

After Edith had gone down, Katherine tossed about restlessly. She knew Ned had come and she did not want to see him. But, after all, it was only putting off the evil day, and it was treating him rather shabbily. She would go down for a minute.

There were two doors to the parlour, and Katherine went by way of the library one, over which a portiere was hanging. Her hand was lifted to draw it back when she heard something that arrested the movement.

A woman was crying in the room beyond. It was Edith—and what was she saying?

"Oh, Ned, it is all perfectly dreadful! I couldn't look Catherine in the face when she came home. I'm so ashamed of myself and I never meant to be so false. We must never let her suspect for a minute."

"It's pretty rough on a fellow," said another voice—Ned's voice—in a choked sort of a way. "Upon my word, Edith, I don't see how I'm going to keep it up."

"You must," sobbed Edith. "It would break her heart—and Sidney's too. We must just make up our minds to forget each other, Ned, and you must marry Katherine."

Just at this point Katherine became aware that she was eavesdropping and she went away noiselessly. She did not look in the least like a person who has received a mortal blow, and she had forgotten her headache altogether.

When Edith came up half an hour later, she found the worn-out invalid sitting up and reading a novel.

"How is your headache, dear?" she asked, carefully keeping her face turned away from Katherine.

"Oh, it's all gone," said Miss Rangely cheerfully.

"Why didn't you come down then? Ned was here."

"Well, Ede, I did go down, but I thought I wasn't particularly wanted, so I came back."

Edith faced her friend in dismay, forgetful of swollen lids and tear-stained cheeks.

"Katherine!"

"Don't look so conscience stricken, my dear child. There is no harm done."

"You heard—"

"Some surprising speeches. So you and Ned have gone and fallen in love with one another?"

"Oh, Katherine," sobbed Edith, "we—we—couldn't help it—but it's all over. Oh, don't be angry with me!"

"Angry? My dear, I'm delighted."

"Delighted?"

"Yes, you dear goose. Can't you guess, or must I tell you? Sidney and I did the very same, and had just such a melancholy parting last night as I suspect you and Ned had tonight."

"Katherine!"

"Yes, it's quite true. And of course we made up our minds to sacrifice ourselves on the altar of duty and all that. But now, thank goodness, there is no need of such wholesale immolation. So just let's forgive each other."

"Oh," sighed Edith happily, "it is almost too good to be true."

"It is really providentially ordered, isn't it?" said Katherine. "Ned and I would never have got on together in the world, and you and Sidney would have bored each other to death. As it is, there will be four perfectly happy people instead of four miserable ones. I'll tell Ned so tomorrow."

Four Winds

Alan Douglas threw down his pen with an impatient exclamation. It was high time his next Sunday's sermon was written, but he could not concentrate his thoughts on his chosen text. For one thing he did not like it and had selected it only because Elder Trewin, in his call of the evening before, had hinted that it was time for a good stiff doctrinal discourse, such as his predecessor in Rexton, the Rev. Jabez Strong, had delighted in. Alan hated doctrines—"the soul's staylaces," he called them—but Elder Trewin was a man to be reckoned with and Alan preached an occasional sermon to please him.

"It's no use," he said wearily. "I could have written a sermon in keeping with that text in November or midwinter, but now, when the whole world is reawakening in a miracle of beauty and love, I can't do it. If a northeast rainstorm doesn't set in before next Sunday, Mr. Trewin will not have his sermon. I shall take as my text instead, 'The flowers appear on the earth, the time of the singing of birds has come.'"

He rose and went to his study window, outside of which a young vine was glowing in soft tender green tints, its small dainty leaves casting quivering shadows on the opposite wall where the portrait of Alan's mother hung. She had a fine, strong, sweet face; the same face, cast in a masculine mould, was repeated in her son, and the resemblance was striking as he stood in the searching evening sunshine. The black hair grew around his forehead in the same way; his eyes were steel blue, like hers, with a similar expression, half brooding, half tender, in their depths. He had the mobile, smiling mouth of the picture, but his chin was deeper and squarer, dented with a dimple which, combined with a certain occasional whimsicality of opinion and glance, had caused Elder Trewin some qualms of doubt regarding the fitness of this young man for his high and holy vocation. The Rev.

Jabez Strong had never indulged in dimples or jokes; but then, as Elder Trewin, being a just man, had to admit, the Rev. Jabez Strong had preached many a time and oft to more empty pews than full ones, while now the church was crowded to its utmost capacity on Sundays and people came to hear Mr. Douglas who had not darkened a church door for years. All things considered, Elder Trewin decided to overlook the dimple. There was sure to be some drawback in every minister.

Alan from his study looked down on all the length of the Rexton valley, at the head of which the manse was situated, and thought that Eden might have looked so in its innocence, for all the orchards were abloom and the distant hills were tremulous and aerial in springtime gauzes of pale purple and pearl. But in any garden, despite its beauty, is an element of tameness and domesticity, and Alan's eyes, after a moment's delighted gazing, strayed wistfully off to the north where the hills broke away into a long sloping lowland of pine and fir. Beyond it stretched the wide expanse of the lake, flashing in the molten gold and crimson of evening. Its lure was irresistible. Alan had been born and bred beside a faraway sea and the love of it was strong in his heart—so strong that he knew he must go back to it sometime. Meanwhile, the great lake, mimicking the sea in its vast expanse and the storms that often swept over it, was his comfort and solace. As often as he could he stole away to its wild and lonely shore, leaving the snug bounds of cultivated home lands behind him with something like a sense of relief. Down there by the lake was a primitive wilderness where man was as naught and man-made doctrines had no place. There one might walk hand in hand with nature and so come very close to God. Many of Alan's best sermons were written after he had come home, rapt-eyed, from some long shore tramp where the wilderness had opened its heart to him and the pines had called to him in their soft, sibilant speech.

With a half guilty glance at the futile sermon, he took his hat and went out. The sun of the cool spring evening was swinging low over the lake as he turned into the unfrequented, deep-rutted road leading to the shore. It was two miles to the lake, but half way there Alan came to where another road branched off and struck down through the pines in a northeasterly direction. He had sometimes wondered where it led but he had never explored it. Now he had a sudden whim to do so and turned into it. It was even rougher and lonelier than the other; between the ruts the grasses grew long and thickly; sometimes the pine boughs met overhead; again, the trees broke away to reveal wonderful glimpses of gleaming water, purple islets, dark feathery coasts. Still, the road seemed to lead nowhere and Alan was half repenting the impulse which had led him to choose it when he suddenly came out from the shadow of the pines and found himself gazing on a sight which amazed him.

Before him was a small peninsula running out into the lake and terminating in a long sandy point. Beyond it was a glorious sweep of sunset water. The peninsula itself seemed barren and sandy, covered for the most part with scrub firs and spruces, through which the narrow road wound on to what was the astonishing; feature in the landscape—a grey and weather-beaten house built almost at the extremity of the point and shadowed from the western light by a thick plantation of tall pines behind it.

It was the house which puzzled Alan. He had never known there was any house near the lake shore—had never heard mention made of any; yet here was one, and one which was evidently occupied, for a slender spiral of smoke was curling upward from it on the chilly spring air. It could not be a fisherman's dwelling, for it was large and built after a quaint tasteful design. The longer Alan looked at it the more his wonder grew. The people living here were in the bounds of his congregation. How then was it that he had never seen or heard of them?

He sauntered slowly down the road until he saw that it led directly to the house and ended in the yard. Then he turned off in a narrow path to the shore. He was not far from the house now and he scanned it observantly as he went past. The barrens swept almost up to its door in front but at the side, sheltered from the lake winds by the pines, was a garden where there was a fine show of gay tulips and golden daffodils. No living creature was visible and, in spite of the blossoming geraniums and muslin curtains at the windows and the homely spiral of smoke, the place had a lonely, almost untenanted, look.

When Alan reached the shore he found that it was of a much more open and less rocky nature than the part which he had been used to frequent. The beach was of sand and the scrub barrens dwindled down to it almost insensibly. To right and left fir-fringed points ran out into the lake, shaping a little cove with the house in its curve.

Alan walked slowly towards the left headland, intending to follow the shore around to the other road. As he passed the point he stopped short in astonishment. The second surprise and mystery of the evening confronted him.

A little distance away a girl was standing—a girl who turned a startled face at his unexpected appearance. Alan Douglas had thought he knew all the girls in Rexton, but this lithe, glorious creature was a stranger to him. She stood with her hand on the head of a huge, tawny collie dog; another dog was sitting on his haunches beside her.

She was tall, with a great braid of shining chestnut hair, showing ruddy burnished tints where the sunlight struck it, hanging over her shoulder. The plain dark dress she wore emphasized the grace and strength of her supple form. Her face was oval and pale, with straight black brows and a finely cut crimson mouth—a face whose beauty bore the indefinable stamp of race and breeding mingled with a wild sweetness, as of a flower growing in some lonely and inaccessible place. None of the Rexton girls looked like that. Who, in the name of all that was amazing, could she be?

As the thought crossed Alan's mind the girl turned, with an air of indifference that might have seemed slightly overdone to a calmer observer than was the young minister at that moment and, with a gesture of command to her dogs, walked quickly away into the scrub spruces. She was so tall that her uncovered head was visible over them as she followed some winding footpath, and Alan stood like a man rooted to the ground until he saw her enter the grey house. Then he went homeward in a maze, all thought of sermons, doctrinal or otherwise, for the moment knocked out of his head.

She is the most beautiful woman I ever saw, he thought. How is it possible that I have lived in Rexton for six months and never heard of her or of that house? Well, I daresay there's some simple explanation of it all. The place may have been unoccupied until lately—probably it is the summer residence of people who have only recently come to it. I'll ask Mrs. Danby. She'll know if anybody will. That good woman knows everything about everybody in Rexton for three generations back.

Alan found Isabel King with his housekeeper when he got home. His greeting was tinged with a slight constraint. He was not a vain man, but he could not help knowing that Isabel looked upon him with a favour that had in it much more than professional interest. Isabel herself showed it with sufficient distinctness. Moreover, he felt a certain personal dislike of her and of her hard, insistent beauty, which seemed harder and more insistent than ever contrasted with his recollection of the girl of the lake shore.

Isabel had a trick of coming to the manse on plausible errands to Mrs. Danby and lingering until it was so dark that Alan was in courtesy bound to see her home. The ruse was a little too patent and amused Alan, although he carefully hid his amusement and treated Isabel with the fine unvarying deference which his mother had engrained into him for womanhood—a deference that flattered Isabel even while it annoyed her with the sense of a barrier which she could not break down or pass. She was the daughter of the richest man in Rexton and inclined to give herself airs on that account, but Alan's gentle indifference always brought home to her an unwelcome feeling of inferiority.

"You've been tiring yourself out again tramping that lake shore, I suppose," said Mrs. Danby, who had kept house for three bachelor ministers and consequently felt entitled to hector them in a somewhat maternal fashion.

"Not tiring myself—resting and refreshing myself rather," smiled Alan. "I was tired when I went out but now I feel like a strong man rejoicing to run a race. By the way, Mrs. Danby, who lives in that quaint old house away down at the very shore? I never knew of its existence before."

Alan's "by the way" was not quite so indifferent as he tried to make it. Isabel King, leaning back posingly among the cushions of the lounge, sat quickly up as he asked his question.

"Dear me, you don't mean to say you've never heard of Captain Anthony—Captain Anthony Oliver?" said Mrs. Danby. "He lives down there at Four Winds, as they call it—he and his daughter and an old cousin."

Isabel King bent forward, her brown eyes on Alan's face.

"Did you see Lynde Oliver?" she asked with suppressed eagerness.

Alan ignored the question—perhaps he did not hear it.

"Have they lived there long?" he asked.

"For eighteen years," said Mrs. Danby placidly. "It's funny you haven't heard them mentioned. But people don't talk much about the Captain now—he's an old story—and of course they never go anywhere, not even to church. The Captain is a rank infidel and they say his daughter is just as bad. To be sure, nobody knows much about her, but it stands to reason that a girl who's had her bringing up must be odd, to say no worse of her. It's not really her fault, I suppose—her wicked old scalawag of a father is to blame for it. She's never darkened a church or school door in her life and they say she's always been a regular tomboy—running wild outdoors with dogs, and fishing and shooting like a man. Nobody ever goes there—the Captain doesn't want visitors. He must have done something dreadful in his time, if it was only known, when he's so set on living like a hermit away down on that jumping-off place. Did you see any of them?"

"I saw Miss Oliver, I suppose," said Alan briefly. "At least I met a young lady on the shore. But where did these people come from? Surely more is known of them than this."

"Precious little. The truth is, Mr. Douglas, folks don't think the Olivers respectable and don't want to have anything to do with them. Eighteen years ago Captain Anthony came from goodness knows where, bought the Four Winds point, and built that house. He said he'd been a sailor all his life and couldn't live away from the water. He brought his wife and child and an old cousin of his with him. This Lynde wasn't more than two years old then. People went to call but they never saw any of the women and the Captain let them see they weren't wanted. Some of the men who'd been working round the place saw his wife and said she was sickly but real handsome and like a lady, but she never seemed to want to see anyone or be seen herself. There was a story that the Captain had been a smuggler and that if he was caught he'd be sent to prison. Oh, there were all sorts of yarns, mostly coming from the men who worked there, for nobody else ever got inside the house. Well, four years ago his wife disappeared—it wasn't known how or when. She just wasn't ever seen again, that's all. Whether she died or was murdered or went away nobody ever knew. There was some talk of an investigation but nothing came of it. As for the girl, she's always lived there with her father. She must be a perfect heathen. He never goes anywhere, but there used to be talk of strangers visiting him—queer sort of characters who came up the lake in vessels from the American side. I haven't heard any reports of such these past few years, though—not since his wife disappeared. He keeps a yacht and goes sailing in it—sometimes he cruises about for weeks—that's about all he ever does. And now you know as much about the Olivers as I do, Mr. Douglas."

Alan had listened to this gossipy narrative with an interest that did not escape Isabel King's observant eyes. Much of it he mentally dismissed as improbable surmise, but the basic facts were probably as Mrs. Danby had reported them. He had known that the girl of the shore could be no commonplace, primly nurtured young woman.

"Has no effort ever been made to bring these people into touch with the church?" he asked absently.

"Bless you, yes. Every minister that's ever been in Rexton has had a try at it. The old cousin met every one of them at the door and told him nobody was at home. Mr. Strong was the most persistent—he didn't like being beaten. He went again and again and finally the Captain sent him word that when he wanted parsons or pill-dosers he'd send for them, and till he did he'd thank them to mind their own business. They say Mr. Strong met Lynde once along shore and wanted to know if she wouldn't come to church, and she laughed in his face and told him she knew more about God now than he did or ever would. Perhaps the story isn't true. Or if it was maybe he provoked her into saying it. Mr. Strong wasn't overly tactful. I believe in judging the poor girl as charitably as possible and making allowances for her, seeing how she's been brought up. You couldn't expect her to know how to behave."

Somehow, Alan resented Mrs. Danby's charity. Then, his sense of humour being strongly developed, he smiled to think of this commonplace old lady "making allowances" for the splendid bit of femininity he had seen on the shore. A plump barnyard fowl might as well have talked of making allowances for a seagull!

Alan walked home with Isabel King but he was very silent as they went together down the long, dark, sweet-smelling country road bordered by its white orchards. Isabel put her own construction on his absent replies to her remarks and presently she asked him, "Did you think Lynde Oliver handsome?"

The question gave Alan an annoyance out of all proportion to its significance. He felt an instinctive reluctance to discuss Lynde Oliver with Isabel King.

"I saw her only for a moment," he said coldly, "but she impressed me as being a beautiful woman."

"They tell queer stories about her—but maybe they're not all true," said Isabel, unable to keep the sneer of malice out of her voice. At that moment Alan's secret contempt for her crystallized into pronounced aversion. He made no reply and they went the rest of the way in silence. At her gate Isabel said, "You haven't been over to see us very lately, Mr. Douglas."

"My congregation is a large one and I cannot visit all my people as often as I might wish," Alan answered, all the more coldly for the personal note in her tone. "A minister's time is not his own, you know."

"Shall you be going to see the Olivers?" asked Isabel bluntly.

"I have not considered that question. Good-night, Miss King."

On his way back to the manse Alan did consider the question. Should he make any attempt to establish friendly relations with the residents of Four Winds? It surprised him to find how much he wanted to, but he finally concluded that he would not. They were not adherents of his church and he did not believe that even a minister had any right to force himself upon people who plainly wished to be let alone.

When he got home, although it was late, he went to his study and began work on a new text—for Elder Trewin's seemed utterly out of the question. Even with the new one he did not get on very well. At last in exasperation he leaned back in his chair.

Why can't I stop thinking of those Four Winds people? Here, let me put these haunting thoughts into words and see if that will lay them. That girl had a beautiful face but a cold one. Would I like to see it lighted up with the warmth of her soul set free? Yes, frankly, I would. She looked upon me with indifference. Would I like to see her welcome me as a friend? I have a conviction that I would, although no doubt everybody in my congregation would look upon her as a most unsuitable friend for me. Do I believe that she is wild, unwomanly, heathenish, as Mrs. Danby says? No, I do not, most emphatically. I believe she is a lady in the truest sense of that much abused word, though she is doubtless unconventional. Having said all this, I do not see what more there is to be said. And—I—am—going—to—write—this—sermon.

Alan wrote it, putting all thought of Lynde Oliver sternly out of his mind for the time being. He had no notion of falling in love with her. He knew nothing of love and imagined that it counted for nothing in his life. He admitted that his curiosity was aflame about the girl, but it never occurred to him that she meant or could mean anything to him but an attractive enigma which once solved would lose its attraction. The young women he knew in Rexton, whose simple, pleasant friendship he valued, had the placid, domestic charm of their own sweet-breathed, windless orchards. Lynde Oliver had the fascination of the lake shore—wild, remote, untamed—the lure of the wilderness and the primitive. There was nothing more personal in his thought of her, and yet when he recalled Isabel King's sneer he felt an almost personal resentment.

During the following fortnight Alan made many trips to the shore—and he always went by the branch road to the Four Winds point. He did not attempt to conceal from himself that he hoped to meet Lynde Oliver again. In this he was unsuccessful. Sometimes he saw her at a distance along the shore but she always disappeared as soon as seen. Occasionally as he crossed the point he saw her working in her garden but he never went very near the house, feeling that he had no right to spy on it or her in any way. He soon became convinced that she avoided him purposely and the conviction piqued him. He felt an odd masterful desire to meet her face to face and make her look at him. Sometimes he called himself a fool and vowed he would go no more to the Four Winds shore. Yet he inevitably went. He did not find in the shore the comfort and inspiration he had formerly found. Something had come between his soul and the soul of the wilderness—something he did not recognize or formulate—a nameless, haunting longing that shaped itself about the memory of a cold sweet face and starry, indifferent eyes, grey as the lake at dawn.

Of Captain Anthony he never got even a glimpse, but he saw the old cousin several times, going and coming about the yard and its environs. Finally one day he met her, coming up a path which led to a spring down in a firry hollow. She was carrying two heavy pails of water and Alan asked permission to help her.

He half expected a repulse, for the tall, grim old woman had a rather stern and forbidding look, but after gazing at him a moment in a somewhat scrutinizing manner she said briefly, "You may, if you like."

Alan took the pails and followed her, the path not being wide enough for two. She strode on before him at a rapid, vigorous pace until they came out into the yard by the house. Alan felt his heart beating foolishly. Would he see Lynde Oliver? Would—

"You may carry the water there," the old woman said, pointing to a little outhouse near the pines. "I'm washing—the spring water is softer than the well water. Thank you"—as Alan set the pails down on a bench—"I'm not so young as I was and bringing the water so far tires me. Lynde always brings it for me when she's home."

She stood before him in the narrow doorway, blocking his exit, and looked at him with keen, deep-set dark eyes. In spite of her withered aspect and wrinkled face, she was not an uncomely old woman and there was about her a dignity of carriage and manner that pleased Alan. It did not occur to him to wonder why it should please him. If he had hunted that feeling down he might have been surprised to discover that it had its origin in a curious gratification over the thought that the woman who lived with Lynde had a certain refinement about her. He preferred her unsmiling dourness to vulgar garrulity.

"Are you the young minister up at Rexton?" she asked bluntly.

"Yes."

"I thought so. Lynde said she had seen you on the shore once. Well"—she cast an uncertain glance over her shoulder at the house—"I'm much obliged to you."

Alan had an idea that that was not what she had thought of saying, but as she had turned aside and was busying herself with the pails, there seemed nothing for him to do but to go.

"Wait a moment." She faced him again, and if Alan had been a vain man he might have thought that admiration looked from her piercing eyes. "What do you think of us? I suppose they've told you tales of us up there?"—with a scornful gesture of her hand in the direction of Rexton. "Do you believe them?"

"I believe no ill of anyone until I have absolute proof of it," said Alan, smiling—he was quite unconscious what a winning smile he had, which was the best of it—"and I never put faith in gossip. Of course you are gossipped about—you know that."

"Yes, I know it"—grimly—"and I don't care what they say about the Captain and me. We are a queer pair—just as queer as they make us out. You can believe what you like about us, but don't you believe a word they say against Lynde. She's sweet and good and beautiful. It's not her fault that she never went to church—it's her father's. Don't you hold that against her."

The fierce yet repressed energy of her tone prevented Alan from feeling any amusement over her simple defence of Lynde. Moreover, it sounded unreasonably sweet in his ears.

"I won't," he promised, "but I don't suppose it would matter much to Miss Oliver if I did. She did not strike me as a young lady who would worry very much about other people's opinions."

If his object were to prolong the conversation about Lynde, he was disappointed, for the old woman had turned abruptly to her work again and, though Alan lingered for a few moments longer, she took no further notice of him. But when he had gone she peered stealthily after him from the door until he was lost to sight among the pines.

"A well-looking man," she muttered. "I wish Lynde had been home. I didn't dare ask him to the house for I knew Anthony was in one of his moods. But it's time something was done. She's woman grown and this is no life for her. And there's nobody to do anything but me and I'm not able, even if I knew what to do. I wonder why she hates men so. Perhaps it's because she never knew any that were real gentlemen. This man is—but then he's a minister and that makes a wide gulf between them in another way. I've seen the love of man and woman bridge some wider gulfs though. But it can't with Lynde, I'm fearing. She's so bitter at the mere speaking of love and marriage. I can't think why. I'm sure her mother and Anthony were happy together, and that was all she's ever seen of marriage. But I thought when she told me of meeting this young man on the shore there was something in her look I'd never noticed before—as if she'd found something in herself she'd never known was there. But she'll never make friends with him and I can't. If the Captain wasn't so queer—"

She stopped abruptly, for a tall lithe figure was coming up from the shore. Lynde waved her hand as she drew near.

"Oh, Emily, I've had such a splendid sail. It was glorious. Bad Emily, you've been carrying water. Didn't I tell you never to do that when I was away?"

"I didn't have to do it. That young minister up at Rexton met me and brought it up. He's nice, Lynde."

Lynde's brow darkened. She turned and walked away to the house without a word.

On his way home that night Alan met Isabel King on the main shore road. She carried an armful of pine boughs and said she wanted the needles for a cushion. Yet the thought came into Alan's mind that she was spying on him and, although he tried to dismiss it as unworthy, it continued to lurk there.

For a week he avoided the shore, but there came a day when its inexplicable lure drew him to it again irresistibly. It was a warm, windy evening and the air was sweet and resinous, the lake misty and blue. There was no sign of life about Four Winds and the shore seemed as lonely and virgin as if human foot had never trodden it. The Captain's yacht was gone from the little harbour where it was generally anchored and, though every flutter of wind in the scrub firs made Alan's heart beat expectantly, he saw nothing of Lynde Oliver. He was on the point of turning homeward, with an unreasoning sense of disappointment, when one of Lynde's dogs broke down through the hedge of spruces, barking loudly.

Alan looked for Lynde to follow, but she did not, and he speedily saw that there was something unusual about the dog's behaviour. The animal circled around him, still barking excitedly, then ran off for a short distance, stopped, barked again, and returned, repeating the manoeuvre. It was plain that he wanted Alan to follow him, and it occurred to the young minister that the dog's mistress must be in danger of some kind. Instantly he set off after him; and the dog, with a final sharp bark of satisfaction, sprang up the low bank into the spruces.

Alan followed him across the peninsula and then along the further shore, which rapidly grew steep and high. Half a mile down the cliffs were rocky and precipitous, while the beach beneath them was heaped with huge boulders. Alan followed the dog along one of the narrow paths with which the barrens abounded until nearly a mile from Four Winds. Then the animal halted, ran to the edge of the cliff and barked.

It was an ugly-looking place where a portion of the soil had evidently broken away recently, and Alan stepped cautiously out to the brink and looked down. He could not repress an exclamation of dismay and alarm.

A few feet below him Lynde Oliver was lying on a mass of mossy soil which was apparently on the verge of slipping over a sloping shelf of rock, below which was a sheer drop of thirty feet to the cruel boulders below. The extreme danger of her position was manifest at a glance; the soil on which she lay was stationary, yet it seemed as if the slightest motion on her part would send it over the brink.

Lynde lay movelessly; her face was white, and both fear and appeal were visible in her large dilated eyes. Yet she was quite calm and a faint smile crossed her pale lips as she saw the man and the dog.

"Good faithful Pat, so you did bring help," she said.

"But how can I help you, Miss Oliver?" said Alan hoarsely. "I cannot reach you—and it looks as if the slightest touch or jar would send that broken earth over the brink."

"I fear it would. You must go back to Four Winds and get a rope."

"And leave you here alone—in such danger?"

"Pat will stay with me. Besides, there is nothing else to do. You will find a rope in that little house where you put the water for Emily. Father and Emily are away. I think I am quite safe here if I don't move at all."

Alan's own common sense told him that, as she said, there was nothing else to do and, much as he hated to leave her alone thus, he realized that he must lose no time in doing it.

"I'll be back as quickly as possible," he said hurriedly.

Alan had been a noted runner at college and his muscles had not forgotten their old training. Yet it seemed to him an age ere he reached Four Winds, secured the rope, and returned. At every flying step he was haunted by the thought of the girl lying on the brink of the precipice and the fear that she might slip over it before he could rescue her. When he reached the scene of the accident he dreaded to look over the broken edge, but she was lying there safely and she smiled when she saw him—a brave smile that softened her tense white face into the likeness of a frightened child's.

"If I drop the rope down to you, are you strong enough to hold to it while the earth goes and then draw yourself up the slope hand over hand?" asked Alan anxiously.

"Yes," she answered fearlessly.

Alan passed down one end of the rope and then braced himself firmly to hold it, for there was no tree near enough to be of any assistance. The next moment the full weight of her body swung from it, for at her first movement the soil beneath her slipped away. Alan's heart sickened; what if she went with it? Could she cling to the rope while he drew her up?

Then he saw she was still safe on the sloping shelf. Carefully and painfully she drew herself to her knees and, dinging to the rope, crept up the rock hand over hand. When she came within his reach he grasped her arms and lifted her up into safety beside him.

"Thank God," he said, with whiter lips than her own.

For a few moments Lynde sat silent on the sod, exhausted with fright and exertion, while her dog fawned on her in an ecstasy of joy. Finally she looked up into Alan's anxious face and their eyes met. It was something more than the physical reaction that suddenly flushed the girl's cheeks. She sprang lithely to her feet.

"Can you walk back home?" Alan asked.

"Oh, yes, I am all right now. It was very foolish of me to get into such a predicament. Father and Emily went down the lake in the yacht this afternoon and I started out for a ramble. When I came here I saw some junebells growing right out on the ledge and I crept out to gather them. I should have known better. It broke away under me and the more I tried to scramble back the faster it slid down, carrying me with it. I thought it would go right over the brink"—she gave a little involuntary shudder—"but just at the very edge it stopped. I knew I must lie very still or it would go right over. It seemed like days. Pat was with me and I told him to go for help, but I knew there was no one at home—and I was horribly afraid," she concluded with another shiver. "I never was afraid in my life before—at least not with that kind of fear."

"You have had a terrible experience and a narrow escape," said Alan lamely. He could think of nothing more to say; his usual readiness of utterance seemed to have failed him.

"You saved my life," she said, "you and Pat—for doggie must have his share of credit."

"A much larger share than mine," said Alan, smiling. "If Pat had not come for me, I would not have known of your danger. What a magnificent fellow he is!"

"Isn't he?" she agreed proudly. "And so is Laddie, my other dog. He went with Father today. I love my dogs more than people." She looked at him with a little defiance in her eyes. "I suppose you think that terrible."

"I think many dogs are much more lovable—and worthy of love—than many people," said Alan, laughing.

How childlike she was in some ways! That trace of defiance—it was so like a child who expected to be scolded for some wrong attitude of mind. And yet there were moments when she looked the tall proud queen. Sometimes, when the path grew narrow, she walked before him, her hand on the dog's head. Alan liked this, since it left him free to watch admiringly the swinging grace of her step and the white curves of her neck beneath the thick braid of hair, which today was wound about her head. When she dropped back beside him in the wider spaces, he could only have stolen glances at her profile, delicately, strongly cut, virginal in its soft curves, childlike in its purity. Once she looked around and caught his glance; again she flushed, and something strange and exultant stirred in Alan's heart. It was as if that maiden blush were the involuntary, unconscious admission of some power he had over her—a power which her hitherto unfettered spirit had never before felt. The cold indifference he had seen in her face at their first meeting was gone, and something told him it was gone forever.

When they came in sight of Four Winds they saw two people walking up the road from the harbour and a few further steps brought them face to face with Captain Anthony Oliver and his old housekeeper.

The Captain's appearance was a fresh surprise to Alan. He had expected to meet a rough, burly sailor, loud of voice and forbidding of manner. Instead, Captain Anthony was a tall, well-built man of perhaps fifty. His face, beneath its shock of iron-grey hair, was handsome but wore a somewhat forbidding expression, and there was something in it, apart from line or feature, which did not please Alan. He had no time to analyze this impression, for Lynde said hurriedly, "Father, this is Mr. Douglas. He has just done me a great service."

She briefly explained her accident; when she had finished, the Captain turned to Alan and held out his hand, a frank smile replacing the rather suspicious and contemptuous scowl which had previously overshadowed it.

"I am much obliged to you, Mr. Douglas," he said cordially. "You must come up to the house and let me thank you at leisure. As a rule I'm not very partial to the cloth, as you may have heard. In this case it is the man, not the minister, I invite."

The front door of Four Winds opened directly into a wide, low-ceilinged living room, furnished with simplicity and good taste. Leaving the two men there, Lynde and the old cousin vanished, and Alan found himself talking freely with the Captain who could, as it appeared, talk well on many subjects far removed from Four Winds. He was evidently a clever, self-educated man, somewhat opinionated and given to sarcasm; he never made any references to his own past life or experiences, but Alan discovered him to be surprisingly well read in politics and science. Sometimes in the pauses of the conversation Alan found the older man looking at him in a furtive way he did not like, but the Captain was such an improvement on what he had been led to expect that he was not inclined to be over critical. At least, this was what he honestly thought. He did not suspect that it was because this man was Lynde's father that he wished to think as well as possible of him.

Presently Lynde came in. She had changed her outdoor dress, stained with moss and soil in her fall, for a soft clinging garment of some pale yellow material, and her long, thick braid of hair hung over her shoulder. She sat mutely down in a dim corner and took no part in the conversation except to answer briefly the remarks which Alan addressed to her. Emily came in and lighted the lamp on the table. She was as grim and unsmiling as ever, yet she cast a look of satisfaction on Alan as she passed out. One dog lay down at Lynde's feet, the other sat on his haunches by her side and laid his head on her lap. Rexton and its quiet round of parish duties seemed thousands of miles away from Alan, and he wondered a little if this were not all a dream.

When he went away the Captain invited him back.

"If you like to come, that is," he said brusquely, "and always as the man, not the priest, remember. I don't want you by and by to be slyly slipping in the thin end of any professional wedges. You'll waste your time if you do. Come as man to man and you'll be welcome, for I like you—and it's few men I like. But don't try to talk religion to me."

"I never talk religion," said Alan emphatically. "I try to live it. I'll not come to your house as a self-appointed missionary, sir, but I shall certainly act and speak at all times as my conscience and my reverence for my vocation demands. If I respect your beliefs, whatever they may be, I shall expect you to respect mine, Captain Oliver."

"Oh, I won't insult your God," said the Captain with a faint sneer.

Alan went home in a tumult of contending feelings. He did not altogether like Captain Anthony—that was very clear to him, and yet there was something about the man that attracted him. Intellectually he was a worthy foeman, and Alan had often longed for such since coming to Rexton. He missed the keen, stimulating debates of his college days and, now there seemed a chance of renewing them, he was eager to grasp it. And Lynde—how beautiful she was! What though she shared—as was not unlikely—in her father's lack of belief? She could not be essentially irreligious—that were impossible in a true woman. Might not this be his opportunity to help her—to lead her into dearer light? Alan Douglas was a sincere man, with himself as well as with others, yet there are some motives that lie, in their first inception, too deep even for the probe of self-analysis. He had not as yet the faintest suspicion as to the real source of his interest in Lynde Oliver—in his sudden forceful desire to be of use and service to her—to rescue her from spiritual peril as he had that day rescued her from bodily danger.

She must have a lonely, unsatisfying life, he thought. It is my duty to help her if I can.

It did not then occur to him that duty in this instance wore a much more pleasing aspect than it had sometimes worn in his experience.

Alan did not mean to be oversoon in going back to Four Winds, but three days later a book came to him which Captain Anthony had expressed a wish to see. It furnished an excuse for an earlier call. After that he went often. He always found the Captain courteous and affable, old Emily grimly cordial, Lynde sometimes remote and demure, sometimes frankly friendly. Occasionally, when the Captain was away in his yacht, he went for a walk with her and her dogs along the shore or through the sweet-smelling pinelands up the lake. He found that she loved books and was avid for more of them than she could obtain; he was glad to take her several and discuss them with her. She liked history and travels best. With novels she had no patience, she said disdainfully. She seldom spoke of herself or her past life and Alan fancied she avoided any personal reference. But once she said abruptly, "Why do you never ask me to go to church? I've always been afraid you would."

"Because I do not think it would do you any good to go if you didn't want to," said Alan gravely. "Souls should not be rudely handled any more than bodies."

She looked at him reflectively, her finger denting her chin in a meditative fashion she had.

"You are not at all like Mr. Strong. He always scolded me, when he got a chance, for not going to church. I would have hated him if it had been worthwhile. I told him one day that I was nearer to God under these pines than I could be in any building fashioned by human hands. He was very much shocked. But I don't want you to misunderstand me. Father does not go to church because he does not believe there is a

God. But I know there is. Mother taught me so. I have never gone to church because Father would not allow me, and I could not go now in Rexton where the people talk about me so. Oh, I know they do—you know it, too—but I do not care for them. I know I'm not like other girls. I would like to be but I can't be—I never can be—now."

There was some strange passion in her voice that Alan did not quite understand—a bitterness and a revolt which he took to be against the circumstances that hedged her in.

"Is not some other life possible for you if your present life does not content you?" he said gently.

"But it does content me," said Lynde imperiously. "I want no other—I wish this life to go on forever—forever, do you understand? If I were sure that it would—if I were sure that no change would ever come to me, I would be perfectly content. It is the fear that a change will come that makes me wretched. Oh!" She shuddered and put her hands over her eyes.

Alan thought she must mean that when her father died she would be alone in the world. He wanted to comfort her—reassure her—but he did not know how.

One evening when he went to Four Winds he found the door open and, seeing the Captain in the living room, he stepped in unannounced. Captain Anthony was sitting by the table, his head in his hands; at Alan's entrance he turned upon him a haggard face, blackened by a furious scowl beneath which blazed eyes full of malevolence.

"What do you want here?" he said, following up the demand with a string of vile oaths.

Before Alan could summon his scattered wits, Lynde glided in with a white, appealing face. Wordlessly she grasped Alan's arm, drew him out, and shut the door.

"Oh, I've been watching for you," she said breathlessly. "I was afraid you might come tonight—but I missed you."

"But your father?" said Alan in amazement. "How have I angered him?"

"Hush. Come into the garden. I will explain there."

He followed her into the little enclosure where the red and white roses were now in full blow.

"Father isn't angry with you," said Lynde in a low shamed voice. "It's just—he takes strange moods sometimes. Then he seems to hate us all—even me—and he is like that for days. He seems to suspect and dread everybody as if they were plotting against him. You—perhaps you think he has been drinking? No, that is not the trouble. These terrible moods come on without any cause that we know of. Even Mother could not do anything with him when he was like that. You must go away now—and do not come back until his dark mood has passed. He will be just as glad to see you as ever then, and this will not make any difference with him. Don't come back for a week at least."

"I do not like to leave you in such trouble, Miss Oliver."

"Oh, it doesn't matter about me—I have Emily. And there is nothing you could do. Please go at once. Father knows I am talking to you and that will vex him still more."

Alan, realizing that he could not help her and that his presence only made matters worse, went away perplexedly. The following week was a miserable one for him. His duties were distasteful to him and meeting his people a positive torture. Sometimes Mrs. Danby looked dubiously at him and seemed on the point of saying something—but never said it. Isabel King watched him when they met, with bold probing eyes. In his abstraction he did not notice this any more than he noticed a certain subtle change which had come over the members of his congregation—as if a breath of suspicion had blown across them and troubled their confidence and trust. Once Alan would have been keenly and instantly conscious of this slight chill; now he was not even aware of it.

When he ventured to go back to Four Winds he found the Captain on the point of starting off for a cruise in his yacht. He was urbane and friendly, utterly ignoring the incident of Alan's last visit and regretting that business compelled him to go down the lake. Alan saw him off with small regret and turned joyfully to Lynde, who was walking under the pines with her dogs. She looked pale and tired and her eyes were still troubled, but she smiled proudly and made no reference to what had happened.

"I'm going to put these flowers on Mother's grave," she said, lifting her slender hands filled with late white roses. "Mother loved flowers and I always keep them near her when I can. You may come with me if you like."

Alan had known Lynde's mother was buried under the pines but he had never visited the spot before. The grave was at the westernmost end of the pine wood, where it gave out on the lake, a beautiful spot, given over to silence and shadow.

"Mother wished to be buried here," Lynde said, kneeling to arrange her flowers. "Father would have taken her anywhere but she said she wanted to be near us and near the lake she had loved so well. Father buried her himself. He wouldn't have anyone else do anything for her.

I am so glad she is here. It would have been terrible to have seen her taken far away—my sweet little mother."

"A mother is the best thing in the world—I realized that when I lost mine," said Alan gently. "How long is it since your mother died?"

"Three years. Oh, I thought I should die too when she did. She was very ill—she was never strong, you know—but I never thought she could die. There was a year then—part of the time I didn't believe in God at all and the rest I hated Him. I was very wicked but I was so unhappy. Father had so many dreadful moods and—there was something else. I used to wish to die."

She bowed her head on her hands and gazed moodily on the ground. Alan, leaning against a pine tree, looked down at her. The sunlight fell through the swaying boughs on her glory of burnished hair and lighted up the curve of cheek and chin against the dark background of wood brown. All the defiance and wildness had gone from her for the time and she seemed like a helpless, weary child. He wanted to take her in his arms and comfort her.

"You must resemble your mother," he said absently, as if thinking aloud. "You don't look at all like your father."

Lynde shook her head.

"No, I don't look like Mother either. She was tiny and dark—she had a sweet little face and velvet-brown eyes and soft curly dark hair. Oh, I remember her look so well. I wish I did resemble her. I loved her so—I would have done anything to save her suffering and trouble. At least, she died in peace."

There was a curious note of fierce self-gratulation in the girl's voice as she spoke the last sentence. Again Alan felt the unpleasant impression that there was much in her that he did not understand—might never understand—although such understanding was necessary to perfect friendship. She had never spoken so freely of her past life to him before, yet he felt somehow that something was being kept back in jealous repression. It must be something connected with her father, Alan thought. Doubtless, Captain Anthony's past would not bear inspection, and his daughter knew it and dwelt in the shadow of her knowledge. His heart filled with aching pity for her; he raged secretly because he was so powerless to help her. Her girlhood had been blighted, robbed of its meed of happiness and joy. Was she likewise to miss her womanhood? Alan's hands clenched involuntarily at the unuttered question.

On his way home that evening he again met Isabel King. She turned and walked back with him but she made no reference to Four

Winds or its inhabitants. If Alan had troubled himself to look, he would have seen a malicious glow in her baleful brown eyes. But the only eyes which had any meaning for him just then were the grey ones of Lynde Oliver.

During Alan's next three visits to Four Winds he saw nothing of Lynde, either in the house or out of it. This surprised and worried him. There was no apparent difference in Captain Anthony, who continued to be suave and friendly. Alan always enjoyed his conversations with the Captain, who was witty, incisive, and pungent; yet he disliked the man himself more at every visit. If he had been compelled to define his impression, he would have said the Captain was a charming scoundrel.

But it occurred to him that Emily was disturbed about something. Sometimes he caught her glance, full of perplexity and—it almost seemed—distrust. She looked as if she felt hostile towards him. But Alan dismissed the idea as absurd. She had been friendly from the first and he had done nothing to excite her disapproval. Lynde's mysterious absence was a far more perplexing problem. She had not gone away, for when Alan asked the Captain concerning her, he responded indifferently that she was out walking. Alan caught a glint of amusement in the older man's eyes as he spoke. He could have sworn it was malicious amusement.

One evening he went to Four Winds around the shore. As he turned the headland of the cove, he saw Lynde and her dogs not a hundred feet away. The moment she saw him she darted up the bank and disappeared among the firs.

Alan was thunderstruck. There was no room for doubt that she meant to avoid him. He walked up to the house in a tumult of mingled feelings which he did not even then understand. He only realized that he felt bitterly hurt and grieved—puzzled as well. What did it all mean?

He met Emily in the yard of Four Winds on her way to the spring and stopped her resolutely.

"Miss Oliver," he said bluntly, "is Miss Lynde angry with me? And why?"

Emily looked at him piercingly.

"Have you no idea why?" she asked shortly.

"None in the world."

She looked at him through and through a moment longer. Then, seeming satisfied with her scrutiny, she picked up her pail.

"Come down to the spring with me," she said.

As soon as they were out of sight of the house, Emily began abruptly.

"If you don't know why Lynde is acting so, I can't tell you, for I don't know either. I don't even know if she is angry. I only thought perhaps she was—that you had done or said something to vex her—plaguing her to go to church maybe. But if you didn't, it may not be anger at all. I don't understand that girl. She's been different ever since her mother died. She used to tell me everything before that. You must go and ask her right out yourself what is wrong. But maybe I can tell you something. Did you write her a letter a fortnight ago?"

"A letter? No."

"Well, she got one then. I thought it came from you—I didn't know who else would be writing to her. A boy brought it and gave it to her at the door. She's been acting strange ever since. She cries at night—something Lynde never did before except when her mother died. And in daytime she roams the shore and woods like one possessed. You must find out what was in that letter, Mr. Douglas."

"Have you any idea who the boy was?" Alan asked, feeling somewhat relieved. The mystery was clearing up, he thought. No doubt it was the old story of some cowardly anonymous letter. His thoughts flew involuntarily to Isabel King.

Emily shook her head.

"No. He was just a half-grown fellow with reddish hair and he limped a little."

"Oh, that is the postmaster's son," said Alan disappointedly. "That puts us further off the scent than ever. The letter was probably dropped in the box at the office and there will consequently be no way of tracing the writer."

"Well, I can't tell you anything more," said Emily. "You'll have to ask Lynde for the truth."

This Alan was determined to do whenever he should meet her. He did not go to the house with Emily but wandered about the shore, watching for Lynde and not seeing her. At length he went home, a prey to stormy emotions. He realized at last that he loved Lynde Oliver. He wondered how he could have been so long blind to it. He knew that he must have loved her ever since he had first seen her. The discovery amazed but did not shock him. There was no reason why he should not love her—should not woo and win her for his wife if she cared for him. She was good and sweet and true. Anything of doubt in her antecedents could not touch her. Probably the world would look upon Captain Anthony as a somewhat undesirable father-in-law for a minister, but that aspect of the question did not disturb Alan. As for the trouble of the letter, he felt sure he would easily be able to clear it away. Probably some malicious busybody had become aware of his frequent calls at Four Winds and chose to interfere in his private affairs thus. For the first time it occurred to him that there had been a certain lack of cordiality among his people of late. If it were really so, doubtless this was the reason. At any other time this would have been of moment to him. But now his thoughts were too wholly taken up with Lynde and the estrangement on her part to attach much importance to anything else. What she thought mattered incalculably more to Alan than what all the people in Rexton put together thought. He had the right, like any other man, to woo the woman of his choice and he would certainly brook no outside interference in the matter.

After a sleepless night he went back to Four Winds in the morning. Lynde would not expect him at that time and he would have more chance of finding her. The result justified his idea, for he met her by the spring.

Alan felt shocked at the change in her appearance. She looked as if years of suffering had passed over her. Her lips were pallid, and hollow circles under her eyes made them appear unnaturally large. He had last left the girl in the bloom of her youth; he found her again a woman on whom life had laid its heavy hand.

A burning flood of colour swept over her face as they met, then receded as quickly, leaving her whiter than before. Without any waste of words, Alan plunged abruptly into the subject.

"Miss Oliver, why have you avoided me so of late? Have I done anything to offend you?"

"No." She spoke as if the word hurt her, her eyes persistently cast down.

"Then what is the trouble?"

There was no answer. She gave an unvoluntary glance around as if seeking some way of escape. There was none, for the spring was set about with thick young firs and Alan blocked the only path.

He leaned forward and took her hands in his.

"Miss Oliver, you must tell me what the trouble is," he said firmly.

She pulled her hands away and flung them up to her face, her form shaken by stormy sobs. In distress he put his arm about her and drew her closer.

"Tell me, Lynde," he whispered tenderly.

She broke away from him, saying passionately, "You must not come to Four Winds any more. You must not have anything more to do with us—any of us. We have done you enough harm already. But I never thought it could hurt you—oh, I am sorry, sorry!"

"Miss Oliver, I want to see that letter you received the other evening. Oh"—as she started with surprise—"I know about it—Emily told me. Who wrote it?"

"There was no name signed to it," she faltered.

"Just as I thought. Well, you must let me see it."

"I cannot—I burned it."

"Then tell me what was in it. You must. This matter must be cleared up—I am not going to have our beautiful friendship spoiled by the malice of some coward. What did that letter say?"

"It said that everybody in your congregation was talking about your frequent visits here—that it had made a great scandal—that it was doing you a great deal of injury and would probably end in your having to leave Rexton."

"That would be a catastrophe indeed," said Alan drily. "Well, what else?"

"Nothing more—at least, nothing about you. The rest was about myself—I did not mind it—much. But I was so sorry to think that I had done you harm. It is not too late to undo it. You must not come here any more. Then they will forget."

"Perhaps—but I should not forget. It's a little too late for me. Lynde, you must not let this venomous letter come between us. I love you, dear—I've loved you ever since I met you and I want you for my wife."

Alan had not intended to say that just then, but the words came to his lips in spite of himself. She looked so sad and appealing and weary that he wanted to have the right to comfort and protect her.

She turned her eyes full upon him with no hint of maidenly shyness or shrinking in them. Instead, they were full of a blank, incredulous horror that swallowed up every other feeling. There was no mistaking their expression and it struck an icy chill to Alan's heart. He had certainly not expected a too ready response on her part—he knew that even if she cared for him he might find it a matter of time to win her avowal of it—but he certainly had not expected to see such evident abject dismay as her blanched face betrayed. She put up her hand as if warding a blow.

"Don't—don't," she gasped. "You must not say that—you must never say it. Oh, I never dreamed of this. If I had thought it possible you could—love me, I would never have been friends with you. Oh, I've made a terrible mistake."

She wrung her hands piteously together, looking like a soul in torment. Alan could not bear to see her pain.

"Don't feel such distress," he implored. "I suppose I've spoken too abruptly—but I'll be so patient, dear, if you'll only try to care for me a little. Can't you, dear?"

"I can't marry you," said Lynde desperately. She leaned against a slim white bole of a young birch behind her and looked at him wretchedly. "Won't you please go away and forget me?"

"I can't forget you," Alan said, smiling a little in spite of his suffering. "You are the only woman I can ever love—and I can't give you up unless I have to. Won't you be frank with me, dear? Do you honestly think you can never learn to love me?"

"It is not that," said Lynde in a hard, unnatural voice. "I am married already."

Alan stared at her, not in the least comprehending the meaning of her words. Everything—pain, hope, fear, passion—had slipped away from him for a moment, as if he had been stunned by a physical blow. He could not have heard aright.

"Married?" he said dully. "Lynde, you cannot mean it?"

"Yes, I do. I was married three years ago."

"Why was I not told this?" Alan's voice was stern, although he did not mean it to be so, and she shrank and shivered. Then she began in a low monotonous tone from which all feeling of any sort seemed to have utterly faded.

"Three years ago Mother was very ill—so ill that any shock would kill her, so the doctor Father brought from the lake told us. A man—a young sea captain—came here to see Father. His name was Frank Harmon and he had known Father well in the past. They had sailed together. Father seemed to be afraid of him—I had never seen him afraid of anybody before. I could not think much about anybody except Mother then, but I knew I did not quite like Captain Harmon, although he was very polite to me and I suppose might have been called handsome. One day Father came to me and told me I must marry Captain Harmon. I laughed at the idea at first but when I looked at Father's face I did not laugh. It was all white and drawn. He implored me to marry Captain Harmon. He said if I did not it would mean shame and disgrace for us all—that Captain Harmon had some hold on him and would tell what he knew if I did not marry him. I don't know what it was but it must have been something dreadful. And he said it would kill Mother. I knew it would, and that was what drove me to consent at last. Oh, I can't tell you what I suffered. I was only seventeen and there was nobody to advise me. One day Father and Captain Harmon and I went down the lake to Crosse Harbour and we were married there. As soon as the ceremony was over, Captain Harmon had to sail in his vessel. He was going to China. Father and I came back home. Nobody knew—not even Emily. He said we must not tell Mother until she was better. But she was never better. She only lived three months more—she lived them happily and at rest. When I think of that, I am not sorry for what I did. Captain Harmon said he would be back in the fall to claim me. I waited, sick at heart. But he did not come—he has never come. We have never heard a word of or about him since. Sometimes I feel sure he cannot be still living. But never a day dawns that I don't say to myself, 'Perhaps he will come today'—and, oh—"

She broke down again, sobbing bitterly. Amid all the daze of his own pain Alan realized that, at any cost, he must not make it harder for her by showing his suffering. He tried to speak calmly, wisely, as a disinterested friend.

"Could it not be discovered whether your—this man—is or is not living? Surely your father could find out."

Lynde shook her head.

"No, he says he has no way of doing so. We do not know if Captain Harmon had any relatives or even where his home was, and it was his own ship in which he sailed. Father would be glad to think that Frank Harmon was dead, but he does not think he is. He says he was always a fickle-minded fellow, one fancy driving another out of his mind. Oh, I can bear my own misery—but to think what I have brought on you! I never dreamed that you could care for me. I was so lonely and your friendship was so pleasant—can you ever forgive me?"

"There is nothing to forgive, as far as you are concerned, Lynde," said Alan steadily. "You have done me no wrong. I have loved you sincerely and such love can be nothing but a blessing to me. I only wish that I could help you. It wrings my heart to think of your position. But I can do nothing—nothing. I must not even come here any more. You understand that?"

"Yes."

There was an unconscious revelation in the girl's mournful eyes as she turned them on Alan. It thrilled him to the core of his being. She loved him. If it were not for that empty marriage form, he could win her, but the knowledge was only an added mocking torment. Alan had not known a man could endure such misery and live. A score of wild questions rushed to his lips but he crushed them back for Lynde's sake and held out his hand.

"Good-bye, dear," he said almost steadily, daring to say no more lest he should say too much.

"Good-bye," Lynde answered faintly.

When he had gone she flung herself down on the moss by the spring and lay there in an utter abandonment of misery and desolation.

Pain and indignation struggled for mastery in Alan's stormy soul as he walked homeward. So this was Captain Anthony's doings! He had sacrificed his daughter to some crime of his dubious past. Alan never dreamed of blaming Lynde for having kept her marriage a secret; he put the blame where it belonged—on the Captain's shoulders. Captain Anthony had never warned him by so much as a hint that Lynde was not free to be won. It had all probably seemed a good joke to him. Alan thought the furtive amusement he had so often detected in the Captain's eyes was explained now.

He found Elder Trewin in his study when he got home. The good Elder's face was stern and anxious; he had called on a distasteful errand—to tell the young minister of the scandal his intimacy with the Four Winds people was making in the congregation and remonstrate with him concerning it. Alan listened absently, with none of the resentment he would have felt at the interference a day previously. A man does not mind a pin-prick when a limb is being wrenched away.

"I can promise you that my objectionable calls at Four Winds will cease," he said sarcastically, when the Elder had finished. Elder Trewin got himself away, feeling snubbed but relieved.

"Took it purty quiet," he reflected. "Don't believe there was much in the yarns after all. Isabel King started them and probably she exaggerated a lot. I suppose he's had some notion like as not of bringing the Captain over to the church. But that's foolish, for he'd never manage it, and meanwhile was giving occasion for gossip. It's just as well to stop it. He's a good pastor and he works hard—too hard, mebbe. He looked real careworn and worried today."

The Rexton gossip soon ceased with the cessation of the young minister's visits to Four Winds. A month later it suffered a brief revival when a tall grim-faced old woman, whom a few recognized as Captain Anthony's housekeeper, was seen to walk down the Rexton road and enter the manse. She did not stay there long—watchers from a dozen different windows were agreed upon that—and nobody, not even Mrs. Danby, who did her best to find out, ever knew why she had called.

Emily looked at Alan with grim reproach when she was shown into his study, and as soon as they were alone she began with her usual abruptness, "Mr. Douglas, why have you given up coming to Four Winds?"

Alan flinched.

"You must ask Lynde that, Miss Oliver," he said quietly.

"I have asked her—and she says nothing."

"Then I cannot tell you."

Anger glowed in Emily's eyes.

"I thought you were a gentleman," she said bitterly. "You are not. You are breaking Lynde's heart. She's gone to a shadow of herself and she's fretting night and day. You went there and made her like you—oh, I've eyes—and then you left her."

Alan bent over his desk and looked the old woman in the face unflinchingly.

"You are mistaken, Miss Oliver," he said earnestly. "I love Lynde and would be only too happy if it were possible that I could marry her. I am not to blame for what has come about—she will tell you that herself if you ask her."

His look and tone convinced Emily.

"Who is to blame then? Lynde herself?"

"No, no."

"The Captain then?"

"Not in the sense you mean. I can tell you nothing more."

A baffled expression crossed the old woman's face. "There's a mystery here—there always has been—and I'm shut out of it. Lynde won't confide in me—in me who'd give my life's blood to help her. Perhaps I can help her—I could tell you something. Have you stopped coming to Four Winds—has she made you stop coming—because she's got such a wicked old scamp for a father? Is that the reason?"

Alan shook his head.

"No, that has nothing to do with it."

"And you won't come back?"

"It is not a question of will. I cannot—must not go."

"Lynde will break her heart then," said Emily in a tone of despair.

"I think not. She is too strong and fine for that. Help her all you can with sympathy but don't torment her with any questions. You may tell her if you like that I advise her to confide the whole story to you, but if she cannot don't tease her to. Be very gentle with her."

"You don't need to tell me that. I'd rather die than hurt her. I came here full of anger against you—but I see now you are not to blame.

You are suffering too—your face tells that. All the same, I wish you'd never set foot in Four Winds. She wasn't happy before but she wasn't so miserable as she is now. Oh, I know Anthony is at the bottom of it all in some way but I won't ask you any more questions since you don't feel free to answer them. But are you sure that nothing can be done to clear up the trouble?"

"Too sure," said Alan's white lips.

The autumn dragged away. Alan found out how much a man may suffer and yet go on living and working. As for that, his work was all that made life possible for him now and he flung himself into it with feverish energy, growing so thin and hollow-eyed over it that even Elder Trewin remonstrated and suggested a vacation—a suggestion at which Alan merely smiled. A vacation which would take him away from Lynde's neighbourhood—the thought was not to be entertained.

He never saw Lynde, for he never went to any part of the shore now; yet he hungered constantly for the sight of her, the sound of her voice, the glance of her luminous eyes. When he pictured her eating her heart out in the solitude of Four Winds, he clenched his hands in despair. As for the possibility of Harmon's return, Alan could never face it for a moment. When it thrust its ugly presence into his thoughts, he put it away desperately. The man was dead—or his fickle fancy had veered elsewhere. Nothing else could explain his absence. But they could never know, and the uncertainty would forever stand between him and Lynde like a spectre. But he thought more of Lynde's pain than his own. He would have elected to bear any suffering if by so doing he could have freed her from the nightmare dread of Harmon's returning to claim her. That dread had always hung over her and now it must be intensified to agony by her love for another man. And he could do nothing—nothing. He groaned aloud in his helplessness.

One evening in late November Alan flung aside his pen and yielded to the impulse that urged him to the lake shore. He did not mean to seek Lynde—he would go to a part of the shore where there would be no likelihood of meeting her. But get away by himself he must. A November storm was raging and there would be a certain satisfaction in breasting its buffets and fighting his way through it. Besides, he knew that Isabel King was in the house and he dreaded meeting her. Since his conviction that she had written that letter to Lynde, he could not tolerate the girl and it tasked his self-control to keep from showing his contempt openly. Perhaps Isabel felt it beneath all his outward courtesy. At least she did not seek his society as she had formerly done.

It was the second day of the storm; a wild northeast gale was blowing and cold rain and freezing sleet fell in frequent showers. Alan shivered as he came out into its full fury on the lake shore. At first he could not see the water through the driving mist. Then it cleared away for a moment and he stopped short, aghast at the sight which met his eyes.

Opposite him was a long low island known as Philip's Point, dwindling down at its northeastern side to two long narrow bars of quicksand. Alan's horrified eyes saw a small schooner sunk between the bars; her hull was entirely under water and in the rigging clung one solitary figure. So much he saw before the Point was blotted out in a renewed downpour of sleet.

Without a moment's hesitation Alan turned and ran for Four Winds, which was only about a quarter of a mile away around a headland. With the Captain's assistance, something might be done. Other help could not be obtained before darkness would fall and then it would be impossible to do anything. He dashed up the steps of Four Winds and met Emily, who had flung the door open. Behind her was Lynde's pale face with its alarmed questioning eyes.

"Where is the Captain?" gasped Alan. "There's a vessel on Philip's Point and one man at least on her."

"The Captain's away on a cruise," said Emily blankly. "He went three days ago."

"Then nothing can be done," said Alan despairingly. "It will be dark long before I can get to the village."

Lynde stepped out, tying a shawl around her head.

"Let us go around to the Point," she said. "Have you matches? No? Emily, get some. We must light a bonfire at least. And bring Father's glass."

"It is not a fit night for you to be out," said Alan anxiously. "You are sheltered here—you don't feel it—but it's a fearful storm down there."

"I am not afraid of the storm. It will not hurt me. Let us hurry. It is growing dark already."

In silence they breasted their way to the shore and around the headland. Arriving opposite Philip's Point, a lull in the sleet permitted them to see the sunken schooner and the clinging figure. Lynde waved her hand to him and they saw him wave back.

"It won't be necessary to light a fire now that he has seen us," said Lynde. "Nothing can be done with village help till morning and that man can never cling there so long. He will freeze to death, for it is growing colder every minute. His only chance is to swim ashore if he can swim. The danger will be when he comes near shore; the undertow of the backwater on the quicksand will sweep him away and in his probably exhausted condition he may not be able to make head against it."

"He knows that, doubtless, and that is why he hasn't attempted to swim ashore before this," said Alan. "But I'll meet him in the backwater and drag him in."

"You—you'll risk your own life," cried Lynde.

"There is a little risk certainly, but I don't think there is a great one. Anyhow, the attempt must be made," said Alan quietly.

Suddenly Lynde's composure forsook her. She wrung her hands.

"I can't let you do it," she cried wildly. "You might be drowned—there's every risk. You don't know the force of that backwater. Alan, Alan, don't think of it."

She caught his arm in her white wet hands and looked into his face with passionate pleading.

Emily, who had said nothing, now spoke harshly.

"Lynde is right, Mr. Douglas. You have no right to risk your life for a stranger. My advice is to go to the village for help, and Lynde and I will make a fire and watch here. That is all that can be expected of you or us."

Alan paid no heed to Emily. Very tenderly he loosened Lynde's hold on his arm and looked into her quivering face.

"You know it is my duty, Lynde," he said gently. "If anything can be done for that poor man, I am the only one who can do it. I will come back safe, please God. Be brave, dear."

Lynde, with a little moan of resignation, turned away. Old Emily looked on with a face of grim disapproval as Alan waded out into the surf that boiled and swirled around him in a mad whirl of foam. The shower of sleet had again slackened, and the wreck half a mile away, with its solitary figure, was dearly visible. Alan beckoned to the man to jump overboard and swim ashore, enforcing his appeal by gestures that commanded haste before the next shower should come. For a few moments it seemed as if the seaman did not understand or lacked the courage or power to obey. The next minute he had dropped from the rigging on the crest of a mighty wave and was being borne onward to the shore.

Speedily the backwater was reached and the man, sucked down by the swirl of the wave, threw up his arms and disappeared. Alan dashed in, groping, swimming; it seemed an eternity before his hand clutched the drowning man and wrenched him from the undertow. And, with the seaman in his arms, he staggered back through the foam and dropped his burden on the sand at Lynde's feet. Alan was reeling from exhaustion and chilled to the marrow, but he thought only of the man he had rescued. The latter was unconscious and, as Alan bent over him, he heard Lynde give a choking little cry.

"He is living still," said Alan. "We must get him up to the house as soon as possible. How shall we manage it?"

"Lynde and I can go and bring the Captain's mattress down," said Emily. Now that Alan was safe she was eager to do all she could. "Then you and I can carry him up to the house."

"That will be best," said Alan. "Go quickly."

He did not look at Lynde or he would have been shocked by the agony on her face. She cast one glance at the prostrate man and followed Emily. In a short time they returned with the mattress, and Alan and Emily carried the sailor on it to Four Winds. Lynde walked behind them, seemingly unconscious of both. She watched the stranger's face as one fascinated.

At Four Winds they carried the man to a room where Emily and Alan worked over him, while Lynde heated water and hunted out stimulants in a mechanical fashion. When Alan came down she asked no questions but looked at him with the same strained horror on her face which it had borne ever since Alan had dropped his burden at her feet.

"Is he—conscious?" asked Lynde, as if she forced herself to ask the question.

"Yes, he has come back to life. But he is delirious and doesn't realize his surroundings at all. He thinks he is still on board the vessel. He'll probably come round all right. Emily is going to watch him and I'll go up to Rexton and send Dr. Ames down."

"Do you know who that man you have saved is?" asked Lynde.

"No. I asked him his name but could not get any sensible answer."

"I can tell you who he is—he is Frank Harmon."

Alan stared at her. "Frank Harmon. Your—your—the man you married? Impossible!"

"It is he. Do you think I could be mistaken?"

Dr. Ames came to Four Winds that night and again the next day. He found Harmon delirious in a high fever.

"It will be several days before he comes to his senses," he said. "Shall I send you help to nurse him?"

"It isn't necessary," said Emily stiffly. "I can look after him—and the Captain ought to be back tomorrow."

"You've no idea who he is, I suppose?" asked the doctor.

"No." Emily was quite sincere. Lynde had not told her, and Emily did not recognize him.

"Well, Mr. Douglas did a brave thing in rescuing him," said Dr. Ames. "I'll be back tomorrow."

Harmon remained delirious for a week. Alan went every day to Four Winds, his interest in a man he had rescued explaining his visits to the Rexton people. The Captain had returned and, though not absolutely uncivil, was taciturn and moody. Alan reflected grimly that Captain Anthony probably owed him a grudge for saving Harmon's life. He never saw Lynde alone, but her strained, tortured face made his heart ache. Old Emily only seemed her natural self. She waited on Harmon and Dr. Ames considered her a paragon of a nurse. Alan thought it was well that Emily knew nothing more of Harmon than that he was an old friend of Captain Anthony's. He felt sure that she would have walked out of the sick room and never reentered it had she guessed that the patient was the man whom, above all others, Lynde dreaded and feared.

One afternoon when Alan went to Four Winds Emily met him at the door.

"He's better," she announced. "He had a good sleep this afternoon and when he woke he was quite himself. You'd better go up and see him. I told him all I could but he wants to see you. Anthony and Lynde are away to Crosse Harbour. Go up and talk to him."

Harmon turned his head as the minister approached and held out his hand with a smile.

"You're the preacher, I reckon. They tell me you were the man who pulled me out of that hurly-burly. I wasn't hardly worth saving but I'm as grateful to you as if I was."

"I only—did—what any man would have done," said Alan, taking the offered hand.

"I don't know about that. Anyhow, it's not every man could have done it. I'd been hanging in that rigging all day and most of the night before. There were five more of us but they dropped off. I knew it was no use to try to swim ashore alone—the backwater would be too much for me. I must have been a lot of trouble. That old woman says I've been raving for a week. And, by the way I feel, I fancy I'll be stretched out here another week before I'll be able to use my pins. Who are these Olivers anyhow? The old woman wouldn't talk about the family."

"Don't you know them?" asked Alan in astonishment. "Isn't your name Harmon?"

"That's right—Harmon—Alfred Harmon, first mate of the schooner, *Annie M.*"

"Alfred! I thought your name was Frank!"

"Frank was my twin brother. We were so much alike our own mammy couldn't tell us apart. Did you know Frank?"

"No. This family did. Miss Oliver thought you were Frank when she saw you."

"I don't feel much like myself but I'm not Frank anyway. He's dead, poor chap—got shot in a spat with Chinese pirates three years ago."

"Dead! Man, are you speaking the truth? Are you certain?"

"Pop sure. His mate told me the whole story. Say, preacher, what's the matter? You look as if you were going to keel over."

Alan hastily drank a glass of water.

"I—I am all right now. I haven't been feeling well of late."

"Guess you didn't do yourself any good going out into that freezing water and dragging me in."

"I shall thank God every day of my life that I did do it," said Alan gravely, new light in his eyes, as Emily entered the room. "Miss Oliver, when will the Captain and Lynde be back?"

"They said they would be home by four."

She looked at Alan curiously.

"I will go and meet her," he said quickly.

He came upon Lynde, sitting on a grey boulder under the shadow of an overhanging fir coppice, with her dogs beside her.

She turned her head indifferently as Alan's footsteps sounded on the pebbles, and then stood slowly up.

"Are you looking for me?" she asked.

"I have some news for you, Lynde," Alan said.

"Has he—has he come to himself?" she whispered.

"Yes, he has come to himself. Lynde, he is not Frank Harmon—he is his twin brother. He says Frank Harmon was killed three years ago in the China seas."

For a moment Lynde's great grey eyes stared into Alan's, questioning. Then, as the truth seized on her comprehension, she sat down on the boulder and put her hands over her face without a word. Alan walked down to the water's edge to give her time to recover herself. When he came back he took her hands and said quietly, "Lynde, do you realize what this means for us—for us? You are free—free to love me—to be my wife."

Lynde shook her head.

"Oh, that can't be. I am not fit to be your wife."

"Don't talk nonsense, dear," he smiled.

"It isn't nonsense. You are a minister and it would ruin you to marry a girl like me. Think what the Rexton people would say of it."

"Rexton isn't the world, dearest. Last week I had a letter from home asking me to go to a church there. I did not think of accepting then—now I will go—we will both go—and a new life will begin for you, clear of the shadows of the old."

"That isn't possible. No, Alan, listen—I love you too well to do you the wrong of marrying you. It would injure you. There is Father. I love him and he has always been very kind to me. But—but—there's something wrong—you know it—some crime in his past—"

"The only man who knew that is dead."

"We do not know that he was the only man. I am the daughter of a criminal and I am no fit wife for Alan Douglas. No, Alan, don't plead, please. I won't think differently—I never can."

There was a ring of finality in her tone that struck dismay to Alan's heart. He prepared to entreat and argue, but before he could utter a word, the boughs behind them parted and Captain Anthony stepped down from the bank.

"I've been listening," he announced coolly, "and I think it high time I took a share in the conversation. You seem to have run up against a snag, Mr. Douglas. You say Frank Harmon is dead. That's good riddance if it's true. Is it true?"

"His brother declares it is."

"Well, then, I'll help you all I can. I like you, Mr. Douglas, and I happen to be fond of Lynde, too—though you mayn't believe it. I'm fond of her for her mother's sake and I'd like to see her happy. I didn't want to give her to Harmon that time three years ago but I couldn't help myself. He had the upper hand, curse him. It wasn't for my own sake, though—it was for my wife's. However, that's all over and done with and I'll do the best I can to atone for it. So you won't marry your minister because your father was not a good man, Lynde? Well, I don't suppose he was a very good man—a man who makes his wife's life a hell, even in a refined way, isn't exactly a saint, to my way of thinking. But that's the worst that could be said of him and it doesn't entail any indelible disgrace on his family, I suppose. I am not your father, Lynde."

"Not my father?" Lynde echoed the words blankly.

"No. Your father was your mother's first husband. She never told you of him. When I said he made her life a hell, I said the truth, no more, no less. I had loved your mother ever since I was a boy, Lynde. But she was far above me in station and I never dreamed it was possible to win her love. She married James Ashley. He was a gentleman, so called—and he didn't kick or beat her. Oh no, he just tormented her refined womanhood to the verge of frenzy, that was all. He died when you were a baby. And a year later I found out your mother could love me, rough sailor and all as I was. I married her and brought her here. We had fifteen years of happiness together. I'm not a good man—but I made your mother happy in spite of her wrecked health and her dark memories. It was her wish that you should be known as my daughter, but under the present circumstances I know she would wish that you should be told the truth. Marry your man, Lynde, and go away with him. Emily will go with you if you like. I'm going back to the sea. I've been hankering for it ever since your mother died. I'll go out of your life. There, don't cry—I hate to see a woman cry. Mr. Douglas, I'll leave you to dry her tears and I'll go up to the house and have a talk with Harmon."

When Captain Anthony had disappeared behind the Point, Alan turned to Lynde. She was sobbing softly and her face was wet with tears. Alan drew her head down on his shoulder.

"Sweetheart, the dark past is all put by. Our future begins with promise. All is well with us, dear Lynde."

Like a child, she put her arms about his neck and their lips met.

Marcella's Reward

Dr. Clark shook his head gravely. "She is not improving as fast as I should like to see," he said. "In fact—er—she seems to have gone backward the past week. You must send her to the country, Miss Langley. The heat here is too trying for her."

Dr. Clark might as well have said, "You must send her to the moon"—or so Marcella thought bitterly. Despair filled her heart as she looked at Patty's white face and transparent hands and listened to the doctor's coolly professional advice. Patty's illness had already swept away the scant savings of three years. Marcella had nothing left with which to do anything more for her.

She did not make any answer to the doctor—she could not. Besides, what could she say, with Patty's big blue eyes, bigger and bluer than ever in her thin face, looking at her so wistfully? She dared not say it was impossible. But Aunt Emma had no such scruples. With a great clatter and racket, that lady fell upon the dishes that held Patty's almost untasted dinner and whisked them away while her tongue kept time to her jerky movements.

"Goodness me, doctor, do you think you're talking to millionaires? Where do you suppose the money is to come from to send Patty to the country? *I* can't afford it, that is certain. I think I do pretty well to give Marcella and Patty their board free, and I have to work my fingers to the bone to do *that.* It's all nonsense about Patty, anyhow. What she ought to do is to make an effort to get better. She doesn't—she just mopes and pines. She won't eat a thing I cook for her. How can anyone expect to get better if she doesn't eat?"

Aunt Emma glared at the doctor as if she were triumphantly sure that she had propounded an unanswerable question. A dull red flush rose to Marcella's face.

"Oh, Aunt Emma, I *can't* eat!" said Patty wearily. "It isn't because I won't—indeed, I can't."

"Humph! I suppose my cooking isn't fancy enough for you—that's the trouble. Well, I haven't the time to put any frills on it. I think I do pretty well to wait on you at all with all that work piling up before me. But some people imagine that they were born to be waited on."

Aunt Emma whirled the last dish from the table and left the room, slamming the door behind her.

The doctor shrugged his shoulders. He had become used to Miss Gibson's tirades during Patty's illness. But Marcella had never got used to them—never, in all the three years she had lived with her aunt. They flicked on the raw as keenly as ever. This morning it seemed unbearable. It took every atom of Marcella's self-control to keep her from voicing her resentful thoughts. It was only for Patty's sake that she was able to restrain herself. It was only for Patty's sake, too, that she did not, as soon as the doctor had gone, give way to tears. Instead, she smiled bravely into the little sister's eyes.

"Let me brush your hair now, dear, and bathe your face."

"Have you time?" said Patty anxiously.

"Yes, I think so."

Patty gave a sigh of content.

"I'm so glad! Aunt Emma always hurts me when she brushes my hair—she is in such a hurry. You're so gentle, Marcella, you don't make my head ache at all. But oh! I'm so tired of being sick. I wish I could get well faster. Marcy, do you think I can be sent to the country?"

"I—I don't know, dear. I'll see if I can think of any way to manage it," said Marcella, striving to speak hopefully.

Patty drew a long breath.

"Oh, Marcy, it would be lovely to see the green fields again, and the woods and brooks, as we did that summer we spent in the country before Father died. I wish we could live in the country always. I'm sure I would soon get better if I could go—if it was only for a little while. It's so hot here—and the factory makes such a noise—my head seems to go round and round all the time. And Aunt Emma scolds so."

"You mustn't mind Aunt Emma, dear," said Marcella. "You know she doesn't really mean it—it is just a habit she has got into. She was really very good to you when you were so sick. She sat up night after night with you, and made me go to bed. There now, dearie, you're fresh and sweet, and I must hurry to the store, or I'll be late. Try and have a little nap, and I'll bring you home some oranges tonight."

Marcella dropped a kiss on Patty's cheek, put on her hat and went out. As soon as she left the house, she quickened her steps almost to a run. She feared she would be late, and that meant a ten-cent fine. Ten cents loomed as large as ten dollars now to Marcella's eyes when every dime meant so much. But fast as she went, her distracted thoughts went faster. She could not send Patty to the country. There was no way, think, plan, worry as she might. And if she could not! Marcella remembered Patty's face and the doctor's look, and her heart sank like lead. Patty was growing weaker every day instead of stronger, and the weather was getting hotter. Oh, if Patty were to—to—but Marcella could not complete the sentence even in thought.

If they were not so desperately poor! Marcella's bitterness overflowed her soul at the thought. Everywhere around her were evidences of wealth—wealth often lavishly and foolishly spent—and she could not get money enough anywhere to save her sister's life! She almost felt that she hated all those smiling, well-dressed people who thronged the streets. By the time she reached the store, poor Marcella's heart was seething with misery and resentment.

Three years before, when Marcella had been sixteen and Patty nine, their parents had died, leaving them absolutely alone in the world except for their father's half-sister, Miss Gibson, who lived in Canning and earned her livelihood washing and mending for the hands employed in the big factory nearby. She had grudgingly offered the girls a home, which Marcella had accepted because she must. She obtained a position in one of the Canning stores at three dollars a week, out of which she contrived to dress herself and Patty and send the latter to school. Her life for three years was one of absolute drudgery, yet until now she had never lost courage, but had struggled bravely on, hoping for better times in the future when she should get promotion and Patty would be old enough to teach school.

But now Marcella's courage and hopefulness had gone out like a spent candle. She was late at the store, and that meant a fine; her head ached, and her feet felt like lead as she climbed the stairs to her department—a hot, dark, stuffy corner behind the shirtwaist counter. It was warm and close at any time, but today it was stifling, and there was already a crowd of customers, for it was the day of a bargain sale. The heat and noise and chatter got on Marcella's tortured nerves. She felt that she wanted to scream, but instead she turned calmly to a waiting customer—a big, handsome, richly dressed woman. Marcella noted with an ever-increasing bitterness that the woman wore a lace collar the price of which would have kept Patty in the country for a year.

She was Mrs. Liddell—Marcella knew her by sight—and she was in a very bad temper because she had been kept waiting. For the next half hour she badgered and worried Marcella to the point of distraction. Nothing suited her. Pile after pile, box after box, of shirtwaists did Marcella take down for her, only to have them flung aside with sarcastic remarks. Mrs. Liddell seemed to hold Marcella responsible for the lack of waists that suited her; her tongue grew sharper and sharper and her comments more trying. Then she mislaid her purse, and was disagreeable about that until it turned up.

Marcella shut her lips so tightly that they turned white to keep back the impatient retort that rose momentarily to her lips. The insolence of some customers was always trying to the sensitive, high-spirited girl, but today it seemed unbearable. Her head throbbed fiercely with the pain of the ever-increasing ache, and—what was the lady on her right saying to a friend?

"Yes, she had typhoid, you know—a very bad form. She rallied from it, but she was so exhausted that she couldn't really recover, and the doctor said—"

"Really," interrupted Mrs. Liddell's sharp voice, "may I ask you to attend to me, if you please? No doubt gossip may be very interesting to you, but I am accustomed to having a clerk pay *some* small attention to my requirements. If you cannot attend to your business, I shall go to the floor walker and ask him to direct me to somebody who can. The laziness and disobligingness of the girls in this store is really getting beyond endurance."

A passionate answer was on the point of Marcella's tongue. All her bitterness and suffering and resentment flashed into her face and eyes. For one moment she was determined to speak out, to repay Mrs. Liddell's insolence in kind. A retort was ready to her hand. Everyone knew that Mrs. Liddell, before her marriage to a wealthy man, had been a working girl. What could be easier than to say contemptuously: "You should be a judge of a clerk's courtesy and ability, madam. You were a shop girl yourself once?"

But if she said it, what would follow? Prompt and instant dismissal. And Patty? The thought of the little sister quelled the storm in Marcella's soul. For Patty's sake she must control her temper—and she did. With an effort that left her white and tremulous she crushed back the hot words and said quietly: "I beg your pardon, Mrs. Liddell. I did not mean to be inattentive. Let me show you some of our new lingerie waists, I think you will like them."

But Mrs. Liddell did not like the new lingerie waists which Marcella brought to her in her trembling hands. For another half hour she examined and found fault and sneered. Then she swept away with the scornful remark that she didn't see a thing there that was fit to wear, and she would go to Markwell Bros. and see if they had anything worth looking at.

When she had gone, Marcella leaned against the counter, pale and exhausted. She must have a breathing spell. Oh, how her head ached! How hot and stifling and horrible everything was! She longed for the country herself. Oh, if she and Patty could only go away to some place where there were green clover meadows and cool breezes and great hills where the air was sweet and pure!

During all this time a middle-aged woman had been sitting on a stool beside the bargain counter. When a clerk asked her if she wished to be waited on, she said, "No, I'm just waiting here for a friend who promised to meet me."

She was tall and gaunt and grey haired. She had square jaws and cold grey eyes and an aggressive nose, but there was something attractive in her plain face, a mingling of common sense and kindliness. She watched Marcella and Mrs. Liddell closely and lost nothing of all that was said and done on both sides. Now and then she smiled grimly and nodded.

When Mrs. Liddell had gone, she rose and leaned over the counter. Marcella opened her burning eyes and pulled herself wearily together.

"What can I do for you?" she said.

"Nothing. I ain't looking for to have anything done for me. You need to have something done for you, I guess, by the looks of you. You seem dead beat out. Aren't you awful tired? I've been listening to that woman jawing you till I felt like rising up and giving her a large and wholesome piece of my mind. I don't know how you kept your patience with her, but I can tell you I admired you for it, and I made up my mind I'd tell you so."

The kindness and sympathy in her tone broke Marcella down. Tears rushed to her eyes. She bowed her head on her hands and said sobbingly, "Oh, I *am* tired! But it's not that. I'm—I'm in such trouble."

"I knew you were," said the other, with a nod of her head. "I could tell that right off by your face. Do you know what I said to myself? I said, 'That girl has got somebody at home awful sick.' *That's* what I said. Was I right?"

"Yes, indeed you were," said Marcella.

"I knew it"—another triumphant nod. "Now, you just tell me all about it. It'll do you good to talk it over with somebody. Here, I'll pretend I'm looking at shirtwaists, so that floor walker won't be coming down on you, and I'll be as hard to please as that other woman was, so's you can take your time. Who's sick—and what's the matter?"

Marcella told the whole story, choking back her sobs and forcing herself to speak calmly, having the fear of the floor walker before her eyes.

"And I can't afford to send Patty to the country—I *can't*—and I know she won't get better if she doesn't go," she concluded.

"Dear, dear, but that's too bad! Something must be done. Let me see—let me put on my thinking cap. What is your name?"

"Marcella Langley."

The older woman dropped the lingerie waist she was pretending to examine and stared at Marcella.

"You don't say! Look here, what was your mother's name before she was married?"

"Mary Carvell."

"Well, I *have* heard of coincidences, but this beats all! Mary Carvell! Well, did you ever hear your mother speak of a girl friend of hers called Josephine Draper?"

"I should think I did! You don't mean—"

"I *do* mean it. I'm Josephine Draper. Your mother and I went to school together, and we were as much as sisters to each other until she got married. Then she went away, and after a few years I lost trace of her. I didn't even know she was dead. Poor Mary! Well, *my* duty is plain—that's one comfort—my duty and my pleasure, too. Your sister is coming out to Dalesboro to stay with me. Yes, and you are too, for the whole summer. You needn't say you're not, because you *are*. I've said so. There's room at Fir Cottage for you both. Yes, Fir Cottage—I guess you've heard your mother speak of *that*. There's her old room out there that we always slept in when she came to stay all night with me. It's all ready for you. What's that? You can't afford to lose your place here? Bless your heart, child, you won't lose it! The owner of this store is my nephew, and he'll do considerable to oblige me, as well he might, seeing as I brought him up. To think that Mary Carvell's daughter has been in his store for three years, and me never suspecting it! And I might never have found you out at all if you hadn't been so patient with that woman. If you'd sassed her back, I'd have thought she deserved it and wouldn't have blamed you a mite, but I wouldn't have bothered coming to talk to you either. Well, well well! Poor child, don't cry. You just pick up and go home. I'll make it all right with Tom. You're pretty near played out yourself, I can see that. But a summer in Fir Cottage, with plenty of cream and eggs and *my* cookery, will soon make another girl of you. Don't you dare to *thank* me. It's a privilege to be able to do something for Mary Carvell's girls. I just loved Mary."

The upshot of the whole matter was that Marcella and Patty went, two days later, to Dalesboro, where Miss Draper gave them a hearty welcome to Fir Cottage—a quaint, delightful little house circled by big Scotch firs and overgrown with vines. Never were such delightful weeks as those that followed. Patty came rapidly back to health and strength. As for Marcella, Miss Draper's prophecy was also fulfilled; she soon looked and felt like another girl. The dismal years of drudgery behind her were forgotten like a dream, and she lived wholly in the beautiful present, in the walks and drives, the flowers and grass slopes, and in the pleasant household duties which she shared with Miss Draper.

"I love housework," she exclaimed one September day. "I don't like the thought of going back to the store a bit."

"Well, you're not going back," calmly said Miss Draper, who had a habit of arranging other people's business for them that might have been disconcerting had it not been for her keen insight and hearty good sense. "You're going to stay here with me—you and Patty. I don't propose to die of lonesomeness losing you, and I need somebody to help me about the house. I've thought it all out. You are to call me Aunt Josephine, and Patty is to go to school. I had this scheme in mind from the first, but I thought I'd wait to see how we got along living in the same house, and how you liked it here, before I spoke out. No, you needn't thank me this time either. I'm doing this every bit as much for my sake as yours. Well, that's all settled. Patty won't object, bless her rosy cheeks!"

"Oh!" said Marcella, with eyes shining through her tears. "I'm so happy, dear Miss Draper—I mean Aunt Josephine. I'll love to stay here—and I *will* thank you."

"Fudge!" remarked Miss Draper, who felt uncomfortably near crying herself. "You might go out and pick a basket of Golden Gems. I want to make some jelly for Patty."

Margaret's Patient

"DID DR. FORBES THINK SHE OUGHT TO GIVE UP HER TRIP?"

Margaret paused a moment at the gate and looked back at the quaint old house under its snowy firs with a thrill of proprietary affection. It was her home; for the first time in her life she had a real home, and the long, weary years of poorly paid drudgery were all behind her. Before her was a prospect of independence and many of the delights she had always craved; in the immediate future was a trip to Vancouver with Mrs. Boyd.

For I shall go, of course, thought Margaret, as she walked briskly down the snowy road. I've always wanted to see the Rockies, and to go there with Mrs. Boyd will double the pleasure. She is such a delightful companion.

Margaret Campbell had been an orphan ever since she could remember. She had been brought up by a distant relative of her father's—that is, she had been given board, lodging, some schooling and indifferent clothes for the privilege of working like a little drudge in the house of the grim cousin who sheltered her. The death of this cousin flung Margaret on her own resources. A friend had procured her employment as the "companion" of a rich, eccentric old lady, infirm of health and temper. Margaret lived with her for five years, and to the young girl they seemed treble the time. Her employer was fault-finding, peevish, unreasonable, and many a time Margaret's patience almost failed her—almost, but not quite. In the end it brought her a more tangible reward than sometimes falls to the lot of the toiler. Mrs. Constance died, and in her will she left to Margaret her little up-country cottage and enough money to provide her an income for the rest of her life.

Margaret took immediate possession of her little house and, with the aid of a capable old servant, soon found herself very comfortable. She realized that her days of drudgery were over, and that henceforth life would be a very different thing from what it had been. Margaret meant to have "a good time." She had never had any pleasure and now she was resolved to garner in all she could of the joys of existence.

"I'm not going to do a single useful thing for a year," she had told Mrs. Boyd gaily. "Just think of it—a whole delightful year of vacation, to go and come at will, to read, travel, dream, rest. After that, I mean to see if I can find something to do for other folks, but I'm going to have this one golden year. And the first thing in it is our trip to Vancouver. I'm so glad I have the chance to go with you. It's a wee bit short notice, but I'll be ready when you want to start."

Altogether, Margaret felt pretty well satisfied with life as she tripped blithely down the country road between the ranks of snow-laden spruces, with the blue sky above and the crisp, exhilarating air all about. There was only one drawback, but it was a pretty serious one.

It's so lonely by spells, Margaret sometimes thought wistfully. All the joys my good fortune has brought me can't quite fill my heart. There's always one little empty, aching spot. Oh, if I had somebody of my very own to love and care for, a mother, a sister, even a cousin. But there's nobody. I haven't a relative in the world, and there are times when I'd give almost anything to have one. Well, I must try to be satisfied with friendship, instead.

Margaret's meditations were interrupted by a brisk footstep behind her, and presently Dr. Forbes came up.

"Good afternoon, Miss Campbell. Taking a constitutional?"

"Yes. Isn't it a lovely day? I suppose you are on your professional rounds. How are all your patients?"

"Most of them are doing well. But I'm sorry to say I have a new one and am very much worried about her. Do you know Freda Martin?"

"The little teacher in the Primary Department who boards with the Wayes? Yes, I've met her once or twice. Is she ill?"

"Yes, seriously. It's typhoid, and she has been going about longer than she should. I don't know what is to be done with her. It seems she is like yourself in one respect, Miss Campbell; she is utterly alone in the world. Mrs. Waye is crippled with rheumatism and can't nurse her, and I fear it will be impossible to get a nurse in Blythefield. She ought to be taken from the Wayes'. The house is overrun with children, is right next door to that noisy factory, and in other respects is a poor place for a sick girl."

"It is too bad, I am very sorry," said Margaret sympathetically.

Dr. Forbes shot a keen look at her from his deep-set eyes. "Are you willing to show your sympathy in a practical form, Miss Campbell?" he said bluntly. "You told me the other day you meant to begin work for others next year. Why not begin now? Here's a splendid chance to befriend a friendless girl. Will you take Freda Martin into your home during her illness?"

"Oh, I couldn't," cried Margaret blankly. "Why, I'm going away next week. I'm going with Mrs. Boyd to Vancouver, and my house will be shut up."

"Oh, I did not know. That settles it, I suppose," said the doctor with a sigh of regret. "Well, I must see what else I can do for poor Freda. If I had a home of my own, the problem would be easily solved, but as

I'm only a boarder myself, I'm helpless in that respect. I'm very much afraid she will have a hard time to pull through, but I'll do the best I can for her. Well, I must run in here and have a look at Tommy Griggs' eyes. Good morning, Miss Campbell."

Margaret responded rather absently and walked on with her eyes fixed on the road. Somehow all the joy had gone out of the day for her, and out of her prospective trip. She stopped on the little bridge and gazed unseeingly at the ice-bound creek. Did Dr. Forbes really think she ought to give up her trip in order to take Freda Martin into her home and probably nurse her as well, since skilled nursing of any kind was almost unobtainable in Blythefield? No, of course, Dr. Forbes did not mean anything of the sort. He had not known she intended to go away. Margaret tried to put the thought out of her mind, but it came insistently back.

She knew—none better—what it was to be alone and friendless. Once she had been ill, too, and left to the ministration of careless servants. Margaret shuddered whenever she thought of that time. She was very, very sorry for Freda Martin, but she certainly couldn't give up her plans for her.

"Why, I'd never have the chance to go with Mrs. Boyd again," she argued with her troublesome inward promptings.

Altogether, Margaret's walk was spoiled. But when she went to bed that night, she was firmly resolved to dismiss all thought of Freda Martin. In the middle of the night she woke up. It was calm and moonlight and frosty. The world was very still, and Margaret's heart and conscience spoke to her out of that silence, where all worldly motives were hushed and shamed. She listened, and knew that in the morning she must send for Dr. Forbes and tell him to bring his patient to Fir Cottage.

The evening of the next day found Freda in Margaret's spare room and Margaret herself installed as nurse, for as Dr. Forbes had feared, he had found it impossible to obtain anyone else. Margaret had a natural gift for nursing, and she had had a good deal of experience in sick rooms. She was skilful, gentle and composed, and Dr. Forbes nodded his head with satisfaction as he watched her.

A week later Mrs. Boyd left for Vancouver, and Margaret, bending over her delirious patient, could not even go to the station to see her off. But she thought little about it. All her hopes were centred on pulling Freda Martin through; and when, after a long, doubtful fortnight, Dr. Forbes pronounced her on the way to recovery, Margaret felt as if she had given the gift of life to a fellow creature. "Oh, I am so glad I stayed," she whispered to herself.

During Freda's convalescence Margaret learned to love her dearly. She was such a sweet, brave little creature, full of a fine courage to face the loneliness and trials of her lot.

"I can never repay you for your kindness, Miss Campbell," she said wistfully.

"I am more than repaid already," said Margaret sincerely. "Haven't I found a dear little friend?"

One day Freda asked Margaret to write a note for her to a certain school chum.

"She will like to know I am getting better. You will find her address in my writing desk."

Freda's modest trunk had been brought to Fir Cottage, and Margaret went to it for the desk. As she turned over the loose papers in search of the address, her eye was caught by a name signed to a faded and yellowed letter—Worth Spencer. Her mother's name!

Margaret gave a little exclamation of astonishment. Could her mother have written that letter? It was not likely another woman would have that uncommon name. Margaret caught up the letter and ran to Freda's room.

"Freda, I couldn't help seeing the name signed to this letter, it is my mother's. To whom was it written?"

"That is one of my mother's old letters," said Freda. "She had a sister, my Aunt Worth. She was a great deal older than Mother. Their parents died when Mother was a baby. Aunt Worth went to her father's people, while Mother's grandmother took her. There was not very good feeling between the two families, I think. Mother said she lost trace of her sister after her sister married, and then, long after, she saw Aunt Worth's death in the papers."

"Can you tell me where your mother and her sister lived before they were separated?" asked Margaret excitedly.

"Ridgetown."

"Then my mother must have been your mother's sister, and, oh, Freda, Freda, you are my cousin."

Eventually this was proved to be the fact. Margaret investigated the matter and discovered beyond a doubt that she and Freda were cousins. It would be hard to say which of the two girls was the more delighted.

"Anyhow, we'll never be parted again," said Margaret happily. "Fir Cottage is your home henceforth, Freda. Oh, how rich I am. I have got somebody who really belongs to me. And I owe it all to Dr. Forbes. If he hadn't suggested you coming here, I should never have found out that we were cousins."

"And I don't think I should ever have got better at all," whispered Freda, slipping her hand into Margaret's.

"I think we are going to be the two happiest girls in the world," said Margaret. "And Freda, do you know what we are going to do when your summer vacation comes? We are going to have a trip through the Rockies, yes, indeedy. It would have been nice going with Mrs. Boyd, but it will be ten times nicer to go with you."

Matthew Insists on Puffed Sleeves

Matthew was having a bad ten minutes of it. He had come into the kitchen, in the twilight of a cold, grey December evening, and had sat down in the wood-box corner to take off his heavy boots, unconscious of the fact that Anne and a bevy of her schoolmates were having a practice of "The Fairy Queen" in the sitting-room. Presently they came trooping through the hall and out into the kitchen, laughing and chattering gaily. They did not see Matthew, who shrank bashfully back into the shadows beyond the wood-box with a boot in one hand and a bootjack in the other, and he watched them shyly for the aforesaid ten minutes as they put on caps and jackets and talked about the dialogue and the concert. Anne stood among them, bright eyed and animated as they; but Matthew suddenly became conscious that there was something about her different from her mates. And what worried Matthew was that the difference impressed him as being something that should not exist. Anne had a brighter face, and bigger, starrier eyes, and more delicate features than the others; even shy, unobservant Matthew had learned to take note of these things; but the difference that disturbed him did not consist in any of these respects. Then in what did it consist?

Matthew was haunted by this question long after the girls had gone, arm in arm, down the long, hard-frozen lane and Anne had betaken herself to her books. He could not refer it to Marilla, who, he felt, would be quite sure to sniff scornfully and remark that the only difference she saw between Anne and the other girls was that they sometimes kept their tongues quiet while Anne never did. This, Matthew felt, would be no great help.

He had recourse to his pipe that evening to help him study it out, much to Marilla's disgust. After two hours of smoking and hard reflection Matthew arrived at a solution of his problem. Anne was not dressed like the other girls!

The more Matthew thought about the matter the more he was convinced that Anne never had been dressed like the other girls—never since she had come to Green Gables. Marilla kept her clothed in plain, dark dresses, all made after the same unvarying pattern. If Matthew knew there was such a thing as fashion in dress it is as much as he did; but he was quite sure that Anne's sleeves did not look at all like the sleeves the other girls wore. He recalled the cluster of little girls he had seen around her that evening—all gay in waists of red and blue and pink and white—and he wondered why Marilla always kept her so plainly and soberly gowned.

Of course, it must be all right. Marilla knew best and Marilla was bringing her up. Probably some wise, inscrutable motive was to be served thereby. But surely it would do no harm to let the child have one pretty dress—something like Diana Barry always wore. Matthew decided that he would give her one; that surely could not be objected to as an unwarranted putting in of his oar. Christmas was only a fortnight off. A nice new dress would be the very thing for a present. Matthew, with a sigh of satisfaction, put away his pipe and went to bed, while Marilla opened all the doors and aired the house.

The very next evening Matthew betook himself to Carmody to buy the dress, determined to get the worst over and have done with it. It would be, he felt assured, no trifling ordeal. There were some things Matthew could buy and prove himself no mean bargainer; but he knew he would be at the mercy of shopkeepers when it came to buying a girl's dress.

After much cogitation Matthew resolved to go to Samuel Lawson's store instead of William Blair's. To be sure, the Cuthberts always had gone to William Blair's; it was almost as much a matter of conscience with them as to attend the Presbyterian church and vote Conservative. But William Blair's two daughters frequently waited on customers there and Matthew held them in absolute dread. He could contrive to deal with them when he knew exactly what he wanted and could point it out; but in such a matter as this, requiring explanation and consultation, Matthew felt that he must be sure of a man behind the counter. So he would go to Lawson's, where Samuel or his son would wait on him.

Alas! Matthew did not know that Samuel, in the recent expansion of his business, had set up a lady clerk also; she was a niece of his wife's and a very dashing young person indeed, with a huge, drooping pompadour, big, rolling brown eyes, and a most extensive and bewildering smile. She was dressed with exceeding smartness and wore several bangle bracelets that glittered and rattled and tinkled with every movement of her hands. Matthew was covered with confusion at finding her there at all; and those bangles completely wrecked his wits at one fell swoop.

"What can I do for you this evening. Mr. Cuthbert?" Miss Lucilla Harris inquired, briskly and ingratiatingly, tapping the counter with both hands.

"Have you any—any—any—well now, say any garden rakes?" stammered Matthew.

Miss Harris looked somewhat surprised, as well she might, to hear a man inquiring for garden rakes in the middle of December.

"I believe we have one or two left over," she said, "but they're upstairs in the lumber-room. I'll go and see."

During her absence Matthew collected his scattered senses for another effort.

When Miss Harris returned with the rake and cheerfully inquired: "Anything else tonight, Mr. Cuthbert?" Matthew took his courage in both hands and replied: "Well now, since you suggest it, I might as well—take—that is—look at—buy some—some hayseed."

Miss Harris had heard Matthew Cuthbert called odd. She now concluded that he was entirely crazy.

"We only keep hayseed in the spring," she explained loftily. "We've none on hand just now."

"Oh, certainly—certainly—just as you say," stammered unhappy Matthew, seizing the rake and making for the door. At the threshold he recollected that he had not paid for it and he turned miserably back. While Miss Harris was counting out his change he rallied his powers for a final desperate attempt.

"Well now—if it isn't too much trouble—I might as well—that is—I'd like to look at—at—some sugar."

"White or brown?" queried Miss Harris patiently.

"Oh—well now—brown," said Matthew feebly.

"There's a barrel of it over there," said Miss Harris, shaking her bangles at it. "It's the only kind we have."

"I'll—I'll take twenty pounds of it," said Matthew, with beads of perspiration standing on his forehead.

Matthew had driven halfway home before he was his own man again. It had been a gruesome experience, but it served him right, he thought, for committing the heresy of going to a strange store. When he reached home he hid the rake in the tool-house, but the sugar he carried in to Marilla.

"Brown sugar!" exclaimed Marilla. "Whatever possessed you to get so much? You know I never use it except for the hired man's porridge or black fruit-cake. Jerry's gone and I've made my cake long ago. It's not good sugar, either—it's coarse and dark—William Blair doesn't usually keep sugar like that."

"I—I thought it might come in handy sometime," said Matthew, making good his escape.

When Matthew came to think the matter over he decided that a woman was required to cope with the situation. Marilla was out of the question. Matthew felt sure she would throw cold water on his project at once. Remained only Mrs. Lynde; for of no other woman in Avonlea would Matthew have dared to ask advice. To Mrs. Lynde he went accordingly, and that good lady promptly took the matter out of the harassed man's hands.

"Pick out a dress for you to give Anne? To be sure I will. I'm going to Carmody tomorrow and I'll attend to it. Have you something particular in mind? No? Well, I'll just go by my own judgment then. I believe a nice rich brown would just suit Anne, and William Blair has some new gloria in that's real pretty. Perhaps you'd like me to make it up for her, too, seeing that if Marilla was to make it Anne would probably get wind of it before the time and spoil the surprise? Well, I'll do it. No, it isn't a mite of trouble. I like sewing. I'll make it to fit my niece, Jenny Gillis, for she and Anne are as like as two peas as far as figure goes."

"Well now, I'm much obliged," said Matthew, "and—and—I dunno—but I'd like—I think they make the sleeves different nowadays to what they used to be. If it wouldn't be asking too much I—I'd like them made in the new way."

"Puffs? Of course. You needn't worry a speck more about it, Matthew. I'll make it up in the very latest fashion," said Mrs. Lynde. To herself she added when Matthew had gone:

"It'll be a real satisfaction to see that poor child wearing something decent for once. The way Marilla dresses her is positively ridiculous, that's what, and I've ached to tell her so plainly a dozen times. I've held my tongue though, for I can see Marilla doesn't want advice and she thinks she knows more about bringing children up than I do for all she's an old maid. But that's always the way. Folks that has brought up children know that there's no hard and fast method in the world that'll suit every child. But them as never have think it's all as plain and easy as Rule of Three—just set your three terms down so fashion, and the sum'll work out correct. But flesh and blood don't come under the head of arithmetic and that's where Marilla Cuthbert makes her mistake. I suppose she's trying to cultivate a spirit of humility in Anne by dressing her as she does: but it's more likely to cultivate envy and discontent. I'm sure the child must feel the difference between her clothes and the other girls'. But to think of Matthew taking notice of it! That man is waking up after being asleep for over sixty years."

Marilla knew all the following fortnight that Matthew had something on his mind, but what it was she could not guess, until Christmas Eve, when Mrs. Lynde brought up the new dress. Marilla behaved pretty well on the whole, although it is very likely she distrusted Mrs. Lynde's diplomatic explanation that she had made the dress because Matthew was afraid Anne would find out about it too soon if Marilla made it.

"So this is what Matthew has been looking so mysterious over and grinning about to himself for two weeks, is it?" she said a little stiffly but tolerantly. "I knew he was up to some foolishness. Well, I must say I don't think Anne needed any more dresses. I made her three good, warm, serviceable ones this fall, and anything more is sheer extravagance. There's enough material in those sleeves alone to make a waist, I declare there is. You'll just pamper Anne's vanity, Matthew, and she's as vain as a peacock now. Well, I hope she'll be satisfied at last, for I know she's been hankering after those silly sleeves ever since they came in, although she never said a word after the first. The puffs have been getting bigger and more ridiculous right along; they're as big as balloons now. Next year anybody who wears them will have to go through a door sideways."

Christmas morning broke on a beautiful white world. It had been a very mild December and people had looked forward to a green Christmas; but just enough snow fell softly in the night to transfigure Avonlea. Anne peeped out from her frosted gable window with delighted eyes. The firs in the Haunted Wood were all feathery and wonderful; the birches and wild cherry trees were outlined in pearl; the ploughed fields were stretches of snowy dimples; and there was a crisp tang in the air that was glorious. Anne ran downstairs singing until her voice re-echoed through Green Gables.

"Merry Christmas, Marilla! Merry Christmas, Matthew! Isn't it a lovely Christmas? I'm so glad it's white. Any other kind of Christmas doesn't seem real, does it? I don't like green Christmases. They're *not* green—they're just nasty faded browns and greys. What makes people call them green? Why—why—Matthew, is that for me? Oh, Matthew!"

Matthew had sheepishly unfolded the dress from its paper swathings and held it out with a deprecatory glance at Marilla, who feigned to be contemptuously filling the teapot, but nevertheless watched the scene out of the corner of her eye with a rather interested air.

Anne took the dress and looked at it in reverent silence. Oh, how pretty it was—a lovely soft brown gloria with all the gloss of silk; a skirt with dainty frills and shirrings; a waist elaborately pin-tucked in the most fashionable way, with a little ruffle of filmy lace at the neck. But the sleeves—they were the crowning glory! Long elbow cuffs, and above them two beautiful puffs divided by rows of shirring and bows of brown silk ribbon.

"That's a Christmas present for you, Anne," said Matthew shyly. "Why—why—Anne, don't you like it? Well now—well now."

For Anne's eyes had suddenly filled with tears.

"*Like* it! Oh, Matthew!" Anne laid the dress over a chair and clasped her hands. "Matthew, it's perfectly exquisite. Oh, I can never thank you enough. Look at those sleeves! Oh, it seems to me this must be a happy dream."

"Well, well, let us have breakfast," interrupted Marilla. "I must say, Anne, I don't think you needed the dress; but since Matthew has got it for you, see that you take good care of it. There's a hair ribbon Mrs. Lynde left for you. It's brown, to match the dress. Come now, sit in."

"I don't see how I'm going to eat breakfast," said Anne rapturously. "Breakfast seems so commonplace at such an exciting moment. I'd rather feast my eyes on that dress. I'm so glad that puffed sleeves are still fashionable. It did seem to me that I'd never get over it if they went out before I had a dress with them. I'd never have felt quite satisfied, you see. It was lovely of Mrs. Lynde to give me the ribbon, too. I feel that I ought to be a very good girl indeed. It's at times like this I'm sorry I'm not a model little girl; and I always resolve that I will be in future. But somehow it's hard to carry out your resolutions when irresistible temptations come. Still, I really will make an extra effort after this."

When the commonplace breakfast was over Diana appeared, crossing the white log bridge in the hollow, a gay little figure in her crimson ulster. Anne flew down the slope to meet her.

"Merry Christmas, Diana! And oh, it's a wonderful Christmas. I've something splendid to show you. Matthew has given me the loveliest dress, with *such* sleeves. I couldn't even imagine any nicer."

"I've got something more for you," said Diana breathlessly. "Here—this box. Aunt Josephine sent us out a big box with ever so many things in it—and this is for you. I'd have brought it over last night, but it didn't come until after dark, and I never feel very comfortable coming through the Haunted Wood in the dark now."

Anne opened the box and peeped in. First a card with "For the Anne-girl and Merry Christmas," written on it; and then, a pair of the daintiest little kid slippers, with beaded toes and satin bows and glistening buckles.

"Oh," said Anne, "Diana, this is too much, I must be dreaming."

"*I* call it providential," said Diana. "You won't have to borrow Ruby's slippers now, and that's a blessing, for they're two sizes too big for you, and it would be awful to hear a fairy shuffling. Josie Pye would be delighted. Mind you, Rob Wright went home with Gertie Pye from the practice night before last. Did you ever hear anything equal to that?"

All the Avonlea scholars were in a fever of excitement that day, for the hall had to be decorated and a last grand rehearsal held.

The concert came off in the evening and was a pronounced success. The little hall was crowded; all the performers did excellently well, but Anne was the bright particular star of the occasion, as even envy, in the shape of Josie Pye, dared not deny.

"Oh, hasn't it been a brilliant evening?" sighed Anne, when it was all over and she and Diana were walking home together under a dark, starry sky.

"Everything went off very well," said Diana practically. "I guess we must have made as much as ten dollars. Mind you, Mr. Allan is going to send an account of it to the Charlottetown papers."

"Oh, Diana, will we really see our names in print? It makes me thrill to think of it. Your solo was perfectly elegant, Diana. I felt prouder than you did when it was encored. I just said to myself, 'It is my dear bosom friend who is so honoured.'"

"Well, your recitations just brought down the house, Anne. That sad one was simply splendid."

"Oh, I was so nervous, Diana. When Mr. Allan called out my name I really cannot tell how I ever got up on that platform. I felt as if a million eyes were looking at me and through me, and for one dreadful moment I was sure I couldn't begin at all. Then I thought of my lovely puffed sleeves and took courage. I knew that I must live up to those sleeves, Diana. So I started in, and my voice seemed to be coming from ever so far away. I just felt like a parrot. It's providential that I practised those recitations so often up in the garret, or I'd never have been able to get through. Did I groan all right?"

"Yes, indeed, you groaned lovely," assured Diana.

"I saw old Mrs. Sloane wiping away tears when I sat down. It was splendid to think I had touched somebody's heart. It's so romantic to take part in a concert isn't it? Oh, it's been a very memorable occasion indeed."

"Wasn't the boys' dialogue fine?" said Diana. "Gilbert Blythe was just splendid. Anne, I do think it's awful mean the way you treat Gil. Wait till I tell you. When you ran off the platform after the fairy dialogue one of your roses fell out of your hair. I saw Gil pick it up and put it in his breast pocket. There now. You're so romantic that I'm sure you ought to be pleased at that."

"It's nothing to me what that person does," said Anne loftily. "I simply never waste a thought on him, Diana."

That night Marilla and Matthew, who had been out to a concert for the first time in twenty years, sat for awhile by the kitchen fire after Anne had gone to bed.

"Well now, I guess our Anne did as well as any of them," said Matthew proudly.

"Yes, she did," admitted Marilla. "She's a bright child, Matthew. And she looked real nice, too. I've been kind of opposed to this concert scheme, but I suppose there's no real harm in it after all. Anyhow, I was proud of Anne tonight, although I'm not going to tell her so."

"Well now, I was proud of her and I did tell her so 'fore she went upstairs," said Matthew. "We must see what we can do for her some of these days, Marilla. I guess she'll need something more than Avonlea school by and by."

"There's time enough to think of that," said Marilla. "She's only thirteen in March. Though tonight it struck me she was growing quite a big girl. Mrs. Lynde made that dress a mite too long, and it makes Anne look so tall. She's quick to learn and I guess the best thing we can do for her will be to send her to Queen's after a spell. But nothing need be said about that for a year or two yet."

"Well now, it'll do no harm to be thinking it over off and on," said Matthew. "Things like that are all the better for lots of thinking over."

Missy's Room

Mrs. Falconer and Miss Bailey walked home together through the fine blue summer afternoon from the Ladies' Aid meeting at Mrs. Robinson's. They were talking earnestly; that is to say, Miss Bailey was talking earnestly and volubly, and Mrs. Falconer was listening. Mrs. Falconer had reduced the practice of listening to a fine art. She was a thin, wistful-faced mite of a woman, with sad brown eyes, and with snow-white hair that was a libel on her fifty-five years and girlish step. Nobody in Lindsay ever felt very well acquainted with Mrs. Falconer, in spite of the fact that she had lived among them forty years. She kept between her and her world a fine, baffling reserve which no one had ever been able to penetrate. It was known that she had had a bitter sorrow in her life, but she never made any reference to it, and most people in Lindsay had forgotten it. Some foolish ones even supposed that Mrs. Falconer had forgotten it.

"Well, I do not know what on earth is to be done with Camilla Clark," said Miss Bailey, with a prodigious sigh. "I suppose that we will simply have to trust the whole matter to Providence."

Miss Bailey's tone and sigh really seemed to intimate to the world at large that Providence was a last resort and a very dubious one. Not that Miss Bailey meant anything of the sort; her faith was as substantial as her works, which were many and praiseworthy and seasonable.

The case of Camilla Clark was agitating the Ladies' Aid of one of the Lindsay churches. They had talked about it through the whole of that afternoon session while they sewed for their missionary box—talked about it, and come to no conclusion.

In the preceding spring James Clark, one of the hands in the lumber mill at Lindsay, had been killed in an accident. The shock had proved nearly fatal to his young wife. The next day Camilla Clark's baby was born dead, and the poor mother hovered for weeks between life and death. Slowly, very slowly, life won the battle, and Camilla came back from the valley of the shadow. But she was still an invalid, and would be so for a long time.

The Clarks had come to Lindsay only a short time before the accident. They were boarding at Mrs. Barry's when it happened, and Mrs. Barry had shown every kindness and consideration to the unhappy young widow. But now the Barrys were very soon to leave Lindsay for the West, and the question was, what was to be done with Camilla Clark? She could not go west; she could not even do work of any sort yet in Lindsay; she had no relatives or friends in the world; and she was absolutely penniless. As she and her husband had joined the church to which the aforesaid Ladies' Aid belonged, the members thereof felt themselves bound to take up her case and see what could be done for her.

The obvious solution was for some of them to offer her a home until such time as she would be able to go to work. But there did not seem to be anyone who could offer to do this—unless it was Mrs. Falconer. The church was small, and the Ladies' Aid smaller. There were only twelve members in it; four of these were unmarried ladies who boarded, and so were helpless in the matter; of the remaining eight seven had large families, or sick husbands, or something else that prevented them from offering Camilla Clark an asylum. Their excuses were all valid; they were good, sincere women who would have taken her in if they could, but they could not see their way clear to do so. However, it was probable they would eventually manage it in some way if Mrs. Falconer did not rise to the occasion.

Nobody liked to ask Mrs. Falconer outright to take Camilla Clark in, yet everyone thought she might offer. She was comfortably off, and though her house was small, there was nobody to live in it except herself and her husband. But Mrs. Falconer sat silent through all the discussion of the Ladies' Aid, and never opened her lips on the subject of Camilla Clark despite the numerous hints which she received.

Miss Bailey made one more effort as aforesaid. When her despairing reference to Providence brought forth no results, she wished she dared ask Mrs. Falconer openly to take Camilla Clark, but somehow she did not dare. There were not many things that could daunt Miss Bailey, but Mrs. Falconer's reserve and gentle aloofness always could.

When Miss Bailey had gone on down the village street, Mrs. Falconer paused for a few moments at her gate, apparently lost in deep thought. She was perfectly well aware of all the hints that had been thrown out for her benefit that afternoon. She knew that the Aids, one and all, thought that she ought to take Camilla Clark. But she had no room to give her—for it was out of the question to think of putting her in Missy's room.

"I couldn't do such a thing," she said to herself piteously. "They don't understand—they can't understand—but I *couldn't* give her Missy's room. I'm sorry for poor Camilla, and I wish I could help her. But I can't give her Missy's room, and I have no other."

The little Falconer cottage, set back from the road in the green seclusion of an apple orchard and thick, leafy maples, was a very tiny one. There were just two rooms downstairs and two upstairs. When Mrs. Falconer entered the kitchen an old-looking man with long white hair and mild blue eyes looked up with a smile from the bright-coloured blocks before him.

"Have you been lonely, Father?" said Mrs. Falconer tenderly.

He shook his head, still smiling.

"No, not lonely. These"—pointing to the blocks—"are so pretty. See my house, Mother."

This man was Mrs. Falconer's husband. Once he had been one of the smartest, most intelligent men in Lindsay, and one of the most trusted employees of the railroad company. Then there had been a train collision. Malcolm Falconer was taken out of the wreck fearfully injured. He eventually recovered physical health, but he was from that time forth merely a child in intellect—a harmless, kindly creature, docile and easily amused.

Mrs. Falconer tried to dismiss the thought of Camilla Clark from her mind, but it would not be dismissed. Her conscience reproached her continually. She tried to compromise with it by saying that she would go down and see Camilla that evening and take her some nice fresh Irish moss jelly. It was so good for delicate people.

She found Camilla alone in the Barry sitting-room, and noticed with a feeling that was almost like self-reproach how thin and frail and white the poor young creature looked. Why, she seemed little more than a child! Her great dark eyes were far too big for her wasted face, and her hands were almost transparent.

"I'm not much better yet," said Camilla tremulously, in response to Mrs. Falconer's inquiries. "Oh, I'm so slow getting well! And I know—I feel that I'm a burden to everybody."

"But you mustn't think that, dear," said Mrs. Falconer, feeling more uncomfortable than ever. "We are all glad to do all we can for you."

Mrs. Falconer paused suddenly. She was a very truthful woman and she instantly realized that that last sentence was not true. She was not doing all she could for Camilla—she would not be glad, she feared, to do all she could.

"If I were only well enough to go to work," sighed Camilla. "Mr. Marks says I can have a place in the shoe factory whenever I'm able to. But it will be so long yet. Oh, I'm so tired and discouraged!"

She put her hands over her face and sobbed. Mrs. Falconer caught her breath. What if Missy were somewhere alone in the world—ill, friendless, with never a soul to offer her a refuge or a shelter? It was so very, very probable. Before she could check herself Mrs. Falconer spoke. "My dear, don't cry! I want you to come and stay with me until you get perfectly well. You won't be a speck of trouble, and I'll be glad to have you for company."

Mrs. Falconer's Rubicon was crossed. She could not draw back now if she wanted to. But she was not at all sure that she did want to. By the time she reached home she was sure she didn't want to. And yet—to give Missy's room to Camilla! It seemed a great sacrifice to Mrs. Falconer.

She went up to it the next morning with firmly set lips to air and dust it. It was just the same as when Missy had left it long ago. Nothing had ever been moved or changed, but everything had always been kept beautifully neat and clean. Snow-white muslin curtains hung before the small square window. In one corner was a little white bed. Missy's pictures hung on the walls; Missy's books and work-basket were lying on the square stand; there was a bit of half-finished fancy work, yellow from age, lying in the basket. On a small bureau before the gilt-framed mirror were several little girlish knick-knacks and boxes whose contents had never been disturbed since Missy went away. One of Missy's gay pink ribbons—Missy had been so fond of pink ribbons—hung over the top of the mirror. On a chair lay Missy's hat, bright with ribbons and roses, just as Missy had laid it there on the night before she left her home.

Mrs. Falconer's lips quivered as she looked about the room, and tears came to her eyes. Oh, how could she put these things away and bring a stranger here—here, where no one save herself had entered for fifteen years, here in this room, sacred to Missy's memory, waiting for her return when she should be weary of wandering? It almost seemed to the mother's vague fancy, distorted by long, silent brooding, that her daughter's innocent girlhood had been kept here for her and would be lost forever if the room were given to another.

"I suppose it's dreadful foolishness," said Mrs. Falconer, wiping her eyes. "I know it is, but I can't help it. It just goes to my heart to think of putting these things away. But I must do it. Camilla is coming here today, and this room must be got ready for her. Oh, Missy, my poor lost child, it's for your sake I'm doing this—because you may be suffering somewhere as Camilla is now, and I'd wish the same kindness to be shown to you."

She opened the window and put fresh linen on the bed. One by one Missy's little belongings were removed and packed carefully away. On the gay, foolish little hat with its faded wreath of roses the mother's tears fell as she put it in a box. She remembered so plainly the first time Missy had worn it. She could see the pretty, delicately tinted face, the big shining brown eyes, and the riotous golden curls under the drooping, lace-edged brim. Oh, where was Missy now? What roof sheltered her? Did she ever think of her mother and the little white cottage under the maples, and the low-ceilinged, dim room where she had knelt to say her childhood's prayer?

Camilla Clark came that afternoon.

"Oh, it is lovely here," she said gratefully, looking out into the rustling shade of the maples. "I'm sure I shall soon get well here. Mrs. Barry was so kind to me—I shall never forget her kindness—but the house is so close to the factory, and there was such a whirring of wheels all the time, it seemed to get into my head and make me wild with nervousness. I'm so weak that sounds like that worry me. But it is so still and green and peaceful here. It just rests me."

When bedtime came, Mrs. Falconer took Camilla up to Missy's room. It was not as hard as she had expected it to be after all. The wrench was over with the putting away of Missy's things, and it did not hurt the mother to see the frail, girlish Camilla in her daughter's place.

"What a dear little room!" said Camilla, glancing around. "It is so white and sweet. Oh, I know I am going to sleep well here, and dream sweet dreams."

"It was my daughter's room," said Mrs. Falconer, sitting down on the chintz-covered seat by the open window.

Camilla looked surprised.

"I did not know you had a daughter," she said.

"Yes—I had just the one child," said Mrs. Falconer dreamily.

For fifteen years she had never spoken of Missy to a living soul except her husband. But now she felt a sudden impulse to tell Camilla about her, and about the room.

"Her name was Isabella, after her father's mother, but we never called her anything but Missy. That was the little name she gave herself when she began to talk. Oh, I've missed her so!"

"When did she die?" asked Camilla softly, sympathy shining, star-like, in her dark eyes.

"She—she didn't die," said Mrs. Falconer. "She went away. She was a pretty girl and gay and fond of fun—but such a good girl. Oh, Missy was always a good girl! Her father and I were so proud of her—too proud, I suppose. She had her little faults—she was too fond of dress and gaiety, but then she was so young, and we indulged her. Then Bert Williams came to Lindsay to work in the factory. He was a handsome fellow, with taking ways about him, but he was drunken and profane, and nobody knew anything about his past life. He fascinated Missy. He kept coming to see her until her father forbade him the house. Then our poor, foolish child used to meet him elsewhere. We found this out afterwards. And at last she ran away with him, and they were married over at Peterboro and went there to live, for Bert had got work there. We—we were too hard on Missy. But her father was so dreadful hurt about it. He'd been so fond and proud of her, and he felt that she had disgraced him. He disowned her, and sent her word never to show her face here again, for he'd never forgive her. And I was angry too. I didn't send her any word at all. Oh, how I've wept over that! If I had just sent her one little word of forgiveness, everything might have been different. But Father forbade me to.

"Then in a little while there was a dreadful trouble. A woman came to Peterboro and claimed to be Bert Williams's wife—and she was—she proved it. Bert cleared out and was never seen again in these parts. As soon as we heard about it Father relented, and I went right down to Peterboro to see Missy and bring her home. But she wasn't there—she had gone, nobody knew where. I got a letter from her the next week. She said her heart was broken, and she knew we would never forgive her, and she couldn't face the disgrace, so she was going away where nobody would ever find her. We did everything we could to trace her, but we never could. We've never heard from her since, and it is fifteen years ago. Sometimes I am afraid she is dead, but then again I feel sure she isn't. Oh, Camilla, if I could only find my poor child and bring her home!

"This was her room. And when she went away I made up my mind I would keep it for her just as she left it, and I have up to now. Nobody has ever been inside the door but myself. I've always hoped that Missy would come home, and I would lead her up here and say, 'Missy, here is your room just as you left it, and here is your place in your mother's heart just as you left it,' But she never came. I'm afraid she never will."

Mrs. Falconer dropped her face in her hands and sobbed softly. Camilla came over to her and put her arms about her.

"I think she will," she said. "I think—I am sure your love and prayers will bring Missy home yet. And I understand how good you have been in giving me her room—oh, I know what it must have cost you! I will pray tonight that God will bring Missy back to you."

When Mrs. Falconer returned to the kitchen to close the house for the night, her husband being already sound asleep; she heard a low, timid knock at the door. Wondering who it could be so late, she opened it. The light fell on a shrinking, shabby figure on the step, and on a pale, pinched face in which only a mother could have recognized the features of her child. Mrs. Falconer gave a cry.

"Missy! Missy! Missy!"

She caught the poor wanderer to her heart and drew her in.

"Oh, Missy, Missy, have you come back at last? Thank God! Oh, thank God!"

"I *had* to come back. I was starving for a glimpse of your face and of the old home, Mother," sobbed Missy. "But I didn't mean you should know—I never meant to show myself to you. I've been sick, and just as soon as I got better I came here. I meant to creep home after dark and look at the dear old house, and perhaps get a glimpse of you and Father through the window if you were still here. I didn't know if you were. And then I meant to go right away on the night train. I was under the window and I heard you telling my story to someone. Oh, Mother, when I knew that you had forgiven me, that you loved me still and had always kept my room for me, I made up my mind that I'd show myself to you."

The mother had got her child into a rocking-chair and removed the shabby hat and cloak. How ill and worn and faded Missy looked! Yet her face was pure and fine, and there was in it something sweeter than had ever been there in her beautiful girlhood.

"I'm terribly changed, am I not, Mother?" said Missy, with a faint smile. "I've had a hard life—but an honest one, Mother. When I went away I was almost mad with the disgrace my wilfulness had brought on you and Father and myself. I went as far as I could get away from you, and I got work in a factory. I've worked there ever since, just making enough to keep body and soul together. Oh, I've starved for a word from you—the sight of your face! But I thought Father would spurn me from his door if I should ever dare to come back."

"Oh, Missy!" sobbed the mother. "Your poor father is just like a child. He got a terrible hurt ten years ago, and never got over it. I don't suppose he'll even know you—he's clean forgot everything. But he forgave you before it happened. You poor child, you're done right out. You're too weak to be travelling. But never mind, you're home now, and I'll soon nurse you up. I'll put on the kettle and get you a good cup of tea first thing. And you're not to do any more talking till the morning. But, oh, Missy, I can't take you to your own room after all. Camilla Clark has it, and she'll be asleep by now; we mustn't disturb her, for she's been real sick. I'll fix up a bed for you on the sofa, though. Missy, Missy, let us kneel down here and thank God for His mercy!"

Late that night, when Missy had fallen asleep in her improvised bed, the wakeful mother crept in to gloat over her.

"Just to think," she whispered, "if I hadn't taken Camilla Clark in, Missy wouldn't have heard me telling about the room, and she'd have gone away again and never have known. Oh, I don't deserve such a blessing when I was so unwilling to take Camilla! But I know one thing: this is going to be Camilla's home. There'll be no leaving it even when she does get well. She shall be my daughter, and I'll love her next to Missy."

Ted's Afternoon Off

Ted was up at five that morning, as usual. He always had to rise early to kindle the fire and go for the cows, but on this particular morning there was no "had to" about it. He had awakened at four o'clock and had sprung eagerly to the little garret window facing the east, to see what sort of a day was being born. Thrilling with excitement, he saw that it was going to be a glorious day. The sky was all rosy and golden and clear beyond the sharp-pointed, dark firs on Lee's Hill. Out to the north the sea was shimmering and sparkling gaily, with little foam crests here and there ruffled up by the cool morning breeze. Oh, it would be a splendid day!

And he, Ted Melvin, was to have a half holiday for the first time since he had come to live in Brookdale four years ago—a whole afternoon off to go to the Sunday School picnic at the beach beyond the big hotel. It almost seemed too good to be true!

The Jacksons, with whom he had lived ever since his mother had died, did not think holidays were necessities for boys. Hard work and cast-off clothes, and three grudgingly allowed months of school in the winter, made up Ted's life year in and year out—his outer life at least. He had an inner life of dreams, but nobody knew or suspected anything about that. To everybody in Brookdale he was simply Ted Melvin, a shy, odd-looking little fellow with big dreamy black eyes and a head of thick tangled curls which could never be made to look tidy and always annoyed Mrs. Jackson exceedingly.

It was as yet too early to light the fire or go for the cows. Ted crept softly to a corner in the garret and took from the wall an old brown fiddle. It had been his father's. He loved to play on it, and his few rare spare moments were always spent in the garret corner or the hayloft, with his precious fiddle. It was his one link with the old life he had lived in a little cottage far away, with a mother who had loved him and a merry young father who had made wonderful music on the old brown violin.

Ted pushed open his garret window and, seating himself on the sill, began to play, with his eyes fixed on the glowing eastern sky. He played very softly, since Mrs. Jackson had a pronounced dislike to being wakened by "fiddling at all unearthly hours."

The music he made was beautiful and would have astonished anybody who knew enough to know how wonderful it really was. But there was nobody to hear this little neglected urchin of all work, and he fiddled away happily, the music floating out of the garret window, over the treetops and the dew-wet clover fields, until it mingled with the winds and was lost in the silver skies of the morning.

Ted worked doubly hard all that forenoon, since there was a double share of work to do if, as Mrs. Jackson said, he was to be gadding to picnics in the afternoon. But he did it all cheerily and whistled for joy as he worked.

After dinner Mrs. Ross came in. Mrs. Ross lived down on the shore road and made a living for herself and her two children by washing and doing days' work out. She was not a very cheerful person and generally spoke as if on the point of bursting into tears. She looked more doleful than ever today, and lost no time in explaining why.

"I've just got word that my sister over at White Sands is sick with pendikis"—this was the nearest Mrs. Ross could get to appendicitis—"and has to go to the hospital. I've got to go right over and see her, Mrs. Jackson, and I've run in to ask if Ted can go and stay with Jimmy till I get back. There's no one else I can get, and Amelia is away. I'll be back this evening. I don't like leaving Jimmy alone."

"Ted's been promised that he could go to the picnic this afternoon," said Mrs. Jackson shortly. "Mr. Jackson said he could go, so he'll have to please himself. If he's willing to stay with Jimmy instead, he can. *I* don't care."

"Oh, I've *got* to go to the picnic," cried Ted impulsively. "I'm awful sorry for Jimmy—but I *must* go to the picnic."

"I s'pose you feel so," said Mrs. Ross, sighing heavily. "I dunno's I blame you. Picnics is more cheerful than staying with a poor little lame boy, I don't doubt. Well, I s'pose I can put Jimmy's supper on the table clost to him, and shut the cat in with him, and mebbe he'll worry through. He was counting on having you to fiddle for him, though. Jimmy's crazy about music, and he don't never hear much of it. Speaking of fiddling, there's a great fiddler stopping at the hotel now. His name is Blair Milford, and he makes his living fiddling at concerts. I knew him well when he was a child—I was nurse in his father's family. He was a taking little chap, and I was real fond of him. Well, I must be getting. Jimmy'll feel bad at staying alone, but I'll tell him he'll just have to put up with it."

Mrs. Ross sighed herself away, and Ted flew up to his garret corner with a choking in his throat. He couldn't go to stay with Jimmy—he couldn't give up the picnic! Why, he had never been at a picnic; and they were going to drive to the hotel beach in wagons, and have swings, and games, and ice cream, and a boat sail to Curtain Island! He had been looking forward to it, waking and dreaming, for a fortnight. He *must* go. But poor little Jimmy! It was too bad for him to be left all alone.

"I wouldn't like it myself," said Ted miserably, trying to swallow a lump that persisted in coming up in his throat. "It must be dreadful to have to lie on the sofa all the time and never be able to run, climb trees or play, or do a single thing. And Jimmy doesn't like reading much. He'll be dreadful lonesome. I'll be thinking of him all the time at the picnic—I know I will. I suppose I *could* go and stay with him, if I just made up my mind to it."

Making up his mind to it was a slow and difficult process. But when Ted was finally dressed in his shabby, "skimpy" Sunday best, he tucked his precious fiddle under his arm and slipped downstairs. "Please, I think I'll go and stay with Jimmy," he said to Mrs. Jackson timidly, as he always spoke to her.

"Well, if you're to waste the afternoon, I s'pose it's better to waste it that way than in going to a picnic and eating yourself sick," was Mrs. Jackson's ungracious response.

Ted reached Mrs. Ross's little house just as that good lady was locking the door on Jimmy and the cat. "Well, I'm real glad," she said, when Ted told her he had come to stay. "I'd have worried most awful if I'd had to leave Jimmy all alone. He's crying in there this minute. Come now, Jimmy, dry up. Here's Ted come to stop with you after all, and he's brought his fiddle, too."

Jimmy's tears were soon dried, and he welcomed Ted joyfully. "I've been thinking awful long to hear you fiddling," said Jimmy, with a sigh of content. "Seems like the ache ain't never half so bad when I'm listening to music—and when it's your music, I forget there's any ache at all."

Ted took his violin and began to play. After all, it was almost as good as a picnic to have a whole afternoon for his music. The stuffy little room, with its dingy plaster and shabby furniture, was filled with wonderful harmonies. Once he began, Ted could play for hours at a stretch and never be conscious of fatigue. Jimmy lay and listened in rapturous content while Ted's violin sang and laughed and dreamed and rippled.

There was another listener besides Jimmy. Outside, on the red sandstone doorstep, a man was sitting—a tall, well-dressed man with a pale, beautiful face and long, supple white hands. Motionless, he sat there and listened to the music until at last it stopped. Then he rose and knocked at the door. Ted, violin in hand, opened it.

An expression of amazement flashed into the stranger's face, but he only said, "Is Mrs. Ross at home?"

"No, sir," said Ted shyly. "She went over to White Sands and she won't be back till night. But Jimmy is here—Jimmy is her little boy. Will you come in?"

"I'm sorry Mrs. Ross is away," said the stranger, entering. "She was an old nurse of mine. I must confess I've been sitting on the step out there for some time, listening to your music. Who taught you to play, my boy?"

"Nobody," said Ted simply. "I've always been able to play."

"He makes it up himself out of his own head, sir," said Jimmy eagerly.

"No, I don't make it—it makes itself—it just *comes*," said Ted, a dreamy gaze coming into his big black eyes.

The caller looked at him closely. "I know a little about music myself," he said. "My name is Blair Milford and I am a professional violinist. Your playing is wonderful. What is your name?"

"Ted Melvin."

"Well, Ted, I think that you have a great talent, and it ought to be cultivated. You should have competent instruction. Come, you must tell me all about yourself."

Ted told what little he thought there was to tell. Blair Milford listened and nodded, guessing much that Ted didn't tell and, indeed, didn't know himself. Then he made Ted play for him again. "Amazing!" he said softly, under his breath.

Finally he took the violin and played himself. Ted and Jimmy listened breathlessly. "Oh, if I could only play like that!" said Ted wistfully.

Blair Milford smiled. "You will play much better some day if you get the proper training," he said. "You have a wonderful talent, my boy, and you should have it cultivated. It will never in the world do to waste such genius. Yes, that is the right word," he went on musingly, as if talking to himself, "'genius.' Nature is always taking us by surprise. This child has what I have never had and would make any sacrifice for. And yet in him it may come to naught for lack of opportunity. But it must not, Ted. You must have a musical training."

"I can't take lessons, if that is what you mean, sir," said Ted wonderingly. "Mr. Jackson wouldn't pay for them."

"I think we needn't worry about the question of payment if you can find time to practise," said Blair Milford. "I am to be at the beach for two months yet. For once I'll take a music pupil. But will you have time to practise?"

"Yes, sir, I'll make time," said Ted, as soon as he could speak at all for the wonder of it. "I'll get up at four in the morning and have an hour's practising before the time for the cows. But I'm afraid it'll be too much trouble for you, sir, I'm afraid—"

Blair Milford laughed and put his slim white hand on Ted's curly head. "It isn't much trouble to train an artist. It is a privilege. Ah, Ted, you have what I once hoped I had, what I know now I never can have. You don't understand me. You will some day."

"Ain't he an awful nice man?" said Jimmy, when Blair Milford had gone. "But what did he mean by all that talk?"

"I don't know exactly," said Ted dreamily. "That is, I seem to *feel* what he meant but I can't quite put it into words. But, oh, Jimmy, I'm so happy. I'm to have lessons—I have always longed to have them."

"I guess you're glad you didn't go to the picnic?" said Jimmy.

"Yes, but I was glad before, Jimmy, honest I was."

Blair Milford kept his promise. He interviewed Mr. and Mrs. Jackson and, by means best known to himself, induced them to consent that Ted should take music lessons every Saturday afternoon. He was a pupil to delight a teacher's heart and, after every lesson, Blair Milford looked at him with kindly eyes and murmured, "Amazing," under his breath. Finally he went again to the Jacksons, and the next day he said to Ted, "Ted, would you like to come away with me—live with me—be my boy and have your gift for music thoroughly cultivated?"

"What do you mean, sir?" said Ted tremblingly.

"I mean that I want you—that I must have you, Ted. I've talked to Mr. Jackson, and he has consented to let you come. You shall be educated, you shall have the best masters in your art that the world affords, you shall have the career I once dreamed of. Will you come, Ted?"

Ted drew a long breath. "Yes, sir," he said. "But it isn't so much because of the music—it's because I love you, Mr. Milford, and I'm so glad I'm to be always with you."

The Doctor's Sweetheart

Just because I am an old woman outwardly it doesn't follow that I am one inwardly. Hearts don't grow old—or shouldn't. Mine hasn't, I am thankful to say. It bounded like a girl's with delight when I saw Doctor John and Marcella Barry drive past this afternoon. If the doctor had been my own son I couldn't have felt more real pleasure in his happiness. I'm only an old lady who can do little but sit by her window and knit, but eyes were made for seeing, and I use mine for that purpose. When I see the good and beautiful things—and a body need never look for the other kind, you know—the things God planned from the beginning and brought about in spite of the counter plans and schemes of men, I feel such a deep joy that I'm glad, even at seventy-five, to be alive in a world where such things come to pass. And if ever God meant and made two people for each other, those people were Doctor John and Marcella Barry; and that is what I always tell folk who come here commenting on the difference in their ages. "Old enough to be her father," sniffed Mrs. Riddell to me the other day. I didn't say anything to Mrs. Riddell. I just looked at her. I presume my face expressed what I felt pretty clearly. How any woman can live for sixty years in the world, as Mrs. Riddell has, a wife and mother at that, and not get some realization of the beauty and general satisfactoriness of a real and abiding love, is something I cannot understand and never shall be able to.

Nobody in Bridgeport believed that Marcella would ever come back, except Doctor John and me—not even her Aunt Sara. I've heard people laugh at me when I said I knew she would; but nobody minds being laughed at when she is sure of a thing and I was sure that Marcella Barry would come back as that the sun rose and set. I hadn't lived beside her for eight years to know so little about her as to doubt her. Neither had Doctor John.

Marcella was only eight years old when she came to live in Bridgeport. Her father, Chester Barry, had just died. Her mother, who was a sister of Miss Sara Bryant, my next door neighbor, had been dead for four years. Marcella's father left her to the guardianship of his brother, Richard Barry; but Miss Sara pleaded so hard to have the little girl that the Barrys consented to let Marcella live with her aunt until she was sixteen. Then, they said, she would have to go back to them, to be properly educated and take the place of her father's daughter in *his* world. For, of course, it is a fact that Miss Sara Bryant's world was and is a very different one from Chester Barry's world. As to which side the difference favors, that isn't for me to say. It all depends on your standard of what is really worth while, you know.

So Marcella came to live with us in Bridgeport. I say "us" advisedly. She slept and ate in her aunt's house, but every house in the village was a home to her; for, with all our little disagreements and diverse opinions, we are really all one big family, and everybody feels an interest in and a good working affection for everybody else. Besides, Marcella was one of those children whom everybody loves at sight, and keeps on loving. One long, steady gaze from those big grayish-blue black-lashed eyes of hers went right into your heart and stayed there.

She was a pretty child and as good as she was pretty. It was the right sort of goodness, too, with just enough spice of original sin in it to keep it from spoiling by reason of over-sweetness. She was a frank, loyal, brave little thing, even at eight, and wouldn't have said or done a mean or false thing to save her life.

She and I were right good friends from the beginning. She loved me and she loved her Aunt Sara; but from the very first her best and deepest affection went out to Doctor John Haven, who lived in the big brick house on the other side of Miss Sara's.

Doctor John was a Bridgeport boy, and when he got through college he came right home and settled down here, with his widowed mother. The Bridgeport girls were fluttered, for eligible young men were scarce in our village; there was considerable setting of caps, I must say that, although I despise ill-natured gossip; but neither the caps nor the wearers thereof seemed to make any impression on Doctor John. Mrs. Riddell said that he was a born old bachelor; I suppose she based her opinion on the fact that Doctor John was always a quiet, bookish fellow, who didn't care a button for society, and had never been guilty of a flirtation in his life. I knew Doctor John's heart far better than Martha Riddell could know anybody's; and I knew there was nothing of the old bachelor in his nature. He just had to wait for the right woman, that was all, not being able to content himself with less as some men can and do. If she never came Doctor John would never marry; but he wouldn't be an old bachelor for all that.

He was thirty when Marcella came to Bridgeport—a tall, broad-shouldered man with a mane of thick brown curls and level, dark hazel eyes. He walked with a little stoop, his hands clasped behind him; and he had the sweetest, deepest voice. Spoken music, if ever a voice was. He was kind and brave and gentle, but a little distant and reserved with most people. Everybody in Bridgeport liked him, but only a very few ever passed the inner gates of his confidence or were admitted to any share in his real life. I am proud to say I was one; I think it is something for an old woman to boast of.

Doctor John was always fond of children, and they of him. It was natural that he and little Marcella should take to each other. He had the most to do with bringing her up, for Miss Sara consulted him in everything. Marcella was not hard to manage for the most part; but she had a will of her own, and when she did set it up in opposition to the powers that were, nobody but the doctor could influence her at all; she never resisted him or disobeyed his wishes.

Marcella was one of those girls who develop early. I suppose her constant association with us elderly folks had something to do with it, too. But, at fifteen, she was a woman, loving, beautiful, and spirited.

And Doctor John loved her—loved the woman, not the child. I knew it before he did—but not, as I think, before Marcella did, for those young, straight-gazing eyes of hers were wonderfully quick to read into other people's hearts. I watched them together and saw the love growing between them, like a strong, fair, perfect flower, whose fragrance was to endure for eternity. Miss Sara saw it, too, and was half-pleased and half-worried; even Miss Sara thought the Doctor too old for Marcella; and besides, there were the Barrys to be reckoned with. Those Barrys were the nightmare dread of poor Miss Sara's life.

The time came when Doctor John's eyes were opened. He looked into his own heart and read there what life had written for him. As he told me long afterwards, it came to him with a shock that left him white-lipped. But he was a brave, sensible fellow and he looked the matter squarely in the face. First of all, he put away to one side all that the world might say; the thing concerned solely him and Marcella, and the world had nothing to do with it. That disposed of, he asked himself soberly if he had a right to try to win Marcella's love. He decided that he had not; it would be taking an unfair advantage of her youth and inexperience. He knew that she must soon go to her father's people—she must not go bound by any ties of his making. Doctor John, for Marcella's sake, gave the decision against his own heart.

So much did Doctor John tell me, his old friend and confidant. I said nothing and gave no advice, not having lived seventy-five years for nothing. I knew that Doctor John's decision was manly and right and fair; but I also knew it was all nullified by the fact that Marcella already loved him.

So much I knew; the rest I was left to suppose. The Doctor and Marcella told me much, but there were some things too sacred to be told, even to me. So that to this day I don't know how the doctor found out that Marcella loved him. All I know is that one day, just a month before her sixteenth birthday, the two came hand in hand to Miss Sara and me, as we sat on Miss Sara's veranda in the twilight, and told us simply that they had plighted their troth to each other.

I looked at them standing there with that wonderful sunrise of life and love on their faces—the doctor, tall and serious, with a sprinkle of silver in his brown hair and the smile of a happy man on his lips—Marcella, such a slip of a girl, with her black hair in a long braid and her lovely face all dewed over with tears and sunned over with smiles—I, an old woman, looked at them and thanked the good God for them and their delight.

Miss Sara laughed and cried and kissed—and forboded what the Barrys would do. Her forebodings proved only too true. When the doctor wrote to Richard Barry, Marcella's guardian, asking his consent to their engagement, Richard Barry promptly made trouble—the very worst kind of trouble. He descended on Bridgeport and completely overwhelmed poor Miss Sara in his wrath. He laughed at the idea of countenancing an engagement between a child like Marcella and an obscure country doctor. And he carried Marcella off with him!

She had to go, of course. He was her legal guardian and he would listen to no pleadings. He didn't know anything about Marcella's character, and he thought that a new life out in the great world would soon blot out her fancy.

After the first outburst of tears and prayers Marcella took it very calmly, as far as outward eye could see. She was as cool and dignified and stately as a young queen. On the night before she went away she came over to say good-bye to me. She did not even shed any tears, but the look in her eyes told of bitter hurt. "It is goodbye for five years, Miss Tranquil," she said steadily. "When I am twenty-one I will come back. That is the only promise I can make. They will not let me write to John or Aunt Sara and I will do nothing underhanded. But I will not forget and I will come back."

Richard Barry would not even let her see Doctor John alone again. She had to bid him good-bye beneath the cold, contemptuous eyes of the man of the world. So there was just a hand-clasp and one long deep look between them that was tenderer than any kiss and more eloquent than any words.

"I will come back when I am twenty-one," said Marcella. And I saw Richard Barry smile.

So Marcella went away and in all Bridgeport there were only two people who believed she would ever return. There is no keeping a secret in Bridgeport, and everybody knew all about the love affair between Marcella and the doctor and about the promise she had made. Everybody sympathized with the doctor because everybody believed he had lost his sweetheart.

"For of course she'll never come back," said Mrs. Riddell to me. "She's only a child and she'll soon forget him. She's to be sent to school and taken abroad and between times she'll live with the Richard Barrys; and they move, as everyone knows, in the very highest and gayest circles. I'm sorry for the doctor, though. A man of his age doesn't get over a thing like that in a hurry and he was perfectly silly over Marcella. But it really serves him right for falling in love with a child."

There are times when Martha Riddell gets on my nerves. She's a good-hearted woman, and she means well; but she rasps—rasps terribly.

Even Miss Sara exasperated me. But then she had her excuse. The child she loved as her own had been torn from her and it almost broke her heart. But even so, I thought she ought to have had a little more faith in Marcella.

"Oh, no, she'll never come back," sobbed Miss Sara. "Yes, I know she promised. But they'll wean her away from me. She'll have such a gay, splendid life she'll not want to come back. Five years is a lifetime at her age. No, don't try to comfort me, Miss Tranquil, because I *won't* be comforted!"

When a person has made up her mind to be miserable you just have to *let* her be miserable.

I almost dreaded to see Doctor John for fear he would be in despair, too, without any confidence in Marcella. But when he came I saw I needn't have worried. The light had all gone out of his eyes, but there was a calm, steady patience in them.

"She will come back to me, Miss Tranquil," he said. "I know what people are saying, but that does not trouble me. They do not know Marcella as I do. She promised and she will keep her word—keep it joyously and gladly, too. If I did not know that I would not wish its fulfilment. When she is free she will turn her back on that brilliant world and all it offers her and come back to me. My part is to wait and believe."

So Doctor John waited and believed. After a little while the excitement died away and people forgot Marcella. We never heard from or about her, except a paragraph now and then in the society columns of the city paper the doctor took. We knew she was sent to school for three years; then the Barrys took her abroad. She was presented at court. When the doctor read this—he was with me at the time—he put his hand over his eyes and sat very silent for a long time. I wondered if at last some momentary doubt had crept into his mind—if he did not fear that Marcella must have forgotten him. The paper told of her triumph and her beauty and hinted at a titled match. Was it probable or even possible that she would be faithful to him after all this?

The doctor must have guessed my thoughts, for at last he looked up with a smile.

"She will come back," was all he said. But I saw that the doubt, if doubt it were, had gone. I watched him as he went away, that tall, gentle, kindly-eyed man, and I prayed that his trust might not be misplaced; for if it should be it would break his heart.

Five years seems a long time in looking forward. But they pass quickly. One day I remembered that it was Marcella's twenty-first birthday. Only one other person thought of it. Even Miss Sara did not. Miss Sara remembered Marcella only as a child that had been loved and lost. Nobody else in Bridgeport thought about her at all. The doctor came in that evening. He had a rose in his buttonhole and he walked with a step as light as a boy's.

"She is free to-day," he said. "We shall soon have her again, Miss Tranquil."

"Do you think she will be the same?" I said.

I don't know what made me say it. I hate to be one of those people who throw cold water on other peoples' hopes. But it slipped out before I thought. I suppose the doubt had been vaguely troubling me always, under all my faith in Marcella, and now made itself felt in spite of me.

But the doctor only laughed.

"How could she be changed?" he said. "Some women might be—most women would be—but not Marcella. Dear Miss Tranquil, don't spoil your beautiful record of confidence by doubting her now. We shall have her again soon—how soon I don't know, for I don't even know where she is, whether in the old world or the new—but just as soon as she can come to us."

We said nothing more—neither of us. But every day the light in the doctor's eyes grew brighter and deeper and tenderer. He never spoke of Marcella, but I knew she was in his thoughts every moment. He was much calmer than I was. I trembled when the postman knocked, jumped when the gate latch clicked, and fairly had a cold chill if I saw a telegraph boy running down the street.

One evening, a fortnight later, I went over to see Miss Sara. She was out somewhere, so I sat down in her little sitting room to wait for her. Presently the doctor came in and we sat in the soft twilight, talking a little now and then, but silent when we wanted to be, as becomes real friendship. It was such a beautiful evening. Outside in Miss Sara's garden the roses were white and red, and sweet with dew; the honeysuckle at the window sent in delicious breaths now and again; a few sleepy birds were twittering; between the trees the sky was all pink and silvery blue and there was an evening star over the elm in my front yard. We heard somebody come through the door and down the hall. I turned, expecting to see Miss Sara—and I saw Marcella! She was standing in the doorway, tall and beautiful, with a ray of sunset light falling athwart her black hair under her travelling hat. She was looking past me at Doctor John and in her splendid eyes was the look of the exile who had come home to her own.

"Marcella!" said the doctor.

I went out by the dining-room door and shut it behind me, leaving them alone together.

The wedding is to be next month. Miss Sara is beside herself with delight. The excitement has been really terrible, and the way people have talked and wondered and exclaimed has almost worn my patience clean out. I've snubbed more persons in the last ten days than I ever did in all my life before.

Nothing of this worries Doctor John or Marcella. They are too happy to care for gossip or outside curiosity. The Barrys are not coming to the wedding, I understand. They refuse to forgive Marcella or countenance her folly, as they call it, in any way. Folly! When I see those two together and realize what they mean to each other I have some humble, reverent idea of what true wisdom is.

The End of the Young Family Feud

A week before Christmas, Aunt Jean wrote to Elizabeth, inviting her and Alberta and me to eat our Christmas dinner at Monkshead. We accepted with delight. Aunt Jean and Uncle Norman were delightful people, and we knew we should have a jolly time at their house. Besides, we wanted to see Monkshead, where Father had lived in his boyhood, and the old Young homestead where he had been born and brought up and where Uncle William still lived. Father never said much about it, but we knew he loved it very dearly, and we had always greatly desired to get at least a glimpse of what Alberta liked to call "our ancestral halls."

Since Monkshead was only sixty miles away, and Uncle William lived there as aforesaid, it may be pertinently asked what there was to prevent us from visiting it and the homestead as often as we wished. We answer promptly: the family feud.

Father and Uncle William were on bad terms, or rather on no terms at all, and had been ever since we could remember. After Grandfather Young's death there had been a wretched quarrel over the property. Father always said that he had been as much to blame as Uncle William, but Great-aunt Emily told us that Uncle William had been by far the most to blame, and that he had behaved scandalously to Father. Moreover, she said that Father had gone to him when cooling-down time came, apologized for what he had said, and asked Uncle William to be friends again; and that William, simply turned his back on Father and walked into the house without saying a word, but, as Great-aunt Emily said, with the Young temper sticking out of every kink and curve of his figure. Great-aunt Emily is our aunt on Mother's side, and she does not like any of the Youngs except Father and Uncle Norman.

This was why we had never visited Monkshead. We had never seen Uncle William, and we always thought of him as a sort of ogre when we thought of him at all. When we were children, our old nurse, Margaret Hannah, used to frighten us into good behaviour by saying ominously, "If you 'uns aint good your Uncle William'll cotch you."

What he would do to us when he "cotched" us she never specified, probably reasoning that the unknown was always more terrible than the known. My private opinion in those days was that he would boil us in oil and pick our bones.

Uncle Norman and Aunt Jean had been living out west for years. Three months before this Christmas they had come east, bought a house in Monkshead, and settled there. They had been down to see us, and Father and Mother and the boys had been up to see them, but we three girls had not; so we were pleasantly excited at the thought of spending Christmas there.

Christmas morning was fine, white as a pearl and clear as a diamond. We had to go by the seven o'clock train, since there was no other before eleven, and we reached Monkshead at eight-thirty.

When we stepped from the train the stationmaster asked us if we were the three Miss Youngs. Alberta pleaded guilty, and he said, "Well, here's a letter for you then."

We took the letter and went into the waiting room with sundry misgivings. What had happened? Were Uncle Norman and Aunt Jean quarantined for scarlet fever, or had burglars raided the pantry and carried off the Christmas supplies? Elizabeth opened and read the letter aloud. It was from Aunt Jean to the following effect:

> DEAR GIRLS: I am so sorry to disappoint you, but I cannot help it. Word has come from Streatham that my sister has met with a serious accident and is in a very critical condition. Your uncle and I must go to Streatham immediately and are leaving on the eight o'clock express. I know you have started before this, so there is no use in telegraphing. We want you to go right to the house and make yourself at home. You will find the key under the kitchen doorstep, and the dinner in the pantry all ready to cook. There are two mince pies on the third shelf, and the plum pudding only needs to be warmed up. You will find a little Christmas remembrance for each of you on the dining-room table. I hope you will make as merry as you possibly can and we will have you down again as soon as we come back.

Your hurried and affectionate,
Aunt Jean

We looked at each other somewhat dolefully. But, as Alberta pointed out, we might as well make the best of it, since there was no way of getting home before the five o'clock train. So we trailed out to the stationmaster, and asked him limply if he could direct us to Mr. Norman Young's house.

He was a rather grumpy individual, very busy with pencil and notebook over some freight; but he favoured us with his attention long enough to point with his pencil and say jerkily, "Young's? See that red house on the hill? That's it."

The red house was about a quarter of a mile from the station, and we saw it plainly. Accordingly, to the red house we betook ourselves. On nearer view it proved to be a trim, handsome place, with nice grounds and very fine old trees.

We found the key under the kitchen doorstep and went in. The fire was black out, and somehow things wore a more cheerless look than I had expected to find. I may as well admit that we marched into the dining room first of all, to find our presents.

There were three parcels, two very small and one pretty big, lying on the table, but when we came to look for names there were none.

"Evidently Aunt Jean, in her hurry and excitement, forgot to label them," said Elizabeth. "Let us open them. We may be able to guess from the contents which belongs to whom."

I must say we were surprised when we opened those parcels. "We had known that Aunt Jean's gifts would be nice, but we had not expected anything like this. There was a magnificent stone marten collar, a dear little gold watch and pearl chatelaine, and a gold chain bracelet set with turquoises.

"The collar must be for you, Elizabeth, because Mary and I have one already, and Aunt Jean knows it," said Alberta; "the watch must be for you, Mary, because I have one; and by the process of exhaustion the bracelet must be for me. Well, they are all perfectly sweet."

Elizabeth put on her collar and paraded in front of the sideboard mirror. It was so dusty she had to take her handkerchief and wipe it before she could see herself properly. Everything in the room was equally dusty. As for the lace curtains, they looked as if they hadn't been washed for years, and one of them had a long ragged hole in it. I couldn't help feeling secretly surprised, for Aunt Jean had the reputation of being a perfect housekeeper. However, I didn't say anything, and neither did the other girls. Mother had always impressed upon us that it was the height of bad manners to criticize anything we might not like in a house where we were guests.

"Well, let's see about dinner," said Alberta, practically, snapping her bracelet on her wrist and admiring the effect.

We went to the kitchen, where Elizabeth proceeded to light the fire, that being one of her specialties, while Alberta and I explored the pantry. We found the dinner supplies laid out as Aunt Jean had explained. There was a nice fat turkey all stuffed, and vegetables galore. The mince pies were in their place, but they were almost the only things about which that could be truthfully said, for the disorder of that pantry was enough to give a tidy person nightmares for a month. "I never in all my life saw—" began Alberta, and then stopped short, evidently remembering Mother's teaching.

"Where is the plum pudding?" said I, to turn the conversation into safer channels.

It was nowhere to be seen, so we concluded it must be in the cellar. But we found the cellar door padlocked good and fast.

"Never mind," said Elizabeth. "You know none of us really likes plum pudding. We only eat it because it is the proper traditional dessert. The mince pies will suit us better."

We hurried the turkey into the oven, and soon everything was going merrily. We had lots of fun getting up that dinner, and we made ourselves perfectly at home, as Aunt Jean had commanded. We kindled a fire in the dining room and dusted everything in sight. We couldn't find anything remotely resembling a duster, so we used our handkerchiefs. When we got through, the room looked like something, for the furnishings were really very handsome, but our handkerchiefs—well!

Then we set the table with all the nice dishes we could find. There was only one long tablecloth in the sideboard drawer, and there were three holes in it, but we covered them with dishes and put a little potted palm in the middle for a centrepiece. At one o'clock dinner was ready for us and we for it. Very nice that table looked, too, as we sat down to it.

Just as Alberta was about to spear the turkey with a fork and begin carving, that being one of *her* specialties, the kitchen door opened and somebody walked in. Before we could move, a big, handsome, bewhiskered man in a fur coat appeared in the dining-room doorway.

I wasn't frightened. He seemed quite respectable, I thought, and I supposed he was some intimate friend of Uncle Norman's. I rose politely and said, "Good day."

You never saw such an expression of amazement as was on that poor man's face. He looked from me to Alberta and from Alberta to

Elizabeth and from Elizabeth to me again as if he doubted the evidence of his eyes.

"Mr. and Mrs. Norman Young are not at home," I explained, pitying him. "They went to Streatham this morning because Mrs. Young's sister is very ill."

"What does all this mean?" said the big man gruffly. "This isn't Norman Young's house ... it is mine. I'm William Young. Who are you? And what are you doing here?"

I fell back into my chair, speechless. My very first impulse was to put up my hand and cover the gold watch. Alberta had dropped the carving knife and was trying desperately to get the gold bracelet off under the table. In a flash we had realized our mistake and its awfulness. As for me, I felt positively frightened; Margaret Hannah's warnings of old had left an ineffaceable impression.

Elizabeth rose to the occasion. Rising to the occasion is another of Elizabeth's specialties. Besides, she was not hampered by the tingling consciousness that she was wearing a gift that had not been intended for her.

"We have made a mistake, I fear," she said, with a dignity which I appreciated even in my panic, "and we are very sorry for it. We were invited to spend Christmas with Mr. and Mrs. Norman Young. When we got off the train we were given a letter from them stating that they were summoned away but telling us to go to their house and make ourselves at home. The stationmaster told us that this was the house, so we came here. We have never been in Monkshead, so we did not know the difference. Please pardon us."

I had got off the watch by this time and laid it on the table, unobserved, as I thought. Alberta, not having the key of the bracelet, had not been able to get it off, and she sat there crimson with shame. As for Uncle William, there was positively a twinkle in his eye. He did not look in the least ogreish.

"Well, it has been quite a fortunate mistake for me," he said. "I came home expecting to find a cold house and a raw dinner, and I find this instead. I'm very much obliged to you."

Alberta rose, went to the mantel piece, took the key of the bracelet therefrom, and unlocked it. Then she faced Uncle William. "Mrs. Young told us in her letter that we would find our Christmas gifts on the table, so we took it for granted that these things belonged to us," she said desperately. "And now, if you will kindly tell us where Mr. Norman Young does live, we won't intrude on you any longer. Come, girls."

Elizabeth and I rose with a sigh. There was nothing else to be done, of course, but we were fearfully hungry, and we did not feel enthusiastic over the prospect of going to another empty house and cooking an-another dinner.

"Wait a bit," said Uncle William. "I think since you have gone to all the trouble of cooking the dinner it's only fair you should stay and help to eat it. Accidents seem to be rather fashionable just now. My housekeeper's son broke his leg down at Weston, and I had to take her there early this morning. Come, introduce yourselves. To whom am I indebted for this pleasant surprise?"

"We are Elizabeth, Alberta, and Mary Young of Green Village," I said; and then I looked to see the ogre creep out if it were ever going to.

But Uncle William merely looked amazed for the first moment, foolish for the second, and the third he was himself again.

"Robert's daughters?" he said, as if it were the most natural thing in the world that Robert's daughters should be there in his house. "So you are my nieces? Well, I'm very glad to make your acquaintance. Sit down and we'll have dinner as soon as I can get my coat off. I want to see if you are as good cooks as your mother used to be long ago."

We sat down, and so did Uncle William. Alberta had her chance to show what she could do at carving, for Uncle William said it was something he never did; he kept a housekeeper just for that. At first we felt a bit stiff and awkward; but that soon wore off, for Uncle William was genial, witty, and entertaining. Soon, to our surprise, we found that we were enjoying ourselves. Uncle William seemed to be, too. When we had finished he leaned back and looked at us.

"I suppose you've been brought up to abhor me and all my works?" he said abruptly.

"Not by Father and Mother," I said frankly. "They never said anything against you. Margaret Hannah did, though. She brought us up in the way we should go through fear of you."

Uncle William laughed.

"Margaret Hannah was a faithful old enemy of mine," he said. "Well, I acted like a fool—and worse. I've been sorry for it ever since. I was in the wrong. I couldn't have said this to your father, but I don't mind saying it to you, and you can tell him if you like."

"He'll be delighted to hear that you are no longer angry with him," said Alberta. "He has always longed to be friends with you again, Uncle William. But he thought you were still bitter against him."

"No—no—nothing but stubborn pride," said Uncle William. "Now, girls, since you are my guests I must try to give you a good time. We'll take the double sleigh and have a jolly drive this afternoon. And about those trinkets there—they are yours. I did get them for some young friends of mine here, but I'll give them something else. I want you to have these. That watch looked very nice on your blouse, Mary, and the bracelet became Alberta's pretty wrist very well. Come and give your cranky old uncle a hug for them."

Uncle William got his hugs heartily; then we washed up the dishes and went for our drive. We got back just in time to catch the evening train home. Uncle William saw us off at the station, under promise to come back and stay a week with him when his housekeeper came home.

"One of you will have to come and stay with me altogether, pretty soon," he said. "Tell your father he must be prepared to hand over one of his girls to me as a token of his forgiveness. I'll be down to talk it over with him shortly."

When we got home and told our story, Father said, "Thank God!" very softly. There were tears in his eyes. He did not wait for Uncle William to come down, but went to Monkshead himself the next day.

In the spring Alberta is to go and live with Uncle William. She is making a supply of dusters now. And next Christmas we are going to have a grand family reunion at the old homestead. Mistakes are not always bad.

The Genesis of the Doughnut Club

When John Henry died there seemed to be nothing for me to do but pack up and go back east. I didn't want to do it, but forty-five years of sojourning in this world have taught me that a body has to do a good many things she doesn't want to do, and that most of them turn out to be for the best in the long run. But I knew perfectly well that it wasn't best for me or anybody else that I should go back to live with William and Susanna, and I couldn't think what Providence was about when things seemed to point that way.

I wanted to stay in Carleton. I loved the big, straggling, bustling little town that always reminded me of a lanky, overgrown schoolboy, all arms and legs, but full to the brim with enthusiasm and splendid ideas. I knew Carleton was bound to grow into a magnificent city, and I wanted to be there and see it grow and watch it develop; and I loved the whole big, breezy golden west, with the rush and tingle of its young life. And, more than all, I loved my boys, and what I was going to do without them or they without me was more than I knew, though I tried to think Providence might know.

But there was no place in Carleton for me; the only thing to do was to go back east, and I knew that all the time, even when I was desperately praying that I might find a way to remain. There's not much comfort, or help either, praying one way and believing another.

I'd lived down east in Northfield all my life—until five years ago—lived with my brother William and his wife. Northfield was a little pinched-up village where everybody knew more about you than you did about yourself, and you couldn't turn around without being commented upon. William and Susanna were kind to me, but I was just the old maid sister, of no importance to anybody, and I never felt as if I were really living. I was simply vegetating on, and wouldn't be missed by a single soul if I died. It is a horrible feeling, but I didn't expect it would ever be any different, and I had made up my mind that when I died I would have the word "Wasted" carved on my tombstone. It wouldn't be conventional at all, but I'd been conventional all my life, and I was determined I'd have something done out of the common even if I had to wait until I was dead to have it.

Then all at once the letter came from John Henry, my brother out west. He wrote that his wife had died and he wanted me to go out and keep house for him. I sat right down and wrote him I'd go and in a week's time I started.

It made quite a commotion; I had that much satisfaction out of it to begin with. Susanna wasn't any too well pleased. I was only the old maid sister, but I was a good cook, and help was scarce in Northfield. All the neighbours shook their heads, and warned me I wouldn't like it. I was too old to change my ways, and I'd be dreadfully homesick, and I'd find the west too rough and boisterous. I just smiled and said nothing.

Well, I came out here to Carleton, and from the time I got here I was perfectly happy. John Henry had a little rented house, and he was as poor as a church mouse, being the ne'er-do-well of our family, and the best loved, as ne'er-do-wells are so apt to be. He'd nearly died of lonesomeness since his wife's death, and he was so glad to see me. That was delightful in itself, and I was just in my element getting that little house fixed up cosy and homelike, and cooking the most elegant meals. There wasn't much work to do, just for me and him, and I got a squaw in to wash and scrub. I never thought about Northfield except to thank goodness I'd escaped from it, and John Henry and I were as happy as a king and queen.

Then after awhile my activities began to sprout and branch out, and the direction they took was *boys*. Carleton was full of boys, like all the western towns, overflowing with them as you might say, young fellows just let loose from home and mother, some of them dying of homesickness and some of them beginning to run wild and get into risky ways, some of them smart and some of them lazy, some ugly and some handsome; but all of them boys, lovable, rollicking boys, with the makings of good men in them if there was anybody to take hold of them and cut the pattern right, but liable to be spoiled just because there wasn't anybody.

Well, I did what I could. It began with John Henry bringing home some of them that worked in his office to spend the evening now and again, and they told other fellows and asked leave to bring them in too. And before long it got to be that there never was an evening there wasn't some of them there, "Aunt-Pattying" me. I told them from the start I would *not* be called Miss. When a woman has been Miss for forty-five years she gets tired of it.

So Aunt Patty it was, and Aunt Patty it remained, and I loved all those dear boys as if they'd been my own. They told me all their troubles, and I mothered them and cheered them up and scolded them, and finally topped off with a jolly good supper; for, talk as you like, you can't preach much good into a boy if he's got an aching void in his stomach. Fill *that* up with tasty victuals, and then you can do something with his spiritual nature. If a boy is well stuffed with good things and then won't listen to advice, you might as well stop wasting your breath on him, because there is something radically wrong with him. Probably his grandfather had dyspepsia. And a dyspeptic ancestor is worse for a boy than predestination, in my opinion.

Anyway, most of my boys took to going to church and Bible class of their own accord, after I'd been their aunt for awhile. The young minister thought it was all his doings, and I let him think so to keep him cheered up. He was a nice boy himself, and often dropped in of an evening too; but I never would let him talk theology until after supper. His views always seemed so much mellower then, and didn't puzzle the other boys more than was wholesome for them.

This went on for five glorious years, the only years of my life I'd ever *lived*, and then came, as I thought, the end of everything. John Henry took typhoid and died. At first that was all I could think of; and when I got so that I could think of other things, there was, as I have said, nothing for me to do but go back east.

The boys, who had been as good as gold to me all through my trouble, felt dreadfully bad over this, and coaxed me hard to stay. They said if I'd start a boarding house I'd have all the boarders I could accommodate; but I knew it was no use to think of that, because I wasn't strong enough, and help was so hard to get. No, there was nothing for it but Northfield and stagnation again, with not a stray boy anywhere to mother. I looked the dismal prospect square in the face and made up my mind to it.

But I was determined to give my boys one good celebration before I went, anyway. It was near Thanksgiving, and I resolved they should have a dinner that would keep my memory green for awhile, a real old-fashioned Thanksgiving dinner such as they used to have at home. I knew it would cost more than I could really afford, but I shut my eyes to that aspect of the question. I was going back to strict eastern economy for the rest of my days, and I meant to indulge in one wild, blissful riot of extravagance before I was cooped up again.

I counted up the boys I must have, and there were fifteen, including the minister. I invited them a fortnight ahead to make sure of getting them, though I needn't have worried, for they all said they would have broken an engagement to dine with the king for one of my dinners. The minister said he had been feeling so homesick he was afraid he wouldn't be able to preach a real thankful sermon, but now he was comfortably sure that his sermon would be overflowing with gratitude.

I just threw myself heart and soul into the preparations for that dinner. I had three turkeys and two sucking pigs, and mince pies and pumpkin pies and apple pies, and doughnuts and fruit cake and cranberry sauce and brown bread, and ever so many other things to fill up the chinks. The night before Thanksgiving everything was ready, and I was so tired I could hardly talk to Jimmy Nelson when he dropped in.

Jimmy had something on his mind, I saw that. So I said, "'Fess up, Jimmy, and then you'll be able to enjoy your call."

"I want to ask a favour of you, Aunt Patty," said Jimmy.

I knew I should have to grant it; nobody could refuse Jimmy anything, he looked so much like a nice, clean, pink-and-white little schoolboy whose mother had just scrubbed his face and told him to be good. At the same time he was one of the wildest young scamps in Carleton, or had been until a year ago. I'd got him well set on the road to reformation, and I felt worse about leaving him than any of the rest of them. I knew he was just at the critical point. With somebody to tide him over the next half year he'd probably go straight for the rest of his life, but if he were left to himself he'd likely just slip back to his old set and ways.

"I want you to let me bring my Uncle Joe to dinner tomorrow," said Jimmy. "The poor old fellow is stranded here for Thanksgiving, and he hates hotels. May I?"

"Of course," I said heartily, wondering why Jimmy seemed to think I mightn't want his Uncle Joe. "Bring him right along."

"Thanks," said Jimmy. "He'll be more than pleased. Your sublime cookery will delight him. He adores the west, but he can't endure its cooking. He's always harping on his mother's pantry and the good old down-east dinners. He's dyspeptic and pessimistic most of the time, and he's got half a dozen cronies just like himself. All they think of is railroads and bills of fare."

"Railroads!" I cried. And then an awful thought assailed me. "Jimmy Nelson, your uncle isn't—isn't—he can't be Joseph P. Nelson, the *rich* Joseph P. Nelson!"

"Oh, he's rich enough," said Jimmy; getting up and reaching for his hat. "In dollars, that is. Some ways he's poor enough. Well, I must be going. Thanks ever so much for letting me bring Uncle Joe."

And that rascal was gone, leaving me crushed. Joseph Nelson was coming to my house to dinner—Joseph P. Nelson, the millionaire railroad king, who kept his own chef and was accustomed to dining with the great ones of the earth!

I was afraid I should never be able to forgive Jimmy. I couldn't sleep a wink that night, and I cooked that dinner next day in a terrible state of mind. Every ring that came at the door made my heart jump,—but in the end Jimmy didn't ring at all, but just walked in with his uncle in tow. The minute I saw Joseph P. I knew I needn't be scared of *him*; he just looked real common. He was little and thin and kind of bored-looking, with grey hair and whiskers, and his clothes were next door to downright shabbiness. If it hadn't been for the thought of that chef, I wouldn't have felt a bit ashamed of my old-fashioned Thanksgiving spread.

When Joseph P. sat down to that table he stopped looking bored. All the time the minister was saying grace that man simply stared at a big plate of doughnuts near my end of the table, as if he'd never seen anything like them before.

All the boys talked and laughed while they were eating, but Joseph P. just *ate*, tucking away turkey and vegetables and keeping an anxious eye on those doughnuts, as if he was afraid somebody else would get hold of them before his turn came. I wished I was sure it was etiquette to tell him not to worry because there were plenty more in the pantry. By the time he'd been helped three times to mince pie I gave up feeling bad about the chef. He finished off with the doughnuts, and I shan't tell how many of them he devoured, because I would not be believed.

Most of the boys had to go away soon after dinner. Joseph P. shook hands with me absently and merely said, "Good afternoon, Miss Porter." I didn't think he seemed at all grateful for his dinner, but that didn't worry me because it was for my boys I'd got it up, and not for dyspeptic millionaires whose digestion had been spoiled by private chefs. And my boys had appreciated it, there wasn't any doubt about that. Peter Crockett and Tommy Gray stayed to help me wash the dishes, and we had the jolliest time ever. Afterward we picked the turkey bones.

But that night I realized that I was once more a useless, lonely old woman. I cried myself to sleep, and next morning I hadn't spunk enough to cook myself a dinner. I dined off some crackers and the remnants of the apple pies, and I was sitting staring at the crumbs when the bell rang. I wiped away my tears and went to the door. Joseph P. Nelson was standing there, and he said, without wasting any words—it was easy to see how that man managed to get railroads built where nobody else could manage it—that he had called to see me on a little matter of business.

He took just ten minutes to make it clear to me, and when I saw the whole project I was the happiest woman in Carleton or out of it. He said he had never eaten such a Thanksgiving dinner as mine, and that I was the woman he'd been looking for for years. He said that he had a few business friends who had been brought up on a down-east farm like himself, and never got over their hankering for old-fashioned cookery.

"That is something we can't get here, with all our money," he said. "Now, Miss Porter, my nephew tells me that you wish to remain in Carleton, if you can find some way of supporting yourself. I have a proposition to make to you. These aforesaid friends of mine and I expect to spend most of our time in Carleton for the next few years. In fact we shall probably make it our home eventually. It's going to be *the* city of the west after awhile, and the centre of a dozen railroads. Well, we mean to equip a small private restaurant for ourselves and we want you to take charge of it. You won't have to do much except oversee the business and arrange the bills of fare. We want plain, substantial old-time meals and cookery. When we have a hankering for doughnuts and apple pies and cranberry tarts, we want to know just where to get them and have them the right kind. We're all horribly tired of hotel fare and fancy fol-de-rols with French names. A place where we could get a dinner such as you served yesterday would be a boon to us. We'd have started the restaurant long ago if we could have got a suitable person to take charge of it."

He named the salary the club would pay and the very sound of it made me feel rich. You may be sure I didn't take long to decide. That was a year ago, and today the Doughnut Club, as they call themselves, is a huge success, and the fame of it has gone abroad in the land, although they are pretty exclusive and keep all their good things close enough to themselves. Joseph P. took a Scotch peer there to dinner one day last week. Jimmy Nelson told me afterward that the man said it was the only satisfying meal he'd had since he left the old country.

As for me, I have my little house, my very own and no rented one, and all my dear boys, and I'm a happy old busybody. You see, Providence did answer my prayers in spite of my lack of faith; but of course He used means, and that Thanksgiving dinner of mine was the earthly instrument of it all.

The Girl Who Drove the Cows

"I wonder who that pleasant-looking girl who drives cows down the beech lane every morning and evening is," said Pauline Palmer, at the tea table of the country farmhouse where she and her aunt were spending the summer. Mrs. Wallace had wanted to go to some fashionable watering place, but her husband had bluntly told her he couldn't afford it. Stay in the city when all her set were out she would not, and the aforesaid farmhouse had been the compromise.

"I shouldn't suppose it could make any difference to you who she is," said Mrs. Wallace impatiently. "I do wish, Pauline, that you were more careful in your choice of associates. You hobnob with everyone, even that old man who comes around buying eggs. It is very bad form."

Pauline hid a rather undutiful smile behind her napkin. Aunt Olivia's snobbish opinions always amused her.

"You've no idea what an interesting old man he is," she said. "He can talk more entertainingly than any other man I know. What is the use of being so exclusive, Aunt Olivia? You miss so much fun. You wouldn't be so horribly bored as you are if you fraternized a little with the 'natives,' as you call them."

"No, thank you," said Mrs. Wallace disdainfully.

"Well, I am going to try to get acquainted with that girl," said Pauline resolutely. "She looks nice and jolly."

"I don't know where you get your low tastes from," groaned Mrs. Wallace. "I'm sure it wasn't from your poor mother. What do you suppose the Morgan Knowles would think if they saw you taking up with some tomboy girl on a farm?"

"I don't see why it should make a great deal of difference what they would think, since they don't seem to be aware of my existence, or even of yours, Aunty," said Pauline, with twinkling eyes. She knew it was her aunt's dearest desire to get in with the Morgan Knowles' "set"—a desire that seemed as far from being realized as ever. Mrs. Wallace could never understand why the Morgan Knowles shut her from their charmed circle. They certainly associated with people much poorer and of more doubtful worldly station than hers—the Markhams, for instance, who lived on an unfashionable street and wore quite shabby clothes. Just before she had left Colchester, Mrs. Wallace had seen Mrs. Knowles and Mrs. Markham together in the former's automobile. James Wallace and Morgan Knowles were associated in business dealings; but in spite of Mrs. Wallace's schemings and aspirations and heart burnings, the association remained a purely business one and never advanced an inch in the direction of friendship.

As for Pauline, she was hopelessly devoid of social ambitions and she did not in the least mind the Morgan Knowles' remote attitude.

"Besides," continued Pauline, "she isn't a tomboy at all. She looks like a very womanly, well-bred sort of girl. Why should you think her a tomboy because she drives cows? Cows are placid, useful animals—witness this delicious cream which I am pouring over my blueberries. And they have to be driven. It's an honest occupation."

"I daresay she is someone's servant," said Mrs. Wallace contemptuously. "But I suppose even that wouldn't matter to you, Pauline?"

"Not a mite," said Pauline cheerfully. "One of the very nicest girls I ever knew was a maid Mother had the last year of her dear life. I loved that girl, Aunt Olivia, and I correspond with her. She writes letters that are ten times more clever and entertaining than those stupid epistles Clarisse Gray sends me—and Clarisse Gray is a rich man's daughter and is being educated in Paris."

"You are incorrigible, Pauline," said Mrs. Wallace hopelessly.

"Mrs. Boyd," said Pauline to their landlady, who now made her appearance, "who is that girl who drives the cows along the beech lane mornings and evenings?"

"Ada Cameron, I guess," was Mrs. Boyd's response. "She lives with the Embrees down on the old Embree place just below here. They're pasturing their cows on the upper farm this summer. Mrs. Embree is her father's half-sister."

"Is she as nice as she looks?"

"Yes, Ada's a real nice sensible girl," said Mrs. Boyd. "There is no nonsense about her."

"That doesn't sound very encouraging," murmured Pauline, as Mrs. Boyd went out. "I like people with a little nonsense about them. But I hope better things of Ada, Mrs. Boyd to the contrary notwithstanding.

She has a pair of grey eyes that can't possibly always look sensible. I think they must mellow occasionally into fun and jollity and wholesome nonsense. Well, I'm off to the shore. I want to get that photo-photograph of the Cove this evening, if possible. I've set my heart on taking first prize at the Amateur Photographers' Exhibition this fall, and if I can only get that Cove with all its beautiful lights and shadows, it will be the gem of my collection."

Pauline, on her return from the shore, reached the beech lane just as the Embree cows were swinging down it. Behind them came a tall, brown-haired, brown-faced girl in a neat print dress. Her hat was hung over her arm, and the low evening sunlight shone redly over her smooth glossy head. She carried herself with a pretty dignity, but when her eyes met Pauline's, she looked as if she would smile on the slightest provocation.

Pauline promptly gave her the provocation.

"Good evening, Miss Cameron," she called blithely. "Won't you please stop a few moments and look me over? I want to see if you think me a likely person for a summer chum."

Ada Cameron did more than smile. She laughed outright and went over to the fence where Pauline was sitting on a stump. She looked down into the merry black eyes of the town girl she had been half envying for a week and said humorously: "Yes, I think you very likely, indeed. But it takes two to make a friendship—like a bargain. If I'm one, you'll have to be the other."

"I'm the other. Shake," said Pauline, holding out her hand.

That was the beginning of a friendship that made poor Mrs. Wallace groan outwardly as well as inwardly. Pauline and Ada found that they liked each other even more than they had expected to. They walked, rowed, berried and picnicked together. Ada did not go to Mrs. Boyd's a great deal, for some instinct told her that Mrs. Wallace did not look favourably on her, but Pauline spent half her time at the little, brown, orchard-embowered house at the end of the beech lane where the Embrees lived. She had never met any girl she thought so nice as Ada.

"She is nice every way," she told the unconvinced Aunt Olivia. "She's clever and well read. She is sensible and frank. She has a sense of humour and a great deal of insight into character—witness her liking for your niece! She can talk interestingly and she can also be silent when silence is becoming. And she has the finest profile I ever saw. Aunt Olivia, may I ask her to visit me next winter?"

"No, indeed," said Mrs. Wallace, with crushing emphasis. "You surely don't expect to continue this absurd intimacy past the summer, Pauline?"

"I expect to be Ada's friend all my life," said Pauline laughingly, but with a little ring of purpose in her voice. "Oh, Aunty, dear, can't you see that Ada is just the same girl in cotton print that she would be in silk attire? She is really far more distinguished looking than any girl in the Knowles' set."

"Pauline!" said Aunt Olivia, looking as shocked as if Pauline had committed blasphemy.

Pauline laughed again, but she sighed as she went to her room. Aunt Olivia has the kindest heart in the world, she thought. What a pity she isn't able to see things as they really are! My friendship with Ada can't be perfect if I can't invite her to my home. And she is such a dear girl—the first real friend after my own heart that I've ever had.

The summer waned, and August burned itself out.

"I suppose you will be going back to town next week? I shall miss you dreadfully," said Ada.

The two girls were in the Embree garden, where Pauline was preparing to take a photograph of Ada standing among the asters, with a great sheaf of them in her arms. Pauline wished she could have said: But you must come and visit me in the winter. Since she could not, she had to content herself with saying: "You won't miss me any more than I shall miss you. But we'll correspond, and I hope Aunt Olivia will come to Marwood again next summer."

"I don't think I shall be here then," said Ada with a sigh. "You see, it is time I was doing something for myself, Pauline. Aunt Jane and Uncle Robert have always been very kind to me, but they have a large family and are not very well off. So I think I'll try for a situation in one of the Remington stores this fall."

"It's such a pity you couldn't have gone to the Academy and studied for a teacher's licence," said Pauline, who knew what Ada's ambitions were.

"I should have liked that better, of course," said Ada quietly. "But it is not possible, so I must do my best at the next best thing. Don't let's talk of it. It might make me feel blueish and I want to look especially pleasant if I'm going to have my photo taken."

"You couldn't look anything else," laughed Pauline. "Don't smile too broadly—I want you to be looking over the asters with a bit of a dream on your face and in your eyes. If the picture turns out as beautiful as I fondly expect, I mean to put it in my exhibition collection under the title 'A September Dream.' There, that's the very expression. When you look like that, you remind me of somebody I have seen, but I can't remember who it is. All ready now—don't move—there, dearie, it is all over."

When Pauline went back to Colchester, she was busy for a month preparing her photographs for the exhibition, while Aunt Olivia renewed her spinning of all the little social webs in which she fondly hoped to entangle the Morgan Knowles and other desirable flies.

When the exhibition was opened, Pauline Palmer's collection won first prize, and the prettiest picture in it was one called "A September Dream"—a tall girl with a wistful face, standing in an old-fashioned garden with her arms full of asters.

The very day after the exhibition was opened the Morgan Knowles' automobile stopped at the Wallace door. Mrs. Wallace was out, but it was Pauline whom stately Mrs. Morgan Knowles asked for. Pauline was at that moment buried in her darkroom developing photographs, and she ran down just as she was—a fact which would have mortified Mrs. Wallace exceedingly if she had ever known it. But Mrs. Morgan Knowles did not seem to mind at all. She liked Pauline's simplicity of manner. It was more than she had expected from the aunt's rather vulgar affectations.

"I have called to ask you who the original of the photograph 'A September Dream' in your exhibit was, Miss Palmer," she said graciously. "The resemblance to a very dear childhood friend of mine is so startling that I am sure it cannot be accidental."

"That is a photograph of Ada Cameron, a friend whom I met this summer up in Marwood," said Pauline.

"Ada Cameron! She must be Ada Frame's daughter, then," exclaimed Mrs. Knowles in excitement. Then, seeing Pauline's puzzled face, she explained: "Years ago, when I was a child, I always spent my summers on the farm of my uncle, John Frame. My cousin, Ada Frame, was the dearest friend I ever had, but after we grew up we saw nothing of each other, for I went with my parents to Europe for several years, and Ada married a neighbour's son, Alec Cameron, and went out west. Her father, who was my only living relative other than my parents, died, and I never heard anything more of Ada until about eight years ago, when somebody told me she was dead and had left no family. That part of the report cannot have been true if this girl is her daughter."

"I believe she is," said Pauline quickly. "Ada was born out west and lived there until she was eight years old, when her parents died and she was sent east to her father's half-sister. And Ada looks like you—she always reminded me of somebody I had seen, but I never could decide who it was before. Oh, I hope it is true, for Ada is such a sweet girl, Mrs. Knowles."

"She couldn't be anything else if she is Ada Frame's daughter," said Mrs. Knowles. "My husband will investigate the matter at once, and if this girl is Ada's child we shall hope to find a daughter in her, as we have none of our own."

"What will Aunt Olivia say!" said Pauline with wickedly dancing eyes when Mrs. Knowles had gone.

Aunt Olivia was too much overcome to say anything. That good lady felt rather foolish when it was proved that the girl she had so despised was Mrs. Morgan Knowles' cousin and was going to be adopted by her. But to hear Aunt Olivia talk now, you would suppose that she and not Pauline had discovered Ada.

The latter sought Pauline out as soon as she came to Colchester, and the summer friendship proved a life-long one and was, for the Wallaces, the open sesame to the enchanted ground of the Knowles' "set."

"So everybody concerned is happy," said Pauline. "Ada is going to college and so am I, and Aunt Olivia is on the same committee as Mrs. Knowles for the big church bazaar. What about my 'low tastes' now, Aunt Olivia?"

"Well, who would ever have supposed that a girl who drove cows to pasture was connected with the Morgan Knowles?" said poor Aunt Olivia piteously.

The Growing Up of Cornelia

January First.

Aunt Jemima gave me this diary for a Christmas present. It's just the sort of gift a person named Jemima would be likely to make.

I can't imagine why Aunt Jemima thought I should like a diary. Probably she didn't think about it at all. I suppose it happened to be the first thing she saw when she started out to do her Christmas duty by me, and so she bought it. I'm sure I'm the last girl in the world to keep a diary. I'm not a bit sentimental and I never have time for soul outpourings. It's jollier to be out skating or snowshoeing or just tramping around. And besides, nothing ever happens to me worth writing in a diary.

Still, since Aunt Jemima gave it to me, I'm going to get the good out of it. I don't believe in wasting even a diary. Father ... it would be easier to write "Dad," but Dad sounds disrespectful in a diary ... says I have a streak of old Grandmother Marshall's economical nature in me. So I'm going to write in this book whenever I have anything that might, by any stretch of imagination, be supposed worth while.

Jen and Alice and Sue would have plenty to write about, I dare say. They certainly seem to have jolly times ... and as for the men ... but there! People say men are interesting. They may be. But I shall never get well enough acquainted with any of them to find out.

Mother says it is high time I gave up my tomboy ways and came "out" too, because I am eighteen. I coaxed off this winter. It wasn't very hard, because no mother with three older unmarried girls on her hands would be very anxious to bring out a fourth. The girls took my part and advised Mother to let me be a child as long as possible. Mother yielded for this time, but said I must be brought out next winter or people would talk. Oh, I hate the thought of it! People might talk about my not being brought out, but they will talk far more about the blunders I shall make.

The doleful fact is, I'm too wretchedly shy and awkward to live. It fills my soul with terror to think of donning long dresses and putting my hair up and going into society. I can't talk and men frighten me to death. I fall over things as it is, and what will it be with long dresses? As far back as I can remember it has been my one aim and object in life to escape company. Oh, if only one need never grow up! If I could only go back four years and stay there!

Mother laments over it muchly. She says she doesn't know what she has done to have such a shy, unpresentable daughter. *I* know. She married Grandmother Marshall's son, and Grandmother Marshall was as shy as she was economical. Mother triumphed over heredity with Jen and Sue and Alice, but it came off best with me. The other girls are noted for their grace and tact. But I'm the black sheep and always will be. It wouldn't worry me so much if they'd leave me alone and stop nagging me. "Oh, for a lodge in some vast wilderness," where there were no men, no parties, no dinners ... just quantities of dogs and horses and skating ponds and woods! I need never put on long dresses then, but just be a jolly little girl forever.

However, I've got one beautiful year before me yet, and I mean to make the most of it.

January Tenth.

It is rather good to have a diary to pour out your woes in when you feel awfully bad and have no one to sympathize with you. I've been used to shutting them all up in my soul and then they sometimes fermented and made trouble.

We had a lot of people here to dinner tonight, and that made me miserable to begin with. I had to dress up in a stiff white dress *with a sash*, and Jen tied two big white fly-away bows on my hair that kept rasping my neck and tickling my ears in a most exasperating way. Then an old lady whom I detest tried to make me talk before everybody, and all I could do was to turn as red as a beet and stammer: "Yes, ma'am," "no, ma'am." It made Mother furious, because it is so old-fashioned to say "ma'am." Our old nurse taught me to say it when I was small, and though it has been pretty well governessed out of me since then, it's sure to pop up when I get confused and nervous.

Sue ... may it be accounted unto her for righteousness ... contrived that I should go out to dinner with old Mr. Grant, because she knew he goes to dinners for the sake of eating and never talks or wants anybody else to. But when we were crossing the hall I stepped on Mrs. Burnett's train and something tore. Mrs. Burnett gave me a furious look and glowered all through dinner. The meal was completely spoiled for me and I could find no comfort, even in the Nesselrode pudding, which is my favourite dessert.

It was just when the pudding came on that I got the most unkindest cut of all. Mrs. Allardyce remarked that Sidney Elliot was coming home to Stillwater.

Everybody exclaimed and questioned and seemed delighted. I saw Mother give one quick, involuntary look at Jen, and then gaze steadfastly at Mr. Grant to atone for it. Jen is twenty-six, and Stillwater is next door to our place!

As for me, I was so vexed that I might as well have been eating chips for all the good that Nesselrode pudding was to me. If Sidney Elliot were coming home everything would be spoiled. There would be no more ramblings in the Stillwater woods, no more delightful skating on the Stillwater lake. Stillwater has been the only place in the world where I could find the full joy of solitude, and now this, too, was to be taken from me. We had no woods, no lake. I hated Sidney Elliot.

It is ten years since Sidney Elliot closed Stillwater and went abroad. He has stayed abroad ever since and nobody has missed him, I'm sure. I remember him dimly as a tall dark man who used to lounge about alone in his garden and was always reading books. Sometimes he came into our garden and teased us children. He is said to be a cynic and to detest society. If this latter item be a fact I almost feel a grim pity for him. He may detest it, but he will be dragged into it. Rich bachelors are few and far between in Riverton, and the mammas will hunt him down.

I feel like crying. If Sidney Elliot comes home I shall be debarred from Stillwater. I have roamed its demesnes for ten beautiful years, and I'm sure I love them a hundredfold better than he does, or can. It is flagrantly unfair. Oh, I hate him!

January Twentieth.

No, I don't. I believe I like him. Yet it's almost unbelievable. I've always thought men so detestable.

I'm tingling all over with the surprise and pleasure of a little unexpected adventure. For the first time I have something really worth writing in a diary ... and I'm glad I have a diary to write it in. Blessings on Aunt Jemima! May her shadow never grow less.

This evening I started out for a last long lingering ramble in my beloved Stillwater woods. The last, I thought, because I knew Sidney Elliot was expected home next week, and after that I'd have to be cooped up on our lawn. I dressed myself comfortably for climbing fences and skimming over snowy wastes. That is, I put on the shortest old tweed skirt I have and a red jacket with sleeves three years behind the fashion, but jolly pockets to put your hands in, and a still redder tam. Thus accoutred, I sallied forth.

It was such a lovely evening that I couldn't help enjoying myself in spite of my sorrows. The sun was low and creamy, and the snow was so white and the shadows so slender and blue. All through the lovely Stillwater woods was a fine frosty stillness. It was splendid to skim down those long wonderful avenues of crusted snow, with the mossy grey boles on either hand, and overhead the lacing, leafless boughs, I just drank in the air and the beauty until my very soul was thrilling, and I went on and on and on until I was most delightfully lost. That is, I didn't know just where I was, but the woods weren't so big but that I'd be sure to come out safely somewhere; and, oh, it was so glorious to be there all alone and never a creature to worry me.

At last I turned into a long aisle that seemed to lead right out into the very heart of a deep-red overflowing winter sunset. At its end I found a fence, and I climbed up on that fence and sat there, so comfortably, with my back against a big beech and my feet dangling.

Then I saw him!

I knew it was Sidney Elliot in a moment. He was just as tall and just as black-eyed; he was still given to lounging evidently, for he was leaning against the fence a panel away from me and looking at me with an amused smile. After my first mad impulse to rush away and bury myself in the wilderness that smile put me at ease. If he had looked grave or polite I would have been as miserably shy as I've always been in a man's presence. But it was the smile of a grandfather for a child, and I just grinned cheerfully back at him.

He ploughed along through the thick drift that was soft and spongy by the fence and came close up to me.

"You must be little Cornelia," he said with another aged smile. "Or rather, you *were* little Cornelia. I suppose you are big Cornelia now and want to be treated like a young lady?"

"Indeed, I don't," I protested. "I'm not grown up and I don't want to be. You are Mr. Elliot, I suppose. Nobody expected you till next week. What made you come so soon?"

"A whim of mine," he said. "I'm full of whims and crotchets. Old bachelors always are. But why did you ask that question in a tone which seemed to imply that you resented my coming so soon, Miss Cornelia?"

"Oh, don't tack the Miss on," I implored. "Call me Cornelia ... or better still, Nic, as Dad does. I *do* resent your coming so soon. I resent your coming at all. And, oh, it is such a satisfaction to tell you so."

He smiled with his eyes ... a deep, black, velvety smile. But he shook his head sorrowfully.

"I must be getting very old," he said. "It's a sign of age when a person finds himself unwelcome and superfluous."

"Your age has nothing to do with it," I retorted. "It is because Stillwater is the only place I have to run wild in ... and running wild is all I'm fit for. It's so lovely and roomy I can lose myself in it. I shall die or go mad if I'm cooped up on our little pocket handkerchief of a lawn."

"But why should you be?" he inquired gravely.

I reflected ... and was surprised.

"After all, I don't know ... now ... why I should be," I admitted. "I thought you wouldn't want me prowling about your domains. Besides, I was afraid I'd meet you ... and I don't like meeting men. I hate to have them around ... I'm so shy and awkward."

"Do you find me very dreadful?" he asked.

I reflected again ... and was again surprised.

"No, I don't. I don't mind you a bit ... any more than if you were Dad."

"Then you mustn't consider yourself an exile from Stillwater. The woods are yours to roam in at will, and if you want to roam them alone you may, and if you'd like a companion once in a while command me. Let's be good friends, little lass. Shake hands on it."

I slipped down from the fence and shook hands with him. I did like him very much ... he was so nice and unaffected and brotherly ... just as if I'd known him all my life. We walked down the long white avenue, where everything was growing dusky, and I had told him all my troubles before we got to the end of it. He was so sympathetic and agreed with me that it was a pity people had to grow up. He promised to come over tomorrow and look at Don's leg. Don is one of my dogs, and he has got a bad leg. I've been doctoring it myself, but it doesn't get any better. Sidney thinks he can cure it. He says I must call him Sidney if I want him to call me Nic.

When we got to the lake, there it lay all gleaming and smooth as glass ... the most tempting thing.

"What a glorious possible slide," he said. "Let us have it, little lass."

He took my hand and we ran down the slope and went skimming over the ice. It *was* glorious. The house came in sight as we reached the other side. It was big and dark and silent.

"So the old place is still standing," said Sidney, looking up at it. In the dusk I thought his face had a tender, reverent look instead of the rather mocking expression it had worn all along.

"Haven't you been there yet?" I asked quickly.

"No. I'm stopping at the hotel over in Croyden. The house will need some fixing up before it's fit to live in. I just came down tonight to look at it and took a short cut through the woods. I'm glad I did. It was worth while to see you come tramping down that long white avenue when you thought yourself alone with the silence. I thought I had never seen a child so full of the pure joy of existence. Hold fast to that, little lass, as long as you can. You'll never find anything to take its place after it goes. You jolly little child!"

"I'm eighteen," I said suddenly. I don't know what made me say it.

He laughed and pulled his coat collar up around his ears.

"Never," he mocked. "You're about twelve ... stay twelve, and always wear red caps and jackets, you vivid thing: Good night."

He was off across the lake, and I came home. Yes, I do like him, even if he is a man.

February Twentieth.

I've found out what diaries are for ... to work off blue moods in, moods that come on without any reason whatever and therefore can't be confided to any fellow creature. You scribble away for a while ... and then it's all gone ... and your soul feels clear as crystal once more.

I always go to Sidney now in a blue mood that has a real cause. He can cheer me up in five minutes. But in such a one as this, which is quite unaccountable, there's nothing for it but a diary.

Sidney has been living at Stillwater for a month. It seems as if he must have lived there always.

He came to our place the next day after I met him in the woods. Everybody made a fuss over him, but he shook them off with an ease I envied and whisked me out to see Don's leg. He has fixed it up so that it is as good as new now, and the dogs like him almost better than they like me.

We have had splendid times since then. We are just the jolliest chums and we tramp about everywhere together and go skating and snowshoeing and riding. We read a lot of books together too, and Sidney always explains everything I don't understand. I'm not a bit shy and I can always find plenty to say to him. He isn't at all like any other man I know.

Everybody likes him, but the women seem to be a little afraid of him. They say he is so terribly cynical and satirical. He goes into society a good bit, although he says it bores him. He says he only goes because it would bore him worse to stay home alone.

There's only one thing about Sidney that I hardly like. I think he rather overdoes it in the matter of treating me as if I were a little girl. Of course, I don't want him to look upon me as grown up. But there is a medium in all things, and he really needn't talk as if he thought I was a child of ten and had no earthly interest in anything but sports and dogs. These *are* the best things ... I suppose ... but I understand lots of other things too, only I can't convince Sidney that I do. I know he is laughing at me when I try to show him I'm not so childish as he thinks me. He's indulgent and whimsical, just as he would be with a little girl who was making believe to be grown up. Perhaps next winter, when I put on long dresses and come out, he'll stop regarding me as a child. But next winter is so horribly far off.

The day we were fussing with Don's leg I told Sidney that Mother said I'd have to be grown up next winter and how I hated it, and I made him promise that when the time came he would use all his influence to beg me off for another year. He said he would, because it was a shame to worry children about society. But somehow I've concluded not to bother making a fuss. I have to come out some time, and I might as well take the plunge and get it over.

Mrs. Burnett was here this evening fixing up some arrangements for a charity bazaar she and Jen are interested in, and she talked most of the time about Sidney ... for Jen's benefit, I suppose, although Jen and Sid don't get on at all. They fight every time they meet, so I don't see why Mrs. Burnett should think things.

"I wonder what he'll do when Mrs. Rennie comes to the Glasgows' next month," said Mrs. Burnett.

"Why should he do anything?" asked Jen.

"Oh, well, you know there was something between them ... an understanding if not an engagement ... before she married Rennie. They met abroad ... my sister told me all about it ... and Mr. Elliot was quite infatuated with her. She was a very handsome and fascinating girl.

Then she threw him over and married old Jacob Rennie ... for his millions, of course, for he certainly had nothing else to recommend him. Amy says Mr. Elliot was never the same man again. But Jacob died obligingly two years ago and Mrs. Rennie is free now; so I dare say they'll make it up. No doubt that is why she is coming to Riverton. Well, it would be a very suitable match."

I'm so glad I never liked Mrs. Burnett.

I wonder if it is true that Sidney did care for that horrid woman ... of course she is horrid! Didn't she marry an old man for his money?... and cares for her still. It is no business of mine, of course, and it doesn't matter to me at all. But I rather hope he doesn't ... because it would spoil everything if he got married. He wouldn't have time to be chums with me then.

I don't know why I feel so dull tonight. Writing in this diary doesn't seem to have helped me as much as I thought it would, either. I dare say it's the weather. It must be the weather. It is a wet, windy night and the rain is thudding against the window. I hate rainy nights.

I wonder if Mrs. Rennie is really as handsome as Mrs. Burnett says. I wonder how old she is. I wonder if she ever cared for Sidney ... no, she didn't. No woman who cared for Sidney could ever have thrown him over for an old moneybag. I wonder if I shall like her. No, I won't. I'm sure I shan't like her.

My head is aching and I'm going to bed.

March Tenth.

Mrs. Rennie was here to dinner tonight. My head was aching again, and Mother said I needn't go down to dinner if I'd rather not; but a dozen headaches could not have kept me back, or a dozen men either, even supposing I'd have to talk to them all. I wanted to see Mrs. Rennie. Nothing has been talked of in Riverton for the last fortnight but Mrs. Rennie. I've heard of her beauty and charm and costumes until I'm sick of the subject. Today I spoke to Sidney about her. Before I thought I said right out, "Mrs. Rennie is to dine with us tonight."

"Yes?" he said in a quiet voice.

"I'm dying to see her," I went on recklessly. "I've heard so much about her. They say she's so beautiful and fascinating. *Is* she? *You* ought to know."

Sidney swung the sled around and put it in position for another coast.

"Yes, I know her," he admitted tranquilly. "She is a very handsome woman, and I suppose most people would consider her fascinating.

Come, Nic, get on the sled. We have just time for one more coast, and then you must go in."

"You were once a good friend ... a very good friend ... of Mrs. Rennie's, weren't you, Sid?" I said.

A little mocking gleam crept into his eyes, and I instantly realized that he was looking upon me as a rather impertinent child.

"You've been listening to gossip, Nic," he said. "It's a bad habit, child. Don't let it grow on you. Come."

I went, feeling crushed and furious and ashamed.

I knew her at once when I went down to the drawing-room. There were three other strange women there, but I knew she was the only one who could be Mrs. Rennie. I felt such a horrible queer sinking feeling at my heart when I saw her. Oh, she was beautiful ... I had never seen anyone so beautiful. And Sidney was standing beside her, talking to her, with a smile on his face, but none in his eyes ... I noticed *that* at a glance.

She was so tall and slender and willowy. Her dress was wonderful, and her bare throat and shoulders were like pearls. Her hair was pale, pale gold, and her eyes long-lashed and sweet, and her mouth like a scarlet blossom against her creamy face. I thought of how I must look beside her ... an awkward little girl in a short skirt with my hair in a braid and too many hands and feet, and I would have given anything then to be tall and grown-up and graceful.

I watched her all the evening and the queer feeling in me somewhere grew worse and worse. I couldn't eat anything. Sidney took Mrs. Rennie in; they sat opposite to me and talked all the time.

I was so glad when the dinner was over and everybody gone. The first thing I did when I escaped to my room was to go to the glass and look myself over just as critically and carefully as if I were somebody else. I saw a great rope of dark brown hair ... a brown skin with red cheeks ... a big red mouth ... a pair of grey eyes. That was all. And when I thought of that shimmering witch woman with her white skin and shining hair I wanted to put out the light and cry in the dark. Only I've never cried since I was a child and broke my last doll, and I've got so out of the habit that I don't know how to go about it.

April Fifth.

Aunt Jemima would not think I was getting the good out of my diary. A whole month and not a word! But there was nothing to write, and I've felt too miserable to write if there had been. I don't know what is the matter with me. I'm just cross and horrid to everyone, even to poor Sidney.

Mrs. Rennie has been queening it in Riverton society for the past month. People rave over her and I admire her horribly, although I don't like her. Mrs. Burnett says that a match between her and Sidney Elliot is a foregone conclusion.

It's plain to be seen that Mrs. Rennie loves Sidney. Even I can see that, and I don't know much about such things. But it puzzles me to know how Sidney regards her. I have never thought he showed any sign of really caring for her. But then, he isn't the kind that would.

"Nic, I wonder if you will ever grow up," he said to me today, laughing, when he caught me racing over the lawn with the dogs.

"I'm grown up now," I said crossly. "Why, I'm eighteen and a half and I'm two inches taller than any of the other girls."

Sidney laughed, as if he were heartily amused at something.

"You're a blessed baby," he said, "and the dearest, truest, jolliest little chum ever a fellow had. I don't know what I'd do without you, Nic. You keep me sane and wholesome. I'm a tenfold better man for knowing you, little girl."

I was rather pleased. It was nice to think I was some good to Sidney.

"Are you going to the Trents' dinner tonight?" I asked.

"Yes," he said briefly.

"Mrs. Rennie will be there," I said.

Sidney nodded.

"Do you think her so very handsome, Sidney?" I said. I had never mentioned Mrs. Rennie to him since the day we were coasting, and I didn't mean to now. The question just asked itself.

"Yes, very; but not as handsome as you will be ten years from now, Nic," said Sidney lightly.

"Do you think I'm handsome, Sidney?" I cried.

"You will be when you're grown up," he answered, looking at me critically.

"Will you be going to Mrs. Greaves' reception after the dinner?" I asked.

"Yes, I suppose so," said Sidney absently. I could see he wasn't thinking of me at all. I wondered if he were thinking of Mrs. Rennie.

April Sixth.

Oh, something so wonderful has happened. I can hardly believe it. There are moments when I quake with the fear that it is all a dream. I wonder if I can really be the same Cornelia Marshall I was yesterday. No, I'm *not* the same ... and the difference is so blessed.

Oh, I'm so happy! My heart bubbles over with happiness and song. It's so wonderful and lovely to be a woman and know it and know that other people know it.

You dear diary, you were made for this moment ... I shall write all about it in you and so fulfil your destiny. And then I shall put you away and never write anything more in you, because I shall not need you ... I shall have Sidney.

Last night I was all alone in the house ... and I was so lonely and miserable. I put my chin on my hands and I thought ... and thought ... and thought. I imagined Sidney at the Greaves', talking to Mrs. Rennie with that velvety smile in his eyes. I could see her, graceful and white, in her trailing, clinging gown, with diamonds about her smooth neck and in her hair. I suddenly wondered what I would look like in evening dress with my hair up. I wondered if Sidney would like me in it.

All at once I got up and rushed to Sue's room. I lighted the gas, rummaged, and went to work. I piled my hair on top of my head, pinned it there, and thrust a long silver dagger through it to hold a couple of pale white roses she had left on her table. Then I put on her last winter's party dress. It was such a pretty pale yellow thing, with touches of black lace, and it didn't matter about its being a little old-fashioned, since it fitted me like a glove. Finally I stepped back and looked at myself.

I saw a woman in that glass ... a tall, straight creature with crimson cheeks and glowing eyes ... and the thought in my mind was so insistent that it said itself aloud: "Oh, I wish Sidney could see me now!"

At that very moment the maid knocked at the door to tell me that Mr. Elliot was downstairs asking for me. I did not hesitate a second. With my heart beating wildly I trailed downstairs to Sidney.

He was standing by the fireplace when I went in, and looked very tired. When he heard me he turned his head and our eyes met.

All at once a terrible thing happened ... at least, I thought it a terrible thing then. *I knew why I had wanted Sidney to realize that I was no longer a child.* It was because I loved him! I knew it the moment I saw that strange, new expression leap into his eyes.

"Cornelia," he said in a stunned sort of voice. "Why ... Nic ... why, little girl ... you're a woman! How blind I've been! And now I've lost my little chum."

"Oh, no, no," I said wildly. I was so miserable and confused I didn't know what I said. "Never, Sidney. I'd rather be a little girl and have you for a friend ... I'll always be a little girl! It's all this hateful dress. I'll go and take it off ... I'll...."

And then I just put my hands up to my burning face and the tears that would never come before came in a flood.

All at once I felt Sidney's arms about me and felt my head drawn to his shoulder.

"Don't cry, dearest," I heard him say softly. "You can never be a little girl to me again ... my eyes are opened ... but I didn't want you to be. I want you to be my big girl ... mine, all mine, forever."

What happened after that isn't to be written in a diary. I won't even write down the things he said about how I looked, because it would seem so terribly vain, but I can't help thinking of them, for I am so happy.

The Old Fellow's Letter

Ruggles and I were down on the Old Fellow. It doesn't matter why and, since in a story of this kind we must tell the truth no matter what happens—or else where is the use of writing a story at all?—I'll have to confess that we had deserved all we got and that the Old Fellow did no more than his duty by us. Both Ruggles and I see that now, since we have had time to cool off, but at the moment we were in a fearful wax at the Old Fellow and were bound to hatch up something to get even with him.

Of course, the Old Fellow had another name, just as Ruggles has another name. He is principal of the Frampton Academy—the Old Fellow, not Ruggles—and his name is George Osborne. We have to call him Mr. Osborne to his face, but he is the Old Fellow everywhere else. He is quite old—thirty-six if he's a day, and whatever possessed Sylvia Grant—but there, I'm getting ahead of my story.

Most of the Cads like the Old Fellow. Even Ruggles and I like him on the average. The girls are always a little provoked at him because he is so shy and absent-minded, but when it comes to the point, they like him too. I heard Emma White say once that he was "so handsome"; I nearly whooped. Ruggles was mad because he's gone on Em. For the idea of calling a thin, pale, dark, dreamy-looking chap like the Old Fellow "handsome" was more than I could stand without guffawing. Em probably said it to provoke Ruggles; she couldn't really have thought it. "Micky," the English professor, now—if she had called him handsome there would have been some sense in it. He is splendid: big six-footer with magnificent muscles, red cheeks, and curly yellow hair. I can't see how he can be contented to sit down and teach mushy English literature and poetry and that sort of thing. It would have been more in keeping with the Old Fellow. There was a rumour running at large in the Academy that the Old Fellow wrote poetry, but he ran the mathematics and didn't make such a foozle of it as you might suppose, either.

Ruggles and I meant to get square with the Old Fellow, if it took all the term; at least, we said so. But if Providence hadn't sent Sylvia Grant walking down the street past our boarding house that afternoon, we should probably have cooled off before we thought of any working plan of revenge.

Sylvia Grant did go down the street, however. Ruggles, hanging halfway out of the window as usual, saw her, and called me to go and look. Of course I went. Sylvia Grant was always worth looking at. There was no girl in Frampton who could hold a candle to her when it came to beauty. As for brains, that is another thing altogether. My private opinion is that Sylvia hadn't any, or she would never have preferred—but there, I'm getting on too fast again. Ruggles should have written this story; he can concentrate better.

Sylvia was the Latin professor's daughter; she wasn't a Cad girl, of course. She was over twenty and had graduated from it two years ago, but she was in all the social things that went on in the Academy; and all the unmarried professors, except the Old Fellow, were in love with her. Micky had it the worst, and we had all made up our minds that Sylvia would marry Micky. He was so handsome, we didn't see how she could help it. I tell you, they made a dandy-looking couple when they were together.

Well, as I said before, I toddled to the window to have a look at the fair Sylvia. She was all togged out in some new fall duds, and I guess she'd come out to show them off. They were brownish, kind of, and she'd a spanking hat on with feathers and things in it. Her hair was shining under it, all purply-black, and she looked sweet enough to eat. Then she saw Ruggles and me and she waved her hand and laughed, and her big blackish-blue eyes sparkled; but she hadn't been laughing before, or sparkling either.

I'd thought she looked kind of glum, and I wondered if she and Micky had had a falling out. I rather suspected it, for at the Senior Prom, three nights before, she had hardly looked at Micky, but had sat in a corner and talked to the Old Fellow. He didn't do much talking; he was too shy, and he looked mighty uncomfortable. I thought it kind of mean of Sylvia to torment him so, when she knew he hated to have to talk to girls, but when I saw Micky scowling at the corner, I knew she was doing it to make him jealous. Girls won't stick at anything when they want to provoke a chap; I know it to my cost, for Jennie Price—but that has nothing to do with this story.

Just across the square Sylvia met the Old Fellow and bowed. He lifted his hat and passed on, but after a few steps he turned and looked back; he caught Sylvia doing the same thing, so he wheeled and came on, looking mighty foolish. As he passed beneath our window Ruggles chuckled fiendishly.

"I've thought of something, Polly," he said—my name is Paul. "Bet you it will make the Old Fellow squirm. Let's write a letter to Sylvia Grant—a love letter—and sign the Old Fellow's name to it. She'll give him a fearful snubbing, and we'll be revenged."

"But who'll write it?" I said doubtfully. "I can't. You'll have to, Ruggles. You've had more practice."

Ruggles turned red. I know he writes to Em White in vacations.

"I'll do my best," he said, quite meekly. "That is, I'll compose it. But you'll have to copy it. You can imitate the Old Fellow's handwriting so well."

"But look here," I said, an uncomfortable idea striking me, "what about Sylvia? Won't she feel kind of flattish when she finds out he didn't write it? For of course he'll tell her. We haven't anything against her, you know."

"Oh, Sylvia won't care," said Ruggles serenely. "She's the sort of girl who can take a joke. I've seen her eyes shine over tricks we've played on the professors before now. She'll just laugh. Besides, she doesn't like the Old Fellow a bit. I know from the way she acts with him. She's always so cool and stiff when he's about, not a bit like she is with the other professors."

Well, Ruggles wrote the letter. At first he tried to pass it off on me as his own composition. But I know a few little things, and one of them is that Ruggles couldn't have made up that letter any more than he could have written a sonnet. I told him so, and made him own up. He had a copy of an old letter that had been written to his sister by her young man. I suppose Ruggles had stolen it, but there is no use inquiring too closely into these things. Anyhow, that letter just filled the bill. It was beautifully expressed. Ruggles's sister's young man must have possessed lots of ability. He was an English professor, something like Micky, so I suppose he was extra good at it. He started in by telling her how much he loved her, and what an angel of beauty and goodness he had always thought her; how unworthy he felt himself of her and how little hope he had that she could ever care for him; and he wound up by imploring her to tell him if she could possibly love him a little bit and all that sort of thing.

I copied the letter out on heliotrope paper in my best imitation of the Old Fellow's handwriting and signed it, "Yours devotedly and imploringly, George Osborne." Then we mailed it that very evening.

The next evening the Cad girls gave a big reception in the Assembly Hall to an Academy alumna who was visiting the Greek professor's wife. It was the smartest event of the term and everybody was there—students and faculty and, of course, Sylvia Grant. Sylvia looked stunning. She was all in white, with a string of pearls about her pretty round throat and a couple of little pink roses in her black hair. I never saw her so smiling and bright; but she seemed quieter than usual, and avoided poor Micky so skilfully that it was really a pleasure to watch her. The Old Fellow came in late, with his tie all crooked, as it always was; I saw Sylvia blush and nudged Ruggles to look.

"She's thinking of the letter," he said.

Ruggles and I never meant to listen, upon my word we didn't. It was pure accident. We were in behind the flags and palms in the Modern Languages Room, fixing up a plan how to get Em and Jennie off for a moonlit stroll in the grounds—these things require diplomacy I can tell you, for there are always so many other fellows hanging about—when in came Sylvia Grant and the Old Fellow arm in arm. The room was quite empty, or they thought it was, and they sat down just on the other side of the flags. They couldn't see us, but we could see them quite plainly. Sylvia still looked smiling and happy, not a bit mad as we had expected, but just kind of shy and radiant. As for the Old Fellow, he looked, as Em White would say, as Sphinx-like as ever. I'd defy any man alive to tell from the Old Fellow's expression what he was thinking about or what he felt like at any time.

Then all at once Sylvia said softly, with her eyes cast down, "I received your letter, Mr. Osborne."

Any other man in the world would have jumped, or said, "My letter!!!" or shown surprise in some way. But the Old Fellow has a nerve. He looked sideways at Sylvia for a moment and then he said kind of drily, "Ah, did you?"

"Yes," said Sylvia, not much above a whisper. "It—it surprised me very much. I never supposed that you—you cared for me in that way."

"Can you tell me how I could help caring?" said the Old Fellow in the strangest way. His voice actually trembled.

"I—I don't think I would tell you if I knew," said Sylvia, turning her head away. "You see—I don't want you to help caring."

"Sylvia!"

You never saw such a transformation as came over the Old Fellow. His eyes just blazed, but his face went white. He bent forward and took her hand.

"Sylvia, do you mean that you—you actually care a little for me, dearest? Oh, Sylvia, do you mean that?"

"Of course I do," said Sylvia right out. "I've always cared—ever since I was a little girl coming here to school and breaking my heart over mathematics, although I hated them, just to be in your class. Why—why—I've treasured up old geometry exercises you wrote out for me just because you wrote them. But I thought I could never make you care for me. I was the happiest girl in the world when your letter came today."

"Sylvia," said the Old Fellow, "I've loved you for years. But I never dreamed that you could care for me. I thought it quite useless to tell you of my love—before. Will you—can you be my wife, darling?"

At this point Ruggles and I differ as to what came next. He asserts that Sylvia turned square around and kissed the Old Fellow. But I'm sure she just turned her face and gave him a look and then he kissed her.

Anyhow, there they both were, going on at the silliest rate about how much they loved each other and how the Old Fellow thought she loved Micky and all that sort of thing. It was awful. I never thought the Old Fellow or Sylvia either could be so spooney. Ruggles and I would have given anything on earth to be out of that. We knew we'd no business to be there and we felt as foolish as flatfish. It was a tremendous relief when the Old Fellow and Sylvia got up at last and trailed away, both of them looking idiotically happy.

"Well, did you ever?" said Ruggles.

It was a girl's exclamation, but nothing else would have expressed his feelings.

"No, I never," I said. "To think that Sylvia Grant should be sweet on the Old Fellow when she could have Micky! It passes comprehension. Did she—did she really promise to marry him, Ruggles?"

"She did," said Ruggles gloomily. "But, I say, isn't that Old Fellow game? Tumbled to the trick in a jiff; never let on but what he wrote the letter, never will let on, I bet. Where does the joke come in, Polly, my boy?"

"It's on us," I said, "but nobody will know of it if we hold our tongues. We'll have to hold them anyhow, for Sylvia's sake, since she's been goose enough to go and fall in love with the Old Fellow. She'd go wild if she ever found out the letter was a hoax. We have made that match, Ruggles. He'd never have got up enough spunk to tell her he wanted her, and she'd probably have married Micky out of spite."

"Well, you know the Old Fellow isn't a bad sort after all," said Ruggles, "and he's really awfully gone on her. So it's all right. Let's go and find the girls."

The Parting of The Ways

Mrs. Longworth crossed the hotel piazza, descended the steps, and walked out of sight down the shore road with all the grace of motion that lent distinction to her slightest movement. Her eyes were very bright, and an unusual flush stained the pallor of her cheek. Two men who were lounging in one corner of the hotel piazza looked admiringly after her.

"She is a beautiful woman," said one.

"Wasn't there some talk about Mrs. Longworth and Cunningham last winter?" asked the other.

"Yes. They were much together. Still, there may have been nothing wrong. She was old Judge Carmody's daughter, you know. Longworth got Carmody under his thumb in money matters and put the screws on. They say he made Carmody's daughter the price of the old man's redemption. The girl herself was a mere child, I shall never forget her face on her wedding day. But she's been plucky since then, I must say. If she has suffered, she hasn't shown it. I don't suppose Longworth ever ill-treats her. He isn't that sort. He's simply a grovelling cad—that's all. Nobody would sympathise much with the poor devil if his wife did run off with Cunningham."

Meanwhile, Beatrice Longworth walked quickly down the shore road, her white skirt brushing over the crisp golden grasses by the way. In a sunny hollow among the sandhills she came upon Stephen Gordon, sprawled out luxuriously in the warm, sea-smelling grasses. The youth sprang to his feet at sight of her, and his big brown eyes kindled to a glow.

Mrs. Longworth smiled to him. They had been great friends all summer. He was a lanky, overgrown lad of fifteen or sixteen, odd and shy and dreamy, scarcely possessing a speaking acquaintance with others at the hotel. But he and Mrs. Longworth had been congenial from their first meeting. In many ways, he was far older than his years, but there was a certain inerradicable boyishness about him to which her heart warmed.

"You are the very person I was just going in search of. I've news to tell. Sit down."

He spoke eagerly, patting the big gray boulder beside him with his slim, brown hand. For a moment Beatrice hesitated. She wanted to be alone just then. But his clever, homely face was so appealing that she yielded and sat down.

Stephen flung himself down again contentedly in the grasses at her feet, pillowing his chin in his palms and looking up at her, adoringly.

"You are so beautiful, dear lady. I love to look at you. Will you tilt that hat a little more over the left eye-brow? Yes—so—some day I shall paint you."

His tone and manner were all simplicity.

"When you are a great artist," said Beatrice, indulgently.

He nodded.

"Yes, I mean to be that. I've told you all my dreams, you know. Now for my news. I'm going away to-morrow. I had a telegram from father to-day."

He drew the message from his pocket and flourished it up at her.

"I'm to join him in Europe at once. He is in Rome. Think of it—in Rome! I'm to go on with my art studies there. And I leave to-morrow."

"I'm glad—and I'm sorry—and you know which is which," said Beatrice, patting the shaggy brown head. "I shall miss you dreadfully, Stephen."

"We *have* been splendid chums, haven't we?" he said, eagerly.

Suddenly his face changed. He crept nearer to her, and bowed his head until his lips almost touched the hem of her dress.

"I'm glad you came down to-day," he went on in a low, diffident voice. "I want to tell you something, and I can tell it better here. I couldn't go away without thanking you. I'll make a mess of it—I can never explain things. But you've been so much to me—you mean so much to me. You've made me believe in things I never believed in before. You—you—I know now that there is such a thing as a good woman, a woman who could make a man better, just because he breathed the same air with her."

He paused for a moment; then went on in a still lower tone:

"It's hard when a fellow can't speak of his mother because he can't say anything good of her, isn't it? My mother wasn't a good woman. When I was eight years old she went away with a scoundrel. It broke father's heart. Nobody thought I understood, I was such a little fellow. But I did. I heard them talking. I knew she had brought shame and disgrace on herself and us. And I had loved her so! Then, somehow, as I grew up, it was my misfortune that all the women I had to do with were mean and base. They were hirelings, and I hated and feared them. There was an aunt of mine—she tried to be good to me in her way. But she told me a lie, and I never cared for her after I found it out. And then, father—we loved each other and were good chums. But he didn't believe in much either. He was bitter, you know. He said all women were alike. I grew up with that notion. I didn't care much for anything—nothing seemed worth while. Then I came here and met you."

He paused again. Beatrice had listened with a gray look on her face. It would have startled him had he glanced up, but he did not, and after a moment's silence the halting boyish voice went on:

"You have changed everything for me. I was nothing but a clod before. You are not the mother of my body, but you are of my soul. It was born of you. I shall always love and reverence you for it. You will always be my ideal. If I ever do anything worth while it will be because of you. In everything I shall ever attempt I shall try to do it as if you were to pass judgment upon it. You will be a lifelong inspiration to me. Oh, I am bungling this! I can't tell you what I feel—you are so pure, so good, so noble! I shall reverence all women for your sake henceforth."

"And if," said Beatrice, in a very low voice, "if I were false to your ideal of me—if I were to do anything that would destroy your faith in me—something weak or wicked—"

"But you couldn't," he interrupted, flinging up his head and looking at her with his great dog-like eyes, "you couldn't!"

"But if I could?" she persisted, gently, "and if I did—what then?"

"I should hate you," he said, passionately. "You would be worse than a murderess. You would kill every good impulse and belief in me. I would never trust anything or anybody again—but there," he added, his voice once more growing tender, "you will never fail me, I feel sure of that."

"Thank you," said Beatrice, almost in a whisper. "Thank you," she repeated, after a moment. She stood up and held out her hand. "I think I must go now. Good-bye, dear laddie. Write to me from Rome. I shall always be glad to hear from you wherever you are. And—and—I shall always try to live up to your ideal of me, Stephen."

He sprang to his feet and took her hand, lifting it to his lips with boyish reverence. "I know that," he said, slowly. "Good-bye, my sweet lady."

When Mrs. Longworth found herself in her room again, she unlocked her desk and took out a letter. It was addressed to Mr. Maurice Cunningham. She slowly tore it twice across, laid the fragments on a tray, and touched them with a lighted match. As they blazed up one line came out in writhing redness across the page: "I will go away with you as you ask." Then it crumbled into gray ashes.

She drew a long breath and hid her face in her hands.

The Promissory Note

Ernest Duncan swung himself off the platform of David White's store and walked whistling up the street. Life seemed good to Ernest just then. Mr. White had given him a rise in salary that day, and had told him that he was satisfied with him. Mr. White was not easy to please in the matter of clerks, and it had been with fear and trembling that Ernest had gone into his store six months before. He had thought himself fortunate to secure such a chance. His father had died the preceding year, leaving nothing in the way of worldly goods except the house he had lived in. For several years before his death he had been unable to do much work, and the finances of the little family had dwindled steadily. After his father's death Ernest, who had been going to school and expecting to go to college, found that he must go to work at once instead to support himself and his mother.

If George Duncan had not left much of worldly wealth behind him, he at least bequeathed to his son the interest of a fine, upright character and a reputation for honesty and integrity. None knew this better than David White, and it was on this account that he took Ernest as his clerk, over the heads of several other applicants who seemed to have a stronger "pull."

"I don't know anything about *you*, Ernest," he said bluntly. "You're only sixteen, and you may not have an ounce of real grit or worth in you. But it will be a queer thing if your father's son hasn't. I knew him all his life. A better man never lived nor, before his accident, a smarter one. I'll give his son a chance, anyhow. If you take after your dad you'll get on all right."

Ernest had not been in the store very long before Mr. White concluded, with a gratified chuckle, that he did take after his father. He was hard-working, conscientious, and obliging. Customers of all sorts, from the rough fishermen who came up from the harbour to the old

Irishwomen from the back country roads, liked him. Mr. White was satisfied. He was beginning to grow old. This lad had the makings of a good partner in him by and by. No hurry; he must serves long apprenticeship first and prove his mettle; no use spoiling him by hinting at future partnerships before need was. That would all come in due time. David White was a shrewd man.

Ernest was unconscious of his employer's plans regarding him; but he knew that he stood well with him and, much to his surprise, he found that he liked the work, and was beginning to take a personal interest and pleasure in the store. Hence, he went home to tea on this particular afternoon with buoyant step and smiling eyes. It was a good world, and he was glad to be alive in it, glad to have work to do and a dear little mother to work for. Most of the folks who met him smiled in friendly fashion at the bright-eyed, frank-faced lad. Only old Jacob Patterson scowled grimly as he passed him, emitting merely a surly grunt in response to Ernest's greeting. But then, old Jacob Patterson was noted as much for his surliness as for his miserliness. Nobody had ever heard him speak pleasantly to anyone; therefore his unfriendliness did not at all dash Ernest's high spirits.

"I'm sorry for him," the lad thought. "He has no interest in life save accumulating money. He has no other pleasure or affection or ambition. When he dies I don't suppose a single regret will follow him. Father died a poor man, but what love and respect went with him to his grave—aye, and beyond it. Jacob Patterson, I'm sorry for you. You have chosen the poorer part, and you are a poor man in spite of your thousands."

Ernest and his mother lived up on the hill, at the end of the straggling village street. The house was a small, old-fashioned one, painted white, set in the middle of a small but beautiful lawn. George Duncan, during the last rather helpless years of his life, had devoted himself to the cultivation of flowers, shrubs, and trees and, as a result, his lawn was the prettiest in Conway. Ernest worked hard in his spare moments to keep it looking as well as in his father's lifetime, for he loved his little home dearly, and was proud of its beauty.

He ran gaily into the sitting-room.

"Tea ready, lady mother? I'm hungry as a wolf. Good news gives one an appetite. Mr. White has raised my salary a couple of dollars per week. We must celebrate the event somehow this evening. What do you say to a sail on the river and an ice cream at Taylor's afterwards? When a little woman can't outlive her schoolgirl hankering for ice cream—why, Mother, what's the matter? Mother, dear!"

Mrs. Duncan had been standing before the window with her back to the room when Ernest entered. When she turned he saw that she had been crying.

"Oh, Ernest," she said brokenly, "Jacob Patterson has just been here—and he says—he says—"

"What has that old miser been saying to trouble you?" demanded Ernest angrily, taking her hands in his.

"He says he holds your father's promissory note for nine hundred dollars, overdue for several years," answered Mrs. Duncan. "Yes—and he showed me the note, Ernest."

"Father's promissory note for nine hundred!" exclaimed Ernest in bewilderment. "But Father paid that note to James Patterson five years ago, Mother—just before his accident. Didn't you tell me he did?"

"Yes, he did," said Mrs. Duncan, "but—"

"Then where is it?" interrupted Ernest. "Father would keep the receipted note, of course. We must look among his papers."

"You won't find it there, Ernest. We—we don't know where the note is. It—it was lost."

"Lost! That is unfortunate. But you say that Jacob Patterson showed you a promissory note of Father's still in existence? How can that be? It can't possibly be the note he paid. And there couldn't have been another note we knew nothing of?"

"I understand how this note came to be in Jacob Patterson's possession," said Mrs. Duncan more firmly, "but he laughed in my face when I told him. I must tell you the whole story, Ernest. But sit down and get your tea first."

"I haven't any appetite for tea now, Mother," said Ernest soberly. "Let me hear the whole truth about the matter."

"Seven years ago your father gave his note to old James Patterson, Jacob's brother," said Mrs. Duncan. "It was for nine hundred dollars. Two years afterwards the note fell due and he paid James Patterson the full amount with interest. I remember the day well. I have only too good reason to. He went up to the Patterson place in the afternoon with the money. It was a very hot day. James Patterson receipted the note and gave it to your father. Your father always remembered that much; he was also sure that he had the note with him when he left the house. He then went over to see Paul Sinclair. A thunderstorm came up while he was on the road. Then, as you know, Ernest, just as he turned in at Paul Sinclair's gate the lightning flash struck and stunned him. It was weeks before he came to himself at all. He never did come completely to himself again. When, weeks afterwards, I thought of the note and asked him about it, we could not find it; and, search as we did, we never found it. Your father could never remember what he did with it when he left James Patterson's. Neither Mr. Sinclair nor his wife could recollect seeing anything of it at the time of the accident. James Patterson had left for California the very morning after, and he never came back. We did not worry much about the loss of the note then; it did not seem of much moment, and your father was not in a condition to be troubled about the matter."

"But, Mother, this note that Jacob Patterson holds—I don't understand about this."

"I'm coming to that. I remember distinctly that on the evening when your father came home after signing the note he said that James Patterson drew up a note and he signed it, but just as he did so the old man's pet cat, which was sitting on the table, upset an ink bottle and the ink ran all over the table and stained one end of the note. Old James Patterson was the fussiest man who ever lived, and a stickler for neatness. 'Tut, tut,' he said, 'this won't do. Here, I'll draw up another note and tear this blotted one up.' He did so and your father signed it. He always supposed James Patterson destroyed the first one, and certainly he must have intended to, for there never was an honester man. But he must have neglected to do so for, Ernest, it was that blotted note Jacob Patterson showed me today. He said he found it among his brother's papers. I suppose it has been in the desk up at the Patterson place ever since James went to California. He died last winter and Jacob is his sole heir. Ernest, that note with the compound interest on it for seven years amounts to over eleven hundred dollars. How can we pay it?"

"I'm afraid that this is a very serious business, Mother," said Ernest, rising and pacing the floor with agitated strides. "We shall have to pay the note if we cannot find the other—and even if we could, perhaps. Your story of the drawing up of the second note would not be worth anything as evidence in a court of law—and we have nothing to hope from Jacob Patterson's clemency. No doubt he believes that he really holds Father's unpaid note. He is not a dishonest man; in fact, he rather prides himself on having made all his money honestly. He will exact every penny of the debt. The first thing to do is to have another thorough search for the lost note—although I am afraid that it is a forlorn hope."

A forlorn hope it proved to be. The note did not turn up. Old Jacob Patterson proved obdurate. He laughed to scorn the tale of the blotted note and, indeed, Ernest sadly admitted to himself that it was not a story anybody would be in a hurry to believe.

"There's nothing for it but to sell our house and pay the debt, Mother," he said at last. Ernest had grown old in the days that had followed Jacob Patterson's demand. His boyish face was pale and haggard. "Jacob Patterson will take the case into the law courts if we don't settle at once. Mr. White offered to lend me the money on a mortgage on the place, but I could never pay the interest out of my salary when we have nothing else to live on. I would only get further and further behind. I'm not afraid of hard work, but I dare not borrow money with so little prospect of ever being able to repay it. We must sell the place and rent that little four-roomed cottage of Mr. Percy's down by the river to live in. Oh, Mother, it half kills me to think of your being turned out of your home like this!"

It was a bitter thing for Mrs. Duncan also, but for Ernest's sake she concealed her feelings and affected cheerfulness. The house and lot were sold, Mr. White being the purchaser thereof; and Ernest and his mother removed to the little riverside cottage with such of their household belongings as had not also to be sold to make up the required sum. Even then, Ernest had to borrow two hundred dollars from Mr. White, and he foresaw that the repayal of this sum would cost him much self-denial and privation. It would be necessary to cut their modest expenses down severely. For himself Ernest did not mind, but it hurt him keenly that his mother should lack the little luxuries and comforts to which she had been accustomed. He saw too, in spite of her efforts to hide it, that leaving her old home was a terrible blow to her. Altogether, Ernest felt bitter and disheartened; his step lacked spring and his face its smile. He did his work with dogged faithfulness, but he no longer found pleasure in it. He knew that his mother secretly pined after her lost home where she had gone as a bride, and the knowledge rendered him very unhappy.

Paul Sinclair, his father's friend and cousin, died that winter, leaving two small children. His wife had died the previous year. When his business affairs came to be settled they were found to be sadly involved. There were debts on all sides, and it was soon only too evident that nothing was left for the little boys. They were homeless and penniless.

"What will become of them, poor little fellows?" said Mrs. Duncan pityingly. "We are their only relatives, Ernest. We must give them a home at least."

"Mother, how can we!" exclaimed Ernest. "We are so poor. It's as much as we can do to get along now, and there is that two hundred to pay Mr. White. I'm sorry for Danny and Frank, but I don't see how we can possibly do anything for them."

Mrs. Duncan sighed.

"I know it isn't right to ask you to add to your burden," she said wistfully.

"It is of *you* I am thinking, Mother," said Ernest tenderly. "I can't have your burden added to. You deny yourself too much and work too hard now. What would it be if you took the care of those children upon yourself?"

"Don't think of me, Ernest," said Mrs. Duncan eagerly. "I wouldn't mind. I'd be glad to do anything I could for them, poor little souls. Their father was your father's best friend, and I feel as if it were our duty to do all we can for them. They're such little fellows. Who knows how they would be treated if they were taken by strangers? And they'd most likely be separated, and that would be a shame. But I leave it for you to decide, Ernest. It is your right, for the heaviest part will fall on you."

Ernest did not decide at once. For a week he thought the matter over, weighing pros and cons carefully. To take the two Sinclair boys meant a double portion of toil and self-denial. Had he not enough to bear now? But, on the other side, was it not his duty, nay, his privilege, to help the children if he could? In the end he said to his mother:

"We'll take the little fellows, Mother. I'll do the best I can for them. We'll manage a corner and a crust for them."

So Danny and Frank Sinclair came to the little cottage. Frank was eight and Danny six, and they were small and lively and mischievous. They worshipped Mrs. Duncan, and thought Ernest the finest fellow in the world. When his birthday came around in March, the two little chaps put their heads together in a grave consultation as to what they could give him.

"You know he gave us presents on our birthdays," said Frank. "So we must give him something."

"I'll div him my pottet-knife," said Danny, taking the somewhat battered and loose-jointed affair from his pocket, and gazing at it affectionately.

"I'll give him one of Papa's books," said Frank. "That pretty one with the red covers and the gold letters."

A few of Mr. Sinclair's books had been saved for the boys, and were stored in a little box in their room. The book Frank referred to was an old *History of the Turks*, and its gay cover was probably the best of it, since its contents were of no particular merit.

On Ernest's birthday both boys gave him their offerings after breakfast.

"Here's a pottet-knife for you," said Danny graciously. "It's a bully pottet-knife. It'll cut real well if you hold it dust the wight way. I'll show you."

"And here's a book for you," said Frank. "It's a real pretty book, and I guess it's pretty interesting reading too. It's all about the Turks."

Ernest accepted both gifts gravely, and after the children had gone out he and his mother had a hearty laugh.

"The dear, kind-hearted little lads!" said Mrs. Duncan. "It must have been a real sacrifice on Danny's part to give you his beloved 'pottet-knife.' I was afraid you were going to refuse it at first, and that would have hurt his little feelings terribly. I don't think the *History of the Turks* will keep you up burning the midnight oil. I remember that book of old—I could never forget that gorgeous cover. Mr. Sinclair lent it to your father once, and he said it was absolute trash. Why, Ernest, what's the matter?"

Ernest had been turning the book's leaves over carelessly. Suddenly he sprang to his feet with an exclamation, his face turning white as marble.

"Mother!" he gasped, holding out a yellowed slip of paper. "Look! It's the lost promissory note."

Mother and son looked at each other for a moment. Then Mrs. Duncan began to laugh and cry together.

"Your father took that book with him when he went to pay the note," she said. "He intended to return it to Mr. Sinclair. I remember seeing the gleam of the red binding in his hand as he went out of the gate. He must have slipped the note into it and I suppose the book has never been opened since. Oh, Ernest—do you think—will Jacob Patterson—"

"I don't know, Mother. I must see Mr. White about this. Don't be too sanguine. This doesn't prove that the note Jacob Patterson found wasn't a genuine note also, you know—that is, I don't think it would serve as proof in law. We'll have to leave it to his sense of justice. If he refuses to refund the money I'm afraid we can't compel him to do so."

But Jacob Patterson did not any longer refuse belief to Mrs. Patterson's story of the blotted note. He was a harsh, miserly man, but he prided himself on his strict honesty; he had been fairly well acquainted with his brother's business transactions, and knew that George Duncan had given only one promissory note.

"I'll admit, ma'am, since the receipted note has turned up, that your story about the blotted one must be true," he said surlily. "I'll pay your money back. Nobody can ever say Jacob Patterson cheated. I took what I believed to be my due. Since I'm convinced it wasn't I'll hand every penny over. Though, mind you, you couldn't make me do it by law. It's my honesty, ma'am, it's my honesty."

Since Jacob Patterson was so well satisfied with the fibre of his honesty, neither Mrs. Duncan nor Ernest was disposed to quarrel with it. Mr. White readily agreed to sell the old Duncan place back to them, and by spring they were settled again in their beloved little home. Danny and Frank were with them, of course.

"We can't be too good to them, Mother," said Ernest. "We really owe all our happiness to them."

"Yes, but, Ernest, if you had not consented to take the homeless little lads in their time of need this wouldn't have come about."

"I've been well rewarded, Mother," said Ernest quietly, "but, even if nothing of the sort had happened, I would be glad that I did the best I could for Frank and Danny. I'm ashamed to think that I was unwilling to do it at first. If it hadn't been for what you said, I wouldn't have. So it is your unselfishness we have to thank for it all, Mother dear."

The Revolt of Mary Isabel

"For a woman of forty, Mary Isabel, you have the least sense of any person I have ever known," said Louisa Irving.

Louisa had said something similar in spirit to Mary Isabel almost every day of her life. Mary Isabel had never resented it, even when it hurt her bitterly. Everybody in Latimer knew that Louisa Irving ruled her meek little sister with a rod of iron and wondered why Mary Isabel never rebelled. It simply never occurred to Mary Isabel to do so; all her life she had given in to Louisa and the thought of refusing obedience to her sister's Mede-and-Persian decrees never crossed her mind. Mary Isabel had only one secret from Louisa and she lived in daily dread that Louisa would discover it. It was a very harmless little secret, but Mary Isabel felt rightly sure that Louisa would not tolerate it for a moment.

They were sitting together in the dim living room of their quaint old cottage down by the shore. The window was open and the sea-breeze blew in, stirring the prim white curtains fitfully, and ruffling the little rings of dark hair on Mary Isabel's forehead—rings which always annoyed Louisa. She thought Mary Isabel ought to brush them straight back, and Mary Isabel did so faithfully a dozen times a day; and in ten minutes they crept down again, kinking defiance to Louisa, who might make Mary Isabel submit to her in all things but had no power over naturally curly hair. Louisa had never had any trouble with her own hair; it was straight and sleek and mouse-coloured—what there was of it.

Mary Isabel's face was flushed and her wood-brown eyes looked grieved and pleading. Mary Isabel was still pretty, and vanity is the last thing to desert a properly constructed woman.

"I can't wear a bonnet yet, Louisa," she protested. "Bonnets have gone out for everybody except really old ladies. I want a hat: one of those pretty, floppy ones with pale blue forget-me-nots."

Then it was that Louisa made the remark quoted above.

"I wore a bonnet before I was forty," she went on ruthlessly, "and so should every decent woman. It is absurd to be thinking so much of dress at your age, Mary Isabel. I don't know what sort of a way you'd bedizen yourself out if I'd let you, I'm sure. It's fortunate you have somebody to keep you from making a fool of yourself. I'm going to town tomorrow and I'll pick you out a suitable black bonnet. You'd look nice starring round in leghorn and forget-me-nots, now, wouldn't you?"

Mary Isabel privately thought she would, but she gave in, of course, although she did hate bitterly that unbought, unescapable bonnet.

"Well, do as you think best, Louisa," she said with a sigh. "I suppose it doesn't matter much. Nobody cares how I look anyhow. But can't I go to town with you? I want to pick out my new silk."

"I'm as good a judge of black silk as you," said Louisa shortly. "It isn't safe to leave the house alone."

"But I don't want a black silk," cried Mary Isabel. "I've worn black so long; both my silk dresses have been black. I want a pretty silver-grey, something like Mrs. Chester Ford's."

"Did anyone ever hear such nonsense?" Louisa wanted to know, in genuine amazement. "Silver-grey silk is the most unserviceable thing in the world. There's nothing like black for wear and real elegance. No, no, Mary Isabel, don't be foolish. You must let me choose for you; you know you never had any judgment. Mother told you so often enough. Now, get your sunbonnet and take a walk to the shore. You look tired. I'll get the tea."

Louisa's tone was kind though firm. She Was really good to Mary Isabel as long as Mary Isabel gave her her own way peaceably. But if she had known Mary Isabel's secret she would never have permitted those walks to the shore.

Mary Isabel sighed again, yielded, and went out. Across a green field from the Irving cottage Dr. Donald Hamilton's big house was hooding itself in the shadows of the thick fir grove that enabled the doctor to have a garden. There was no shelter at the cottage, so the Irving "girls" never tried to have a garden. Soon after Dr. Hamilton had come there to live he had sent a bouquet of early daffodils over by his housekeeper. Louisa had taken them gingerly in her extreme fingertips, carried them across the field to the lawn fence, and cast them over it, under the amused grey eyes of portly Dr. Hamilton, who was looking out of his office window. Then Louisa had come back to the porch door and ostentatiously washed her hands.

"I guess that will settle Donald Hamilton," she told the secretly sorry Mary Isabel triumphantly, and it did settle him—at least as far as any farther social advances were concerned.

Dr. Hamilton was an excellent physician and an equally excellent man. Louisa Irving could not have picked a flaw in his history or character. Indeed, against Dr. Hamilton himself she had no grudge, but he was the brother of a man she hated and whose relatives were consequently taboo in Louisa's eyes. Not that the brother was a bad man either; he had simply taken the opposite side to the Irvings in a notable church feud of a dozen years ago, and Louisa had never since held any intercourse with him or his fellow sinners.

Mary Isabel did not look at the Hamilton house. She kept her head resolutely turned away as she went down the shore lane with its wild sweet loneliness of salt-withered grasses and piping sea-winds. Only when she turned the corner of the fir-wood, which shut her out from view of the houses, did she look timidly over the line-fence. Dr. Hamilton was standing there, where the fence ran out to the sandy shingle, smoking his little black pipe, which he took out and put away when Mary Isabel came around the firs. Men did things like that instinctively in Mary Isabel's company. There was something so delicately virginal about her, in spite of her forty years, that they gave her the reverence they would have paid to a very young, pure girl.

Dr. Hamilton smiled at the little troubled face under the big sunbonnet. Mary Isabel had to wear a sunbonnet. She would never have done it from choice.

"What is the matter?" asked the doctor, in his big, breezy, old-bachelor voice. He had another voice for sick-beds and rooms of bereavement, but this one suited best with the purring of the waves and winds.

"How do you know that anything is the matter?" Mary Isabel parried demurely.

"By your face. Come now, tell me what it is."

"It is really nothing. I have just been foolish, that is all. I wanted a hat with forget-me-nots and a grey silk, and Louisa says I must have black and a bonnet."

The doctor looked indignant but held his peace. He and Mary Isabel had tacitly agreed never to discuss Louisa, because such discussion would not make for harmony. Mary Isabel's conscience would not let the doctor say anything uncomplimentary of Louisa, and the doctor's conscience would not let him say anything complimentary. So they left her out of the question and talked about the sea and the boats and poetry and flowers and similar non-combustible subjects.

These clandestine meetings had been going on for two months, ever since the day they had just happened to meet below the firs. It never occurred to Mary Isabel that the doctor meant anything but friendship; and if it had occurred to the doctor, he did not think there would be much use in saying so. Mary Isabel was too hopelessly under Louisa's thumb. She might keep tryst below the firs occasionally—so long as Louisa didn't know—but to no farther lengths would she dare go. Besides, the doctor wasn't quite sure that he really wanted anything more. Mary Isabel was a sweet little woman, but Dr. Hamilton had been a bachelor so long that it would be very difficult for him to get out of the habit; so difficult that it was hardly worth while trying when such an obstacle as Louisa Irving's tyranny loomed in the way. So he never tried to make love to Mary Isabel, though he probably would have if he had thought it of any use. This does not sound very romantic, of course, but when a man is fifty, romance, while it may be present in the fruit, is assuredly absent in blossom.

"I suppose you won't be going to the induction of my nephew Thursday week?" said the doctor in the course of the conversation.

"No. Louisa will not permit it. I had hoped," said Mary Isabel with a sigh, as she braided some silvery shore-grasses nervously together, "that when old Mr. Moody went away she would go back to the church here. And I think she would if—if—"

"If Jim hadn't come in Mr. Moody's place," finished the doctor with his jolly laugh.

Mary Isabel coloured prettily. "It is not because he is your nephew, doctor. It is because—because—"

"Because he is the nephew of my brother who was on the other side in that ancient church fracas? Bless you, I understand. What a good hater your sister is! Such a tenacity in holding bitterness from one generation to another commands admiration of a certain sort. As for Jim, he's a nice little chap, and he is coming to live with me until the manse is repaired."

"I am sure you will find that pleasant," said Mary Isabel primly.

She wondered if the young minister's advent would make any difference in regard to these shore-meetings; then decided quickly that it would not; then more quickly still that it wouldn't matter if it did.

"He will be company," admitted the doctor, who liked company and found the shore road rather lonesome. "I had a letter from him to-day saying that he'd come home with me from the induction. By the way, they're tearing down the old post office today. And that reminds me—by Jove, I'd all but forgotten. I promised to go up and see Mollie Marr this evening; Mollie's nerves are on the rampage again. I must rush."

With a wave of his hand the doctor hurried off. Mary Isabel lingered for some time longer, leaning against the fence, looking dreamily out to sea. The doctor was a very pleasant companion. If only Louisa would allow neighbourliness! Mary Isabel felt a faint, impotent resentment. She had never had anything other girls had: friends, dresses, beaus, and it was all Louisa's fault—Louisa who was going to make her wear a bonnet for the rest of her life. The more Mary Isabel thought of that bonnet the more she hated it.

That evening Warren Marr rode down to the shore cottage on horseback and handed Mary Isabel a letter; a strange, scrumpled, soiled, yellow letter. When Mary Isabel saw the handwriting on the envelope she trembled and turned as deadly pale as if she had seen a ghost:

"Here's a letter for you," said Warren, grinning. "It's been a long time on the way—nigh fifteen years. Guess the news'll be rather stale. We found it behind the old partition when we tore it down today."

"It is my brother Tom's writing," said Mary Isabel faintly. She went into the room trembling, holding the letter tightly in her clasped hands. Louisa had gone up to the village on an errand; Mary Isabel almost wished she were home; she hardly felt equal to the task of opening Tom's letter alone. Tom had been dead for ten years and this letter gave her an uncanny sensation; as of a message from the spirit-land.

Fifteen years, ago Thomas Irving had gone to California and five years later he had died there. Mary Isabel, who had idolized her brother, almost grieved herself to death at the time.

Finally she opened the letter with ice-cold fingers. It had been written soon after Tom reached California. The first two pages were filled with descriptions of the country and his "job."

On the third Tom began abruptly:

Look here, Mary Isabel, you are not to let Louisa boss you about as she was doing when I was at home. I was going to speak to you about it before I came away, but I forgot. Lou is a fine girl, but she is too domineering, and the more you give in to her the worse it makes her. You're far too easy-going for your own welfare, Mary Isabel, and for your own sake I Wish you had more spunk. Don't let Louisa live your life for you; just you live it yourself. Never mind if there is some friction at first; Lou will give in when she finds she has to, and you'll both be the better for it, I want you to be real happy, Mary Isabel, but you won't be if you don't assert your independence. Giving in the way you do is bad for both you and Louisa. It will make her a tyrant and you a poor-spirited creature of no account in the world. Just brace up and stand firm.

When she had read the letter through Mary Isabel took it to her own room and locked it in her bureau drawer. Then she sat by her window, looking out into a sea-sunset, and thought it over. Coming in the strange way it had, the letter seemed a message from the dead, and Mary Isabel had a superstitious conviction that she must obey it. She had always had a great respect for Tom's opinion. He was right—oh, she felt that he was right. What a pity she had not received the letter long ago, before the shackles of habit had become so firmly riveted. But it was not too late yet. She would rebel at last and—how had Tom phrased it—oh, yes, assert her independence. She owed it to Tom; It had been his wish—and he was dead—and she would do her best to fulfil it.

"I shan't get a bonnet," thought Mary Isabel determinedly. "Tom wouldn't have liked me in a bonnet. From this out I'm just going to do exactly as Tom would have liked me to do, no matter how afraid I am of Louisa. And, oh, I am horribly afraid of her."

Mary Isabel was every whit as much afraid the next morning after breakfast but she did not look it, by reason of the flush on her cheeks and the glint in her brown eyes. She had put Tom's letter in the bosom of her dress and she pressed her fingertips on it that the crackle might give her courage.

"Louisa," she said firmly, "I am going to town with you."

"Nonsense," said Louisa shortly.

"You may call it nonsense if you like, but I am going," said Mary Isabel unquailingly. "I have made up my mind on that point, Louisa, and nothing you can say will alter it."

Louisa looked amazed. Never before had Mary Isabel set her decrees at naught.

"Are you crazy, Mary Isabel?" she demanded.

"No, I am not crazy. But I am going to town and I am going to get a silver-grey silk for myself and a new hat. I will not wear a bonnet and you need never mention it to me again, Louisa."

"If you are going to town I shall stay home," said Louisa in a cold, ominous tone that almost made Mary Isabel quake. If it had not been for that reassuring crackle of Tom's letter I fear Mary Isabel would have given in. "This house can't be left alone. If you go, I'll stay."

Louisa honestly thought that would bring the rebel to terms. Mary Isabel had never gone to town alone in her life. Louisa did not believe she would dare to go. But Mary Isabel did not quail. Defiance was not so hard after all, once you had begun.

Mary Isabel went to town and she went alone. She spent the whole delightful day in the shops, unhampered by Louisa's scorn and criticism in her examination of all the pretty things displayed. She selected a hat she felt sure Tom would like—a pretty crumpled grey straw with forget-me-nots and ribbons. Then she bought a grey silk of a lovely silvery shade.

When she got back home she unwrapped her packages and showed her purchases to Louisa. But Louisa neither looked at them nor spoke to Mary Isabel. Mary Isabel tossed her head and went to her own room. Her draught of freedom had stimulated her, and she did not mind Louisa's attitude half as much as she would have expected. She read Tom's letter over again to fortify herself and then she dressed her hair in a fashion she had seen that day in town and pulled out all the little curls on her forehead.

The next day she took the silver-grey silk to the Latimer dressmaker and picked out a fashionable design for it. When the silk dress came home, Louisa, who had thawed out somewhat in the meantime, unbent sufficiently to remark that it fitted very well.

"I am going to wear it to the induction tomorrow," Mary Isabel said, boldly to all appearances, quakingly in reality. She knew that she was throwing down the gauntlet for good and all. If she could assert and maintain her independence in this matter Louisa's power would be broken forever.

Twelve years before this, the previously mentioned schism had broken out in the Latimer church. The minister had sided with the faction which Louisa Irving opposed. She had promptly ceased going to his church and withdrew all financial support. She paid to the Marwood church, fifteen miles away, and occasionally she hired a team and drove over there to service. But she never entered the Latimer church again nor allowed Mary Isabel to do so. For that matter, Mary Isabel did not wish to go. She had resented the minister's attitude almost as bitterly as Louisa. But when Mr. Moody accepted a call elsewhere Mary Isabel hoped that she and Louisa might return to their old church home. Possibly they might have done so had not the congregation called the young, newly fledged James Anderson. Mary Isabel would not have cared for this, but Louisa sternly said that neither she nor any of hers should ever darken the doors of a church where the nephew of Martin Hamilton preached. Mary Isabel had regretfully acquiesced at the time, but now she had made up her mind to go to church and she meant to begin with the induction service.

Louisa stared at her sister incredulously.

"Have you taken complete leave of your senses, Mary Isabel?"

"No. I've just come to them," retorted Mary Isabel recklessly, gripping a chair-back desperately so that Louisa should not see how she was trembling. "It is all foolishness to keep away from church just because of an old grudge. I'm tired of staying home Sundays or driving fifteen miles to Marwood to hear poor old Mr. Grattan. Everybody says Mr. Anderson is a splendid young man and an excellent preacher, and I'm going to attend his services regularly."

Louisa had taken Mary Isabel's first defiance in icy disdain. Now she lost her temper and raged. The storm of angry words beat on Mary Isabel like hail, but she fronted it staunchly. She seemed to hear Tom's voice saying, "Live your own life, Mary Isabel; don't let Louisa live it for you," and she meant to obey him.

"If you go to that man's induction I'll never forgive you," Louisa concluded.

Mary Isabel said nothing. She just primmed up her lips very determinedly, picked up the silk dress, and carried it to her room.

The next day was fine and warm. Louisa said no word all the morning. She worked fiercely and slammed things around noisily. After dinner Mary Isabel went to her room and came down presently, fine and dainty in her grey silk, with the forget-me-not hat resting on the soft loose waves of her hair. Louisa was blacking the kitchen stove.

She shot one angry glance at Mary Isabel, then gave a short, contemptuous laugh, the laugh of an angry woman who finds herself robbed of all weapons except ridicule.

Mary Isabel flushed and walked with an unfaltering step out of the house and up the lane. She resented Louisa's laughter. She was sure there was nothing so very ridiculous about her appearance. Women far older than she, even in Latimer, wore light dresses and fashionable hats. Really, Louisa was very disagreeable.

"I have put up with her ways too long," thought Mary Isabel, with a quick, unwonted rush of anger. "But I never shall again—no, never, let her be as vexed and scornful as she pleases."

The induction services were interesting, and Mary Isabel enjoyed them. Doctor Hamilton was sitting across from her and once or twice she caught him looking at her admiringly. The doctor noticed the hat and the grey silk and wondered how Mary Isabel had managed to get her own way concerning them. What a pretty woman she was! Really, he had never realized before how very pretty she was. But then, he had never seen her except in a sunbonnet or with her hair combed primly back.

But when the service was over Mary Isabel was dismayed to see that the sky had clouded over and looked very much like rain. Everybody hurried home, and Mary Isabel tripped along the shore road filled with anxious thoughts about her dress. That kind of silk always spotted, and her hat would be ruined if it got wet. How foolish she had been not to bring an umbrella!

She reached her own doorstep panting just as the first drop of rain fell.

"Thank goodness," she breathed.

Then she tried to open the door. It would not open.

She could see Louisa sitting by the kitchen window, calmly reading.

"Louisa, open the door quick," she called impatiently.

Louisa never moved a muscle, although Mary Isabel knew she must have heard.

"Louisa, do you hear what I say?" she cried, reaching over and tapping on the pane imperiously. "Open the door at once. It is going to rain—it is raining now. Be quick."

Louisa might as well have been a graven image for all the response she gave. Then did Mary Isabel realize her position. Louisa had locked her out purposely, knowing the rain was coming. Louisa had no intention of letting her in; she meant to keep her out until the dress and hat of her rebellion were spoiled. This was Louisa's revenge.

Mary Isabel turned with a gasp. What should she do? The padlocked doors of hen-house and well-house and wood-house: revealed the thoroughness of Louisa's vindictive design. Where should she go? She would go somewhere. She would not have her lovely new dress and hat spoiled!

She caught her ruffled skirts up in her hand and ran across the yard. She climbed the fence into the field and ran across that. Another drop of rain struck her cheek. She never glanced back or she would have seen a horrified face peering from the cottage kitchen window. Louisa had never dreamed that Mary Isabel would seek refuge over at Dr. Hamilton's.

Dr. Hamilton, who had driven home from church with the young minister, saw her coming and ran to open the door for her. Mary Isabel dashed up the verandah steps, breathless, crimson-cheeked, trembling with pent-up indignation and sense of outrage.

"Louisa locked me out, Dr. Hamilton," she cried almost hysterically. "She locked me out on purpose to spoil my dress. I'll never forgive her, I'll never go back to her, never, never, unless she asks me to. I had to come here. I was not going to have my dress ruined to please Louisa."

"Of course not—of course not," said Dr. Hamilton soothingly, drawing her into his big cosy living room. "You did perfectly right to come here, and you are just in time. There is the rain now in good earnest."

Mary Isabel sank into a chair and looked at Dr. Hamilton with tears in her eyes.

"Wasn't it an unkind, unsisterly thing to do?" she asked piteously. "Oh, I shall never feel the same towards Louisa again. Tom was right—I didn't tell you about Tom's letter but I will by and by. I shall not go back to Louisa after her locking me out. When it stops raining I'll go straight up to my cousin Ella's and stay with her until I arrange my plans. But one thing is certain, I shall not go back to Louisa."

"I wouldn't," said the doctor recklessly. "Now, don't cry and don't worry. Take off your hat—you can go to the spare room across the hall, if you like. Jim has gone upstairs to lie down; he has a bad headache and says he doesn't want any tea. So I was going to get up a bachelor's snack for myself. My housekeeper is away. She heard, at church that her mother was ill and went over to Marwood."

When Mary Isabel came back from the spare room, a little calmer but with traces of tears on her pink cheeks, the doctor had as good a tea-table spread as any woman could have had. Mary Isabel thought it was fortunate that the little errand boy, Tommy Brewster, was there, or she certainly would have been dreadfully embarrassed, now that the flame of her anger had blown out. But later on, when tea was over and she and the doctor were left alone, she did not feel embarrassed after all. Instead, she felt delightfully happy and at home. Dr. Hamilton put one so at ease.

She told him all about Tom's letter and her subsequent revolt. Dr. Hamilton never once made the mistake of smiling. He listened and approved and sympathized.

"So I'm determined I won't go back," concluded Mary Isabel, "unless she asks me to—and Louisa will never do that. Ella will be glad enough to have me for a while; she has five children and can't get any help."

The doctor shrugged his shoulders. He thought of Mary Isabel as unofficial drudge to Ella Kemble and her family. Then he looked at the little silvery figure by the window.

"I think I can suggest a better plan," he said gently and tenderly. "Suppose you stay here—as my wife. I've always wanted to ask you that but I feared it was no use because I knew Louisa would oppose it and I did not think you would consent if she did not. I think," the doctor leaned forward and took Mary Isabel's fluttering hand in his, "I think we can be very happy here, dear."

Mary Isabel flushed crimson and her heart beat wildly. She knew now that she loved Dr. Hamilton—and Tom would have liked it—yes, Tom would. She remembered how Tom hated the thought of his sisters being old maids.

"I—think—so—too," she faltered shyly.

"Then," said the doctor briskly, "what is the matter with our being married right here and now?"

"Married!"

"Yes, of course. Here we are in a state where no licence is required, a minister in the house, and you all dressed in the most beautiful wedding silk imaginable. You must see, if you just look at it calmly, how much better it will be than going up to Mrs. Kemble's and thereby publishing your difference with Louisa to all the village. I'll give you fifteen minutes to get used to the idea and then I'll call Jim down."

Mary Isabel put her hands to her face.

"You—you're like a whirlwind," she gasped. "You take away my breath."

"Think it over," said the doctor in a businesslike voice.

Mary Isabel thought—thought very hard for a few moments.

What would Tom have said?

Was it probable that Tom would have approved of such marrying in haste?

Mary Isabel came to the decision that he would have preferred it to having family jars bruited abroad. Moreover, Mary Isabel had never liked Ella Kemble very much. Going to her was only one degree better than going back to Louisa.

At last Mary Isabel took her hands down from her face. "Well?" said the doctor persuasively as she did so.

"I will consent on one condition," said Mary Isabel firmly. "And that is, that you will let me send word over to Louisa that I am going to be married and that she may come and see the ceremony if she will. Louisa has behaved very unkindly in this matter, but after all she is my sister—and she has been good to me in some ways—and I am not going to give her a chance to say that I got married in this—this headlong-fashion and never let her know."

"Tommy can take the word over," said the doctor.

Mary Isabel went to the doctor's desk and wrote a very brief note.

Dear Louisa:

> I am going to be married to Dr. Hamilton right away. I've seen him often at the shore this summer. I would like you to be present at the ceremony if you choose.

Mary Isabel.

Tommy ran across the field with the note.

It had now ceased raining and the clouds were breaking. Mary Isabel thought that a good omen. She and the doctor watched Tommy from the window. They saw Louisa come to the door, take the note, and shut the door in Tommy's face. Ten minutes later she reappeared, habited in her mackintosh, with her second-best bonnet on.

"She's—coming," said Mary Isabel, trembling.

The doctor put his arm protectingly about the little lady.

Mary Isabel tossed her head. "Oh, I'm not—I'm only excited. I shall never be afraid of Louisa again."

Louisa came grimly over the field, up the verandah steps, and into the room without knocking.

"Mary Isabel," she said, glaring at her sister and ignoring the doctor entirely, "did you mean what you said in that letter?"

"Yes, I did," said Mary Isabel firmly.

"You are going to be married to that man in this shameless, indecent haste?"

"Yes."

"And nothing I can say will have the least effect on you?"

"Not the slightest."

"Then," said Louisa, more grimly than ever, "all I ask of you is to come home and be married from under your father's roof. Do have that much respect for your parents' memory, at least."

"Of course I will," cried Mary Isabel impulsively, softening at once. "Of course we will—won't we?" she asked, turning prettily to the doctor.

"Just as you say," he answered gallantly.

Louisa snorted. "I'll go home and air the parlour," she said. "It's lucky I baked that fruitcake Monday. You can come when you're ready."

She stalked home across the field. In a few minutes the doctor and Mary Isabel followed, and behind them came the young minister, carrying his blue book under his arm, and trying hard and not altogether successfully to look grave.

The Twins and a Wedding

Sometimes Johnny and I wonder what would really have happened if we had never started for Cousin Pamelia's wedding. I think that Ted would have come back some time; but Johnny says he doesn't believe he ever would, and Johnny ought to know, because Johnny's a boy. Anyhow, he couldn't have come back for four years. However, we *did* start for the wedding and so things came out all right, and Ted said we were a pair of twin special Providences.

Johnny and I fully expected to go to Cousin Pamelia's wedding because we had always been such chums with her. And she did write to Mother to be sure and bring us, but Father and Mother didn't want to be bothered with us. That is the plain truth of the matter. They are good parents, as parents go in this world; I don't think we could have picked out much better, all things considered; but Johnny and I have always known that they never want to take us with them anywhere if they can get out of it. Uncle Fred says that it is no wonder, since we are a pair of holy terrors for getting into mischief and keeping everybody in hot water. But I think we are pretty good, considering all the temptations we have to be otherwise. And, of course, twins have just twice as many as ordinary children.

Anyway, Father and Mother said we would have to stay home with Hannah Jane. This decision came upon us, as Johnny says, like a bolt from the blue. At first we couldn't believe they were not joking. Why, we felt that we simply *had* to go to Pamelia's wedding. We had never been to a wedding in our lives and we were just aching to see what it would be like. Besides, we had written a marriage ode to Pamelia and we wanted to present it to her. Johnny was to recite it, and he had been practising it out behind the carriage house for a week. I wrote the most of it. I can write poetry as slick as anything. Johnny helped me hunt out the rhymes. That is the hardest thing about writing poetry, it is so difficult to find rhymes. Johnny would find me a rhyme and then I would write a line to suit it, and we got on swimmingly.

When we realized that Father and Mother meant what they said we were just too miserable to live. When I went to bed that night I simply pulled the clothes over my face and howled quietly. I couldn't help it when I thought of Pamelia's white silk dress and tulle veil and flower girls and all the rest. Johnny said it was the wedding dinner *he* thought about. Boys are like that, you know.

Father and Mother went away on the early morning train, telling us to be good twins and not bother Hannah Jane. It would have been more to the point if they had told Hannah Jane not to bother us. She worries more about our bringing up than Mother does.

I was sitting on the front doorstep after they had gone when Johnny came around the corner, looking so mysterious and determined that I knew he had thought of something splendid.

"Sue," said Johnny impressively, "if you have any real sporting blood in you now is the time to show it. If you've enough grit we'll get to Pamelia's wedding after all."

"How?" I said as soon as I was able to say anything.

"We'll just go. We'll take the ten o'clock train. It will get to Marsden by eleven-thirty and that'll be in plenty of time. The wedding isn't until twelve."

"But we've never been on the train alone, and we've never been to Marsden at all!" I gasped.

"Oh, of course, if you're going to hatch up all sorts of difficulties!" said Johnny scornfully. "I thought you had more spunk!"

"Oh, I have, Johnny," I said eagerly. "I'm *all* spunk. And I'll do anything you'll do. But won't Father and Mother be perfectly savage?"

"Of course. But we'll be there and they can't send us home again, so we'll see the wedding. We'll be punished afterwards all right, but we'll have had the fun, don't you see?"

I saw. I went right upstairs to dress, trusting everything blindly to Johnny. I put on my best pale blue shirred silk hat and my blue organdie dress and my high-heeled slippers. Johnny whistled when he saw me, but he never said a word; there are times when Johnny is a duck.

We slipped away when Hannah Jane was feeding the hens.

"I'll buy the tickets," explained Johnny. "I've got enough money left out of my last month's allowance because I didn't waste it all on candy as you did. You'll have to pay me back when you get your next month's jink, remember. I'll ask the conductor to tell us when we get to

Marsden. Uncle Fred's house isn't far from the station, and we'll be sure to know it by all the cherry trees round it."

It sounded easy, and it *was* easy. We had a jolly ride, and finally the conductor came along and said, "Here's your jumping-off place, kiddies."

Johnny didn't like being called a kiddy, but I saw the conductor's eye resting admiringly on my blue silk hat and I forgave him.

Marsden was a pretty little village, and away up the road we saw Uncle Fred's place, for it was fairly smothered in cherry trees all white with lovely bloom. We started for it as fast as we could go, for we knew we had no time to lose. It is perfectly dreadful trying to hurry when you have on high-heeled shoes, but I said nothing and just tore along, for I knew Johnny would have no sympathy for me. We finally reached the house and turned in at the open gate of the lawn. I thought everything looked very peaceful and quiet for a wedding to be under way and I had a sickening idea that it was too late and it was all over.

"Nonsense!" said Johnny, cross as a bear, because he was really afraid of it too. "I suppose everybody is inside the house. No, there are two people over there by that bench. Let us go and ask them if this is the right place, because if it isn't we have no time to lose."

We ran across the lawn to the two people. One of them was a young lady, the very prettiest young lady I had ever seen. She was tall and stately, just like the heroine in a book, and she had lovely curly brown hair and big blue eyes and the most dazzling complexion. But she looked very cross and disdainful and I knew the minute I saw her that she had been quarrelling with the young man. He was standing in front of her and he was as handsome as a prince. But he looked angry too. Altogether, you never saw a crosser-looking couple. Just as we came up we heard the young lady say, "What you ask is ridiculous and impossible, Ted. I *can't* get married at two days' notice and I don't mean to be."

And he said, "Very well, Una, I am sorry you think so. You would not think so if you really cared anything for me. It is just as well I have found out you don't. I am going away in two days' time and I shall not return in a hurry, Una."

"I do not care if you never return," she said.

That was a fib and well I knew it. But the young man didn't—men are so stupid at times. He swung around on one foot without replying and he would have gone in another second if he had not nearly fallen over Johnny and me.

"Please, sir," said Johnny respectfully, but hurriedly. "We're looking for Mr. Frederick Murray's place. Is this it?"

"No," said the young man a little gruffly. "This is Mrs. Franklin's place. Frederick Murray lives at Marsden, ten miles away."

My heart gave a jump and then stopped beating. I know it did, although Johnny says it is impossible.

"Isn't this Marsden?" cried Johnny chokily.

"No, this is Harrowsdeane," said the young man, a little more mildly.

I couldn't help it. I was tired and warm and so disappointed. I sat right down on the rustic seat behind me and burst into tears, as the story-books say.

"Oh, don't cry, dearie," said the young lady in a very different voice from the one she had used before. She sat down beside me and put her arms around me. "We'll take you over to Marsden if you've got off at the wrong station."

"But it will be too late," I sobbed wildly. "The wedding is to be at twelve—and it's nearly that now—and oh, Johnny, I do think you might try to comfort me!"

For Johnny had stuck his hands in his pockets and turned his back squarely on me. I thought it so unkind of him. I didn't know then that it was because he was afraid he was going to cry right there before everybody, and I felt deserted by all the world.

"Tell me all about it," said the young lady.

So I told her as well as I could all about the wedding and how wild we were to see it and why we were running away to it.

"And now it's all no use," I wailed. "And we'll be punished when they find out just the same. I wouldn't mind being punished if we hadn't missed the wedding. We've never seen a wedding—and Pamelia was to wear a white silk dress—and have flower girls—and oh, my heart is just broken. I shall never get over this—never—if I live to be as old as Methuselah."

"What can we do for them?" said the young lady, looking up at the young man and smiling a little. She seemed to have forgotten that they had just quarrelled. "I can't bear to see children disappointed. I remember my own childhood too well."

"I really don't know what we can do," said the young man, smiling back, "unless we get married right here and now for their sakes. If it is a wedding they want to see and nothing else will do them, that is the only idea I can suggest."

"Nonsense!" said the young lady. But she said it as if she would rather like to be persuaded it wasn't nonsense.

I looked up at her. "Oh, if you have any notion of being married I wish you would right off," I said eagerly. "Any wedding would do just as well as Pamelia's. Please do."

The young lady laughed.

"One might just as well be married at two hours' notice as two days'," she said.

"Una," said the young man, bending towards her, "will you marry me here and now? Don't send me away alone to the other side of the world, Una."

"What on earth would Auntie say?" said Una helplessly.

"Mrs. Franklin wouldn't object if you told her you were going to be married in a balloon."

"I don't see how we could arrange—oh, Ted, it's absurd."

"'Tisn't. It's highly sensible. I'll go straight to town on my wheel for the licence and ring and I'll be back in an hour. You can be ready by that time."

For a moment Una hesitated. Then she said suddenly to me, "What is your name, dearie?"

"Sue Murray," I said, "and this is my brother, Johnny. We're twins. We've been twins for ten years."

"Well, Sue, I'm going to let you decide for me. This gentleman here, whose name is Theodore Prentice, has to start for Japan in two days and will have to remain there for four years. He received his orders only yesterday. He wants me to marry him and go with him. Now, I shall leave it to you to consent or refuse for me. Shall I marry him or shall I not?"

"Marry him, of course," said I promptly. Johnny says she knew I would say that when she left it to me.

"Very well," said Una calmly. "Ted, you may go for the necessaries. Sue, you must be my bridesmaid and Johnny shall be best man. Come, we'll go into the house and break the news to Auntie."

I never felt so interested and excited in my life. It seemed too good to be true. Una and I went into the house and there we found the sweetest, pinkest, plumpest old lady asleep in an easy-chair. Una wakened her and said, "Auntie, I'm going to be married to Mr. Prentice in an hour's time."

That was a most wonderful old lady! All she said was, "Dear me!" You'd have thought Una had simply told her she was going out for a walk.

"Ted has gone for licence and ring and minister," Una went on. "We shall be married out under the cherry trees and I'll wear my new white organdie. We shall leave for Japan in two days. These children are Sue and Johnny Murray who have come out to see a wedding—*any* wedding. Ted and I are getting married just to please them."

"Dear me!" said the old lady again. "This is rather sudden. Still—if you must. Well, I'll go and see what there is in the house to eat."

She toddled away, smiling, and Una turned to me. She was laughing, but there were tears in her eyes.

"You blessed accidents!" she said, with a little tremble in her voice. "If you hadn't happened just then Ted would have gone away in a rage and I might never have seen him again. Come now, Sue, and help me dress."

Johnny stayed in the hall and I went upstairs with Una. We had such an exciting time getting her dressed. She had the sweetest white organdie you ever saw, all frills and laces. I'm sure Pamelia's silk couldn't have been half so pretty. But she had no veil, and I felt rather disappointed about that. Then there was a knock at the door and Mrs. Franklin came in, with her arms full of something all fine and misty like a lacy cobweb.

"I've brought you my wedding veil, dearie," she said. "I wore it forty years ago. And God bless you, dearie. I can't stop a minute. The boy is killing the chickens and Bridget is getting ready to broil them. Mrs. Jenner's son across the road has just gone down to the bakery for a wedding cake."

With that she toddled off again. She was certainly a wonderful old lady. I just thought of Mother in her place. Well, Mother would simply have gone wild entirely.

When Una was dressed she looked as beautiful as a dream. The boy had finished killing the chickens, and Mrs. Franklin had sent him up with a basket of roses for us, and we had each the loveliest bouquet. Before long Ted came back with the minister, and the next thing we knew we were all standing out on the lawn under the cherry trees and Una and Ted were being married.

I was too happy to speak. I had never thought of being a bridesmaid in my wildest dreams and here I was one. How thankful I was that I had put on my blue organdie and my shirred hat! I wasn't a bit nervous and I don't believe Una was either. Mrs. Franklin stood at one side with a smudge of flour on her nose, and she had forgotten to take off her apron. Bridget and the boy watched us from the kitchen garden. It was all like a beautiful, bewildering dream. But the ceremony was horribly solemn. I am sure I shall never have the courage to go through with anything of the sort, but Johnny says I will change my mind when I grow up.

When it was all over I nudged Johnny and said "Ode" in a fierce whisper. Johnny immediately stepped out before Una and recited it. Pamelia's name was mentioned three times and of course he should have put Una in place of it, but he forgot. You can't remember everything.

"You dear funny darlings!" said Una, kissing us both. Johnny didn't like *that*, but he said he didn't mind it in a bride.

Then we had dinner, and I thought Mrs. Franklin more wonderful than ever. I couldn't have believed any woman could have got up such a spread at two hours' notice. Of course, some credit must be given to Bridget and the boy. Johnny and I were hungry enough by this time and we enjoyed that repast to the full.

We went home on the evening train. Ted and Una came to the station with us, and Una said she would write me when she got to Japan, and Ted said he would be obliged to us forever and ever.

When we got home we found Hannah Jane and Father and Mother—who had arrived there an hour before us—simply distracted. They were so glad to see us safe and sound that they didn't even scold us, and when Father heard our story he laughed until the tears came into his eyes.

"Some are born to luck, some achieve luck, and some have luck thrust upon them," he said.

The Complete Richard Hannay - 39 Steps, Greenmantle, Mr Steadfast, Three Hostages, Island of Sheep.
John Buchan
Benediction Classics, 2012
908 pages
ISBN: 978-1-78139-203-4

Available from www.amazon.com, www.amazon.co.uk

The Complete Richard Hannay includes the five John Buchan novels that feature the hero: 39 Steps, Greenmantle, Mr Steadfast, Three Hostages, Island of Sheep. Richard Hannay was one of the first modern spy thriller heroes and has shaped the genre. Hannay is strong and silent, combining the Scottish dourness with the English "stiff upper lip". He is tough and shrewd, courageous and resourceful. However, unlike later spy thrillers he has a greater breadth of emotion. He is philosophical and refuses to demonise his enemies, he falls in love, he is dependent upon his friends and he is religious. These books are exciting, with Richard Hannay being chased over moor and glen, they are page turning thrillers.

The Blanket of the Dark
John Buchan
Benediction Classics, 2012
236 pages
ISBN: 978-1-78139-162-4

Available from www.amazon.com, www.amazon.co.uk

The Blanket of the Dark is a compelling story. A young clerk, Peter Pentecost, find that he is a descendent of Henry of Buckingham and has a claim to the throne. Buchan spins a beautifully woven tale of intrigue around the king, where 'under the blanket of the dark all men are alike and all are nameless'. Henry VIII is portrayed as an ogre, his description of the monarch is vivid and persuasive. Buchan takes us into the world in which the people of the early sixteenth-century England lived, under perhaps the most repellant figure to sit on the English throne.

The Complete Sherlock Holmes - unabridged and illustrated - A Study In Scarlet, The Sign Of The Four, The Hound Of The Baskervilles, The Valley Of Fear, The Adventures Of Sherlock Holmes, The Memoirs Of Sherlock Holmes, The Return Of Sherlock Holmes, His Last Bow, and The Case-Book Of Sherlock Holmes
Arthur Conan Doyle
Benediction Classics, 2012
1108 pages
ISBN: 978-1-78139-210-2

Available from www.amazon.com, www.amazon.co.uk

The Complete Sherlock Holmes - Illustrated. This edition brings together the four Sherlock Holmes Novels: A Study In Scarlet, The Sign Of The Four, The Hound Of The Baskervilles and The Valley Of Fear. In addition, it includes the five Sherlock Holmes Collections, bringing together the 56 short stories: The Adventures Of Sherlock Holmes, The Memoirs Of Sherlock Holmes, The Return Of Sherlock Holmes, His Last Bow and The Case-Book Of Sherlock Holmes. This book is a must have for any Sherlock Holmes lover.

Woman: Her Charm and Power
Robert P. Downes
Benediction Classics, 2011
366 pages
ISBN: 978-1-78139-009-2

Available from www.amazon.com, www.amazon.co.uk

This is a book written in 1900, describing the status and treatment of women. It is a culturally important book, as well as being both interesting and a pleasure to read. This book shows in stark contrast how far women have come since it was first published.

Also from Benediction Books ...

Wandering Between Two Worlds: Essays on Faith and Art
Anita Mathias
Benediction Books, 2007
152 pages
ISBN: 0955373700

Available from www.amazon.com, www.amazon.co.uk

In these wide-ranging lyrical essays, Anita Mathias writes, in lush, lovely prose, of her naughty Catholic childhood in Jamshedpur, India; her large, eccentric family in Mangalore, a sea-coast town converted by the Portuguese in the sixteenth century; her rebellion and atheism as a teenager in her Himalayan boarding school, run by German missionary nuns, St. Mary's Convent, Nainital; and her abrupt religious conversion after which she entered Mother Teresa's convent in Calcutta as a novice. Later rich, elegant essays explore the dualities of her life as a writer, mother, and Christian in the United States-- Domesticity and Art, Writing and Prayer, and the experience of being "an alien and stranger" as an immigrant in America, sensing the need for roots.

About the Author

Anita Mathias is the author of *Wandering Between Two Worlds: Essays on Faith and Art*. She has a B.A. and M.A. in English from Somerville College, Oxford University, and an M.A. in Creative Writing from the Ohio State University, USA. Anita won a National Endowment of the Arts fellowship in Creative Nonfiction in 1997. She lives in Oxford, England with her husband, Roy, and her daughters, Zoe and Irene.

Anita's website:
http://www.anitamathias.com, and
Anita's blog Dreaming Beneath the Spires:
http://dreamingbeneaththespires.blogspot.com

The Church That Had Too Much
Anita Mathias
Benediction Books, 2010
52 pages
ISBN: 9781849026567

Available from www.amazon.com, www.amazon.co.uk

The Church That Had Too Much was very well-intentioned. She wanted to love God, she wanted to love people, but she was both hampered by her muchness and the abundance of her possessions, and beset by ambition, power struggles and snobbery. Read about the surprising way The Church That Had Too Much began to resolve her problems in this deceptively simple and enchanting fable.

About the Author

Anita Mathias is the author of *Wandering Between Two Worlds: Essays on Faith and Art*. She has a B.A. and M.A. in English from Somerville College, Oxford University, and an M.A. in Creative Writing from the Ohio State University, USA. Anita won a National Endowment of the Arts fellowship in Creative Nonfiction in 1997. She lives in Oxford, England with her husband, Roy, and her daughters, Zoe and Irene.

Anita's website:
    http://www.anitamathias.com, and
Anita's blog Dreaming Beneath the Spires:
    http://dreamingbeneaththespires.blogspot.com

www.ingramcontent.com/pod-product-compliance
Lightning Source LLC
Chambersburg PA
CBHW030342310726
48979CB00001B/158
* 9 7 8 1 7 8 1 3 9 2 4 3 0 *